Hotel O

CLARISSA WILD

PROLOGUE

DECLAN

Pleasure is business. That's our motto here at Hotel O.

No-strings-attached gratification is what we provide. *Nothing* is off-limits. And all of it stays within these walls.

My job as the organizer of these events requires a personal sacrifice. Girlfriends are a liability I can't afford, so I get my satisfaction elsewhere.

Online. Anonymous. Nothing beyond a one-night stand … No one has to know. No one will find out.

And the more time I spend on this chat site tonight, the more I'm starting to think I've found the perfect toy to play with.

ONE

Kat

Name: NaughtyKitten.

Age: Twenty-seven.

Currently Wearing: Blue tank top.

My profile is blank with the exception of two small tidbits.

As dirty as can be. Humiliate me.

It might sound wrong, but that's what these chat sites are for. People don't discuss the weather or work here. No one cares who you are in real life, and no one wants to get to know you. Everyone just wants to have fun. That's why I love this site so much.

Being cooped up in my tiny one-story house with little breathing room in my private life has made me eager to try new things, and *this* … this little gem right here is proving to be one of my favorite things to do late at night.

Or any time of day really.

I'm a sucker for exciting things. Or rather … dicks.

I can't help myself. Growing up so sheltered has me wanting to try literally everything out since I've been living on my own. Nothing's too thrilling for me, and I haven't yet found a line I don't want to cross.

That's what you get when you're not allowed to date, and your parents are protective as hell. You resort to being a sneaky bitch and having boyfriends climb up to your room in the middle of the night. But all that fades compared to what I really want. To what I'm thinking of when I play with myself.

I want to be taken. Used. In every way possible.

I've wanted it for so long, but no man who came into my life after I moved out was ever up to the task. Most men shy away when I tell them my dirtiest wishes. Guess I'm a lot of maintenance in the bedroom. Or maybe they're just not into experimenting. Who knows. So I resort to online stuff instead. It makes it easier to quit without even having to say a word.

I can just exit the window and be done with it or hop on to the next. Quiet and under the radar.

Privacy is a big thing on this chat site. No one will ever know it was me who was on there, which is the most important factor. If my friends and family ever discovered what I really liked, they'd run for the hills. Hell, if my boss found out, she'd probably fire me on the spot for lewd behavior.

Especially if she knew I sometimes go to this chatroom at work. But no one has to find out. It's my dirty little secret.

And now it will be *his* too.

Because someone has already pinged me for a private conversation … and when I check out his profile, I'm pleasantly surprised.

Name: D.

Age: Thirty-three.

Currently Wearing: Suit. Commando underneath.

Description: No commitment. No strings. Just pleasure … and you doing everything I tell you to.

A wicked grin spreads on my lips as I take a sip of my coffee and press the accept button.

His picture appears too now. Second surprise of the day. It's not a dick pic. It's a picture of him buttoning up his sharply creased shirt.

Well, now I've seen it all.

A man who won't show off his dick the very first chance he gets? Color me intrigued.

And not only that, but he looks rather … buff too. Because I can definitely see those pecs underneath his shirt.

My mouth is already watering.

But I have to remind myself that this is only a fantasy. Once I close the laptop, he'll be gone forever.

With a smirk on my face, I start typing. If he won't be the first to say something, I'll break the ice. I'm not that shy … but maybe he is.

NaughtyKitten: Hey.

No response.

I can see him typing, though. What kind of greeting takes so long to write?

D: Take off your clothes.

I frown. What's this then? Going all out right away?

NaughtyKitten: No 'hi' first? Maybe we should talk first? See if we match up?

D: I take no pleasure in formalities. Are you here to play or not?

I take another sip of my coffee and narrow my eyes. He's very straightforward. I haven't decided yet whether I like it, but I'll play along. See where it goes.

NaughtyKitten: Yes. What are you here for?

D: To get off.

NaughtyKitten: Then we have a mutual interest.

D: My interest is you. Now take off your clothes.

NaughtyKitten: What gave you the impression I'll do what you say?

I lick my lips and set my coffee down as I wait for his answer.

D: Because you want to. Because you asked for it.

NaughtyKitten: Where?

It takes him a while to respond.

It's not a text.

It's a picture of my profile description.

D: Was this a lie?

NaughtyKitten: It wasn't. But I like to know who I'm speaking to as well. What do you like?

D: You. Naked. Fingering yourself for me on camera.

I'm not gonna lie, that actually made my pussy clench.

NaughtyKitten: Okay. But what makes you think I will trust you with pictures?

D: You don't have to trust me. I'm just here to humiliate you. Now do as I say.

I swallow away the lump in my throat as my finger hovers over the touchpad. I'm tempted to close the chat right then, but something stops me. The curious side in me refuses to let go of this opportunity. I've never talked to a man like him, so straightforward with what he wants. It's almost … scary.

Scary exciting. Too exciting.

But then I remember I've been living the norm because other people want me to. Not because I want to.

I want to be filthy. I want to be someone's plaything. I want this. Now.

So I smile and start to type again.

NaughtyKitten: Tell me what to do.

D: Send me a picture of your tits.

I rub my lips and contemplate it for a few seconds.

Should I? It's not as if I haven't sent them to a dude before. I always make sure to blur out or cut off my face, of course. I don't want anyone to recognize me. There's really no reason not to. Except ... I normally talk with a guy before immediately jumping into the sex chats with them.

But I guess this guy likes things to move along.

Okay. No problem. Challenging myself to push my boundaries is fun.

I check my laptop for any pics I already took and find one of my boobs, which I send to him.

It doesn't take him long to respond.

D: That's not from today.

My brows draw together. How can he tell?

D: Wrong shirt.

Oh ... right. I forgot you had to enter what you're wearing.

D: Are you trying to fool me?

NaughtyKitten: No.

D: How will I know if you really look like the picture on your profile?

NaughtyKitten: It's me. Promise.

D: You're really a naughty kitten ... playing dirty.

It's a picture of my boobs covered by a small pink bra, which is enough to lure the men without giving away my best asset. Obviously, he paid attention. Smart.

D: I won't accept a pre-made picture. I need the real deal. Now. Write the letter D on your left tit. Make your nipples nice and hard. Twist your right nipple.

9

Send me a picture. Nude.

Holy shit. He really is demanding. I like it.

I lift my tank top to expose my boobs and grab a marker, penning the letter down on my left one. Then I make my nipples hard and twist the right one, taking a picture with my phone. I immediately upload it to my laptop where I edit it until my face is no longer visible.

One ... two ... three seconds of doubt. It's sent.

My whole body trembles with delicious electrical vibes as I wait for his response. I don't know why I always like this moment so much or what excites me about a man seeing me for the first time. Maybe it's the forbidden aspect ... that makes me feel really, really dirty.

D: Good ... Now this is what I wanted to see.

NaughtyKitten: Do you like my tits?

D: Oh, yes. I'm already hard as a rock.

My pussy thumps again at the thought. I wonder what he looks like. How long and thick he is.

NaughtyKitten: Send me a pic.

D: You listen to me. Not the other way around. Remember what you came here for.

I frown. Well, isn't he cheerful. Though, I suppose he's right ... in a way.

D: But I'll humor you this time. Because I like you.

Not too long after, he sends me a picture ... but not of his dick. No, it's his button-up shirt, the same one from his profile picture, pulled up all the way to the top of his neck. All I see are ... abs ... but my God, do they look lickable. A small trail of hair leads downward from his navel, past his V-line, right to where I want to put my mouth.

D: Like what you see?

NaughtyKitten: Oh, yes. Although I was hoping for more.

D: Patience is a virtue.

NaughtyKitten: I'm not patient. Or good, for that matter.

D: A true naughty kitten then …

I take another sip of my coffee, which isn't even hot anymore. Shit. I completely forgot about it in the heat of the moment. Guess I'm a sucker for a filthy fuck … and this guy certainly strikes me as one.

D: But how naughty are you?

Is this a trick question?

NaughtyKitten: As naughty as you want me to be.

D: Do you have a video camera?

Well, this could get interesting.

NaughtyKitten: I have my phone. Is that good?

D: Film yourself while you play with your pussy. I want to see it all. Up. Close.

I jump up from my seat and grab my phone, then take off my panties. They're already soaked. Jesus, am I this easy? Apparently I am, and I don't even care.

I sit down and place the camera near my legs, so it only films my pussy and not any higher. I don't want to expose my face. But before I start, I send him another message.

NaughtyKitten: Ready.

11

D: Open your legs as wide as you can. Touch your clit. Make yourself wet.

Fuck, I already am. But I still rub myself anyway. I can't help it; the thought of someone watching soon makes me so goddamn horny. I can't wait for him to see it … I wonder if it'll make him come.

The camera is recording as I flick my clit and moan out loud. I hope it picks up my sounds. I'm already soaked and swollen when he types more.

D: Finger yourself. First with one. Then with two. And when you do, think about how dirty you're being. How bad you are.

Fuck, yes. I love it when they talk dirty. It only makes me moan louder.

I shove a finger in and imagine he's doing it while he claims my mouth. I imagine him making me come and then shoving his dick into my mouth, forcing me to swallow him down. God, I want it all. Every inch of filth.

D: Finger yourself until you come all over the chair and show me the wetness on your fingers. I want to see how much of a filthy slut you really are.

Fuck me, when they start calling me names, I'm begging for mercy.

I don't know what it is about being humiliated that turns me on so much, but it does.

D: Come like the slut you are. Come all over your hands and the camera.

One second is all it takes for the explosions to fill my

body and take over. And I sink into the chair as my body convulses, my legs quaking with need. Fuck … what I wouldn't do for a dick right about now.

NaughtyKitten: Fuck … Yes.
D: Did you come? Show me.

I hold my fingers in front of the camera and then turn it off with my other hand. Then I wash my hands and get back to my seat. I contemplate shutting off the chat. I got my fill. Then again … I haven't met many dudes like him online. I don't want this to stop.

So I upload the video from my phone to my laptop and play it to make sure it doesn't show my face before I send it to him. When I click the button to send, my heart begins to race.

What if he finds out who I am? What if he uses it against me? Makes me lose my job? Or worse …

A shiver runs down my spine.

No way he can find out who I am from just a video of my pussy.

Besides, it's already too late. I already pressed the button. He's already downloading it as we speak.

I just have to believe in him and stop worrying about the consequences. I wanted this. I needed the excitement. So I'll have to accept whatever happens. It's part of the thrill.

When he starts typing again, I blow out a sigh of relief.

D: Tell me what you thought of when you fucked yourself like that.

NaughtyKitten: You.

D: What did you imagine me doing to you?

NaughtyKitten: I thought of your fingers, pushing inside me. You, making me come. And you ... shoving your dick down my throat until I can't breathe.

D: You like that, filthy slut?

NaughtyKitten: I love being used.

D: You're still wet, aren't you?

NaughtyKitten: Yes. And I'm greedy for more.

D: You're even more perfect than I thought.

Perfect? What does he mean? Does he intend to make this into more than a one-time thing? God, I hope so, even though it goes against unofficial chat rules ...

D: I'm rubbing my cock right now ... watching you play with yourself. Does that turn you on?

NaughtyKitten: Fuck, yes. I want to see.

D: If you're naughty enough, I might show it to you.

NaughtyKitten: I'll do anything. Just give it to me.

D: Anything?

NaughtyKitten: Yes.

D: Then let's make this a rain check.

I suck in a breath and pause. Where is he going with this?

NaughtyKitten: ??

D: Next time you log on, you contact me. We'll see how much you want to see this.

NaughtyKitten: Next time?

D: Do you work?

NaughtyKitten: Yes. But we're not supposed to talk about that.

This is so strange … I've never talked with a guy who wants to do this again. Also, it's not advised because it could put members in jeopardy if they keep in contact. Yet I can't stop talking to him. I want more. I want so much more.

D: Right, but do you have a lunch break?

NaughtyKitten: Yes. Twelve thirty, every day.

God, I'm so easy. Too easy.

D: Good.

D: Monday. Twelve thirty. Same names. Same outfit. And bring a dildo or a vibrator.

NaughtyKitten: But I'm wearing inappropriate stuff. And a dildo? At work?

D: You will wear this and bring the dildo because I want you to.

NaughtyKitten: But …

D: Humiliation, remember? It's in your profile.

Well, he isn't wrong. I just don't know if I can do it.

D: Do what I want, and I'll give it to you. Every … inch.

Oh, God… Just the thought makes me drool.

But before I can even say yes or no, he's already closed the chat and gone offline.

TWO

CHASE

Scrolling through my phone, I take a sip of my coffee. I can't stop looking at the video of her fingering herself. This kitten is naughty, all right …

She agreed so easily to everything I asked of her. With a snap of a finger or a stern command, I could make her do anything I wanted.

It's as if she was waiting for me and me alone.

I wonder how far she'll go and how far I'm willing to take this. Because it's so goddamn exciting. I can't even stop staring at her sweet, wet pussy, getting my cock rock hard in my pants.

"Declan?"

I immediately gaze up in the direction of the voice and will my cock back down. "Hmm?"

My boss and several other employees are all staring at me. For a moment there, I completely forgot I was in a meeting. Oh, well. Guess her pussy will have to come later. Literally.

"Yes?" I reply, clearing my throat.

"Your plan? Is it ready to go?" my boss asks.

"Yes," I say, nodding. "I'm working on the final details, but everything's set to go."

"So the event can be announced?" Sarah asks, tapping her pencil on her notepad.

"Yes." I tap my phone and send my co-workers the email I've prepared. "Check your inbox. I've sent you all the details concerning the theme and setting. My department has worked hard to provide our clients with the best experience."

"Great," my boss says. "I don't need to know the exact details. Just get it done." He gets up from his chair with his coffee and laptop in his hands and says, "That's all."

Everyone gets up after he's left the room, and we shake hands and agree on our meeting. It's a busy week, but I'm used to it. Here at Hotel O, business is booming, and my job is to make sure that everything goes according to plan.

"Thanks, Declan," Sarah says. "I appreciate the update."

"Yeah, no problem. You still good to go with the marketing?"

She nods. "I've got everything set up to go out to our regular clients today."

"Great. If you need any help, you know where to find me." I wink and drink the last drops of my coffee before getting up.

She briefly touches my arm. "You know you can always ask me for help too, right? I know it can get busy." She smiles, tucking a strand of her hair behind her ear. "I just wanted you to know. In case things get too hectic."

I smile back, but I'm way too distracted to even keep that in mind. "Of course."

"Okay," she mutters as I turn around and start scrolling through my phone again.

"See you next Monday!" she calls. She's been trying to get my attention for a while now, but I'm not interested in dating co-workers. Nothing personal. I just like to keep things strictly business.

So I just raise my hand and wave as I leave the room. My eyes refuse to leave my phone. That's how obsessed I am with the images in front of me, the screenshots I took of her video.

What? She sent it to me; she should know that could happen.

But I'm not an asshole. I'll take good care of them, and I won't ever share them. Unless she likes that sort of thing. Maybe I'll ask ... or not.

It doesn't really matter anyway. Our play is only for a limited time. As long as it's fun, I'll let it continue, but I

18

can't let it go too far. This job requires a hundred percent of my attention. I don't have time for relationships, nor am I interested in them. Relationships only make things difficult, and I'm not interested in losing my job over a bit of sex.

That's why I'm only looking for quick hookups that are mutually beneficial. Steamy encounters enough to satiate me. And I don't ever stray off that path.

I have three strict rules when it comes to girls like NaughtyKitten.

One: Never expose your real identity.

Two: Don't hook up more than once.

Three: Cut it off before she falls in love.

The company I work for employs these same rules when it comes to protecting its clients.

Following these guidelines has kept me and the company safe from exposure to the public. After all … exclusivity and privacy are key to Hotel O's success. And I intend to maintain those at top level.

But right now, I need some private time.

I go down with the elevator, walk into my office on the second floor, and sit down behind my desk. I zip down my pants and pull it down far enough to expose myself while I watch her video once again. I'm quickly hard enough and take a picture of my cock.

I take out my laptop and check the time while starting the chat. Perfect.

When I get online, I type in the exact details as before and wait until she's online.

The moment her name pops online, she immediately begins a conversation with me.

NaughtyKitten: I'm here.

D: So it seems. And on time too. Well done.

NaughtyKitten: It took some effort, but I got it done.

D: I don't have to know the specifics. I just want you to do exactly as I ask.

NaughtyKitten: And what is it that you want, exactly?

I grin at the thought of all the fun we're going to have. Her showing me her pussy was merely the start. I can't wait to see where this will go.

***

Kat

D: I promised you something ...

I raise a brow. Does this mean what I think it means?

Before I can reply, he's already sent me a picture. And holy fucking shit ... I have to do a double take. That is one big, juicy dick. My mouth waters just from looking at it.

NaughtyKitten: I'm licking my lips right now.

D: Good. Keep them wet. I want an up-close picture later.

Hmm … that depends on whether he delivers. If he's not gonna send me a video of him jerking off, then I might not even comply.

After all, I'm naughty, and a naughty kitten sometimes likes to break the rules if she's not getting her fill.

D: Brought the dildo?

NaughtyKitten: Yes! And it has a suction cup at the bottom.

D: Send me a picture of you holding it next to your breasts.

I roll my eyes. Of course, he'd think I lie, but where's the fun in that? I like the excitement of doing something totally irresponsible and immoral. I mean, I'm literally sexting with a stranger in my office. It can't get more indecent than that.

But I do what he asks anyway. I remove the jacket I'd layered on top and take the dildo from my purse, holding it close to my boobs while one of my nipples peeks out … just for fun. Then I send it to him.

D: Good girl.

Seconds later, another image pops up. In this one, he's holding his dick with both hands. It's firm and long and very much erect … only after staring at it for a while do I notice the watch on his wrist. It shows today's date and time. So it's really him.

Well, fuck. Well-endowed isn't even adequate to

describe him. I'm honestly flabbergasted.

NaughtyKitten: Nice.

D: There's more for you if you play nice.

NaughtyKitten: What do you want me to do?

D: Take off your panties. Play with yourself for a while. Use the picture I sent you to warm up.

I bite my lip as I pull down my panties from underneath my skirt and tuck them in my purse. I'm already warm and wet down below just from thinking about this all day. During breakfast, my first cup of coffee, driving to work, talking with co-workers … I couldn't get him off my mind. Hell, I even dreamed about him last night. That's how horny I am. Literally all the time. And I've finally found the proper man to take care of it.

I giggle as I take a picture of my wet fingers and send it to him.

NaughtyKitten: What now?

D: I want you on the edge. Push the dildo into your pussy. Make it nice and wet. Film it going all the way in.

Blushing, I pick up my phone and press the video button on my camera as I push the dildo inside, thrusting it in and out my pussy until I'm scorching hot. I imagine it's his huge dick entering me, and oh God …

I'm almost ready to climax.

Instead, I type again.

NaughtyKitten: Can I come?

D: No.

Well, fuck.

D: Not yet, Kitten. Send me the video.

NaughtyKitten: But I haven't seen anything from you yet.

It's quiet for a few seconds.

D: You do what I say, not the other way around.

I sigh. So much for a good jerk-off vid.

D: If you behave, I'll send a video later.

My heart immediately begins to jump up and down in my chest at the thought. Fuck, what a tease.

NaughtyKitten: Fine.

I open the site on my phone and send him the video I made and wait for his reply.

D: Delectable.

I raise a brow. *Delectable? Who says that?*

Within seconds, I get something back. This time, it's a video. I'm almost too scared to click it, but the temptation grows too strong after few seconds. And fuck me … is it good.

He's jerking off right in front of the camera, which is tilted down toward his crotch. I can't see a face or a body … only a pair of pants and his hard dick hanging out as he rubs himself.

Fuck me. I'd give my left kidney to have that inside me.

D: There you go, Kitten. You make me hard. And your play makes me want to come all over you.

NaughtyKitten: I'm drooling.

D: Maybe I'll let you lick it some time.

NaughtyKitten: My tongue is waiting.

Is that slutty? Whatever, I don't even care. I'll be his slut. It doesn't matter anyway. It's just sex, and sex is good.

D: Now … stuff that dildo inside you. I want it deep, all the way to the base. Then put on your panties again.

I narrow my eyes. *What is he asking here? That I walk around with it?*

Still, I grasp my panties and shove the dildo deep inside until I feel it every time I move, and then I slide my panties back on.

NaughtyKitten: I don't understand why?
D: Keep it in your pussy for the rest of the day.
My eyes widen.

NaughtyKitten: But I'm at work.
D: So?
Of course, he'd say that.

I rub my lips together. If I protest, he'll probably say the same thing as before—that this is what I asked for. Humiliation. And to be honest, I did. And I do like it. I'm just not sure how far I'm willing to take it.

D: Doubting your own needs?
NaughtyKitten: Maybe.
D: Don't. Just do it. Have fun.

I take a deep breath and adjust in my seat. The dildo moves inside me, teasing all my senses. Fuck. I was supposed to do some work today. But with this thing inside me? No way that's gonna work.

24

D: Try to concentrate. Send me pics when you can. Every hour. I want to see if you can commit.

NaughtyKitten: And what if I don't?

D: Oh … I know you will.

A smirk spreads across my lips. This guy … God, this guy.

D: Now, spread your pussy lips and rub your clit while you think of me. But don't come.

Fuck, he's really going down and dirty this time. Still, I can't resist shoving my hands down my panties and circling my clit.

D: Can you feel the dick inside you? Imagine it's me.

NaughtyKitten: Oh yes, I want it.

D: Turn on the camera. Show me and moan for me. I wanna hear you enjoy yourself.

Fuck yes. I quickly grab my phone and hold it close to my panties as I turn on the camera, showing him the wetness pooling right in the fabric and my fingers going crazy down there.

I know he can hear me.

The video is live this time, and I don't even care.

All I want is for him to fuck me and make me come again and again. Fuck, that'd be nice.

D: Stop.

Well, fuck. I was this close to actually doing it even though I know he said I couldn't.

When I pull my fingers back, my clit is engorged and

throbbing, and the dildo inside me feels so tight.

But the picture he sends me when I turn off the live video is what makes me gasp.

It's a black napkin … covered in cum. *His* cum.

I swallow down the lump in my throat.

D: If you were here, I'd make you lick it … then shove it into your mouth and fuck you in the ass.

NaughtyKitten: Oh my God … Yes, please.

I immediately save the picture to my drive for keepsake in my secret treasure trove. Jesus, I'm going to come so hard to that image.

Suddenly, someone jerks the door handle. I pull my fingers from my panties, aimlessly chuck the phone into my purse, and close my laptop quickly.

"Kat, did you have those notes for—" Crystal busts into my office and immediately looks befuddled. "Sorry, did I interrupt something?"

Fuck.

Did I forget to lock my door? Why? Why the hell did I forget?

A blush spreads on my cheeks as I try to hide the evidence, randomly picking up a cup of coffee, which was already empty, just to pretend to slurp, and a pen to tap on my notebook. "No, no, I was just … emailing."

She frowns, gazing around the room, clearly noticing the closed blinds.

"I have a headache," I explain, shrugging. "Happens."

"Oh yeah …" She smiles awkwardly, but I feel as if I

just avoided a mother lode of trouble.

She isn't my boss, but I hate leaving bad impressions on fellow co-workers. And this would definitely get me into trouble.

"The meeting's about to begin. Do you have the notes?" she asks, approaching my desk.

The moment I shift in my seat, the dildo moves inside me, and I freeze.

"Are you okay?" she asks.

"Yeah, yeah," I reply, trying to play it cool by rubbing my back. "Aches. You know how it goes. That time of the month." I roll my eyes.

"Oh, I see. If you need anything, let me know." She winks. "I've got plenty of spare pads."

"Ah no, I'm fine, thanks," I mumble, cringing at the thought.

I scan my desk and quickly grasp the notebook, tearing off the pages she needs. "Here."

"No, it's fine. You can keep them. I only wanted to make sure you had them so we can actually show Ellen something." She chuckles.

I frown. Why would she even ask? Is this why she disturbed my awesome time with D for? For *this*?

"Here. I insist," I say, shoving them into her hands. "I don't want them anyway."

"But they're your notes …" she stammers.

"I already know what I want and what I'm going to say," I say. "Just take them. Maybe you can fill in Ellen while I

27

take care of this ... monthly *thing*."

"Okay, if you're sure." The chuckle she adds at the end gets on my nerves.

Or maybe it's because I was *this* fucking close to coming ... and she ruined it all.

She glances at her watch and then says, "Oh! Almost time. Gotta run. Grabbing some coffee on the way. Don't be late!" She rushes out and slams the door shut behind her, leaving me in peace.

I lower my head until it hits the desk, planting my face against the wood, groaning out loud.

All I can think of is him and how I left our whole conversation hanging in thin air.

And that I'll have to wait the entire day until I'm home again before I can finally release this pent-up need.

Great.

THREE

DECLAN

I stare at the screen and the two words in front of me.

Chat ended.

What? Did she really just ...

I sigh. I can't believe she actually closed the goddamn chat.

Did she get off when she wasn't supposed to? Or did something happen?

I make a fist. This wasn't the deal. She was to do everything I told her. I never told her she was allowed to stop the chat when I wasn't finished with her yet. And I definitely had more cum in store for her.

Fuck. Why does this make my blood boil so much?

Someone knocking on my door pulls me from my thoughts.

"Come in," I growl, quickly chucking the dirty napkin in the trash as I zip up my pants and close the laptop.

"Sorry, someone said we were supposed to come here …"

It's a long-legged girl in a short skirt. More appear behind her, peeking over her shoulders.

I almost forgot they were coming in today. Damn distracting chats …

"Yeah, this is the place," I say to the girls, beckoning them when they give me the side-eye. "Don't be shy. I don't bite."

The door opens wide and in step three girls, all of different heights and with different shades of hair and skin. But all equally beautiful, as requested.

"Over there," I say, nodding at the middle of the room as I go to lock the door.

When I sit back down again, they stand in line and wait for instructions, as told beforehand. Good. They know the drill.

I narrow my eyes and say, "Turn."

All the girls do what I ask, showing me their rear, which I inspect thoroughly.

"Turn," I say again, and they turn to face me.

This repeats again and again until I'm satisfied and have seen enough, after which I hold my finger up in the air.

A wicked smile spreads on my lips. This is the part when things become … interesting.

"Strip."

One of the girls blankly stares at me, her jaw dropping as my face remains rigid.

It's not a joke even though she's probably wishing it is.

"Well?" I say.

The other two girls begin taking off their clothes piece by piece, but not the girl on the left. "But …"

"Did you not read the instructions?" I inquire.

"Yes, but—"

"Then you know what's expected of you," I interrupt.

"But you're not one of the clients, right?" she asks with a befuddled look on her face.

"I'm here to assess the value you can add to this company. It's simple really," I reply. I don't ask for my personal pleasure. This is strictly business. "If I don't like what I see, then you don't get in."

She swallows, and a few seconds pass before she finally decides to remove her clothes.

They all do, eventually.

All it takes is that little nudge.

They knew what they were in for when they came here looking for a job. These aren't your run-of-the-mill girls. They were trained for years. Although some do retain their questioning attitudes, like the girl on the left, all of them eventually … agree.

Hotel O is a special kind of exclusive club. One that

requires excellence and obedience.

Do what is asked of you. No ifs. No buts.

That's what these girls are hired for.

And in exchange, they'll be able to pay for whatever their hearts desire.

***

Kat

With my thighs clenched together, I make my way through the building as fast as possible. It's not big, by any means; we're not a huge magazine, but I still feel as though everyone's watching me. Even though I try my hardest to avoid any eye contact whatsoever, I swear some of them are staring. Am I flushing? Probably. Does my walk look weird? Most likely.

Will they notice I actually have a dildo shoved up my pussy right now?

God, I hope not.

"Hey, Kat!" one of my co-workers says cheerfully as I pass him.

Swallowing away the lump in my throat, I glance at him over my shoulder. "Hey."

"Got a minute?"

"Sorry, can't talk right now," I say. The look on his face makes me want to squirm. "Meeting."

"Oh, right."

"Send an email," I say, moving on. I hope he won't see how awkward I'm behaving.

"Will do," he calls out after me.

But I've already disappeared through a hallway.

I'm sure he won't mind. I just hope he didn't notice, and that no one else talks to me.

As I get to the other end of the building and close the door behind me, I breathe a sigh of relief.

"Finally," someone says, breaking my calm.

When I spin on my heels and see five others sitting around the big desk in the middle of the room, I have a slight panic attack.

Today, out of all days, I had to have a meeting … and a stranger telling me to wear a dildo the entire day. Fuck.

I should've ran to the toilet and pulled it out.

Why am I doing this again?

"You're late," my boss, Ellen, hums.

"Sorry," I say, my cheeks warming up as I clutch my laptop and pretend nothing's going on. "Forgot the time."

"Sit," she says, which I do, immediately.

It doesn't feel any better. At all.

In fact, it's only more prominent, right there, in the middle of my crotch, pushing heavily into my pussy. All my senses are focused on that single object of desire.

And the more I move, the more I feel my pussy thump in response.

Fuck.

"You sure you're okay?" Crystal whispers into my ear. "I've got tampons too if you need one."

"No, I'm fine. I got it covered," I say, brushing it off.

She shrugs. "If there's anything else you need, you know you can always come to me, right?"

"Of course. Thanks," I say.

But I don't think I'd *ever* want her help with this.

"So back to business," Ellen interjects. "Crystal, those notes you mentioned?"

"Oh, yes," Crystal says, pulling mine up and placing them on the table. "We're almost done with the piece on the Laren Twins. Just finishing the edits and then we'll send it to Jade for the final touches."

"Good, and what about that other article?" Ellen asks. "The one about the school lunches?"

Crystal's lips part, but seeing as nothing comes out, I take over for her. "We're working on it."

"And the column?" Ellen asks.

"I've answered most of the reader's questions, so the column is good to go."

"Great. I expect all three to be done tomorrow." Ellen clears her throat. "Elections. Front and center. Judy and Dale, got it covered?"

"Got it," Judy says, penning down a few notes.

"Carter, help them out if needed."

"Aye aye, captain," he says, saluting her.

She gives him the side-eye but then continues. "Anything else?"

"Well …" I mutter, but the moment I shift in my seat, I pause and suck in a breath. Damn dildo, always reminding me what a filthy girl I am. Why did I agree to do this again?

"Yes?" Ellen says. Everyone's staring at me now.

"Um … I was thinking … maybe …" God, why is it so hard to put my thoughts into words?

Then again, it's no surprise I'm stammering, considering the length of that *thing* currently crammed up my vagina.

Crystal gives me a soft nudge against the shoulder, and I snap out of it.

"I was thinking of writing something bigger too," I say.

Ellen's eyes narrow.

"Like not just a column about people's questions and answers, but more along the line of an opinion piece. Something exciting and maybe shocking. Not just couples."

"About …?" Ellen mumbles, cocking her head.

"Well, I had this idea about exploring the various nuances of sex."

She looks puzzled. "Sex?"

Not good?

Not good. I can tell from the face she's making.

"Every week, I could try out something new. A new game, a new toy, a new experience somewhere. Then write about it."

"No," Ellen says sternly.

"But we're already skirting the edges with this magazine."

"Yes, well … small editorials about erotic experiences people had are different than feature articles, don't you think?"

"No … I think it would do the magazine good. Especially for our female readers."

She takes a deep breath. "For now, my answer is still no. The column you're doing is going great. I don't want to jeopardize that."

She turns her head and focuses on another employee sitting at the table.

So … that's it. My idea's shot dead right away.

I sigh and try not to let it get to me as I focus on the notes in front of me. We still have a lot of work to do if we're going to finish all three of these topics by tomorrow.

Still, I can't help but feel a little disappointed at how this all went.

When the meeting is over, everyone grabs their stuff. I'm the only one who remains seated. Not because I need to contemplate something or because I want to finish up, but because I literally don't want anyone staring at my ass while I make my way toward the door.

Things could get ugly. And by that, I mean this dildo could fall out at any moment and flop down on the floor.

Now that's a nightmarish scene I wouldn't ever want to see, let alone play out for anyone else to see.

Before she leaves, Crystal pats me on the shoulder and

says, "You'll get it one day. I just know it."

"Thanks, Crys," I say, smiling at her.

If I want this opinion piece at least once—no, on a regular basis—I have to pull my big girl panties up and show Ellen it will be awesome. It's the only way to change her mind.

"Good. You keep working at it. And in the meantime, we'll produce the most amazing responses to the reader's questions." She winks.

"See you tomorrow!" I muse as she walks out.

When she's gone, I pack up my things and get up from my chair. Every movement I make reminds me of the fake flesh snuggly fit between my folds. I wiggle around a little, adjusting the feel before I walk out the door. The exit isn't too far up ahead. Even as I walk, I'm constantly reminded of how wet I still am.

Fuck. I can't wait to get home.

After a day like this, I really need a big dose of D. *Mr. Big Dick.*

I smirk to myself, thinking about the images and the video he sent me. Maybe that's why he calls himself D. It wouldn't surprise me at all. With equipment like that, who wouldn't boast about it?

Suddenly, my phone buzzes, and I grab it to check what's going on.

It's a message from my telephone company. I have reached the mobile plan limit and have to pay or else this phone will get shut off from the internet for the rest of this pay cycle. Great. Just what I needed.

I sigh and throw it back in my purse.

I would pay it if I could, but money's tight when you live on your own and on a tight budget. Which is why I tried to shoot for a bigger project today … and failed.

Oh well, my time will come. I refuse to give up.

One day, I'm going to write this article, and Ellen will be amazed, and the readership will be amazing, and I'm gonna get a raise, and my life will be fantastic.

I nod at my own dreams. If I work hard enough, they won't remain fantasies but will actually become real life. And I'll stick with that mantra for as long as I can.

Why? Because it keeps me from running back to my parents for things I want to do on my own. Things I know I should be able to do without their help.

My life is my own to rule. And as long as I'm happy with doing what I want, when I want it, that's all I'll ever need.

FOUR

Kat

The first thing I do when I get home is chuck my bag in a corner and sit down with my laptop. It's been a rough day, and I don't want to wait any longer to get online.

Besides, D is probably pissed that I left so abruptly. I wonder if he'll even talk to me. Only one way to find out and it's happening right now.

Thank God, he's actually online. And he didn't block me.

I open the chat and immediately begin to type.

NaughtyKitten: *Sorry. Someone came into my*

office. I had to close the chat.

It takes him a while to type back.

D: You didn't lock the door? Bad kitten.

NaughtyKitten: I'm really sorry about that.

D: What happened to the updates you'd send?

Updates? Crap, that's right. He asked for pictures and stuff. I completely forgot.

NaughtyKitten: Fuck. I forgot. I'm sorry.

D: You didn't do what I asked.

NaughtyKitten: I'm here now. Home. I'll do whatever you want.

D: Is the dildo still inside your pussy?

Everything throbs the moment he mentions it, causing me to giggle.

NaughtyKitten: Yup, and keeping me horny.

D: Good. I like you horny. And wet.

NaughtyKitten: My panties are soaked.

I bring my fingers down between my legs. Yep. Drenched.

D: And now you'd like to come, wouldn't you?

NaughtyKitten: Oh … yes, please.

D: But you left me hanging too. So I'm going to make you wait a little longer too.

Fuck. Is this his idea of punishment? I guess he really does hate it when things don't go according to his plans. Or maybe he just loves tormenting me.

A picture suddenly pops onto my screen. It's his dick, fully erect, with pre-cum dripping down onto his fingers. I lick my lips as my mouth waters.

D: I've been waiting all day for you. Don't make me wait any longer.

NaughtyKitten: I won't.

D: Then make me come ... and maybe I'll let you come too.

NaughtyKitten: What do you want me to do?

D: Anything and everything I ask you to. Do you agree?

NaughtyKitten: Yes.

I don't even have to think about it.

It takes him a while to respond, but then I see a notification in the corner of the screen. He wants to turn on the microphone on the laptop. Not mine. *His.*

I suck in a breath. Then I push the accept button.

"Good girl." His voice sounds buttery smooth. Like delicious whipped cream I want to lather all over my body.

NaughtyKitten: I love your voice.

Jesus, why did I even say that? I sound like a drooling teen.

He chuckles. Dark. Sinfully. The sound of it covers my skin in goose bumps.

"Are you interested in my suggestion?" he asks.

God, I love his voice already. I don't know if I'll ever want to quit knowing he sounds like this.

NaughtyKitten: Fuck yes.

"Turn on the camera. Take the dildo from your pussy ... stick it to the laptop ... and suck it off until we both come."

My eyes widen.

I'm staring at the laptop, hearing his voice repeat the words over and over in my mind. Does he really want me to go on camera? With my face showing? But that's against the chat rules, right?

NaughtyKitten: You sure ask a lot.

"Tell me you're not wet just thinking about it."

He's right. I am.

Soaking wet, actually.

"Put on a mask if you're worried about your identity. Either way, you're doing this for me because you like pleasing me ... and I like seeing you squirm."

He's completely right. I am just as filthy as he describes me.

Admitting that only turns me on. And hearing his voice is the final trigger.

***

DECLAN

Will she or will she not?

I tap my fingers on the keyboard as I wait for her to reply. My request was outrageous and completely out of line. Exactly what I crave ... and precisely what I shouldn't have.

I enjoy pushing boundaries. It gives me a kick.

But maybe this time I went too far.

These girls aren't like anything else.

It's real. Raw. Uncensored.

Not like porn, where you get only a quarter of the story. It's all scripted. All an act.

But this? I'm talking to a real person. Someone with emotions and needs. Someone who can be just as filthy. And it's much more exhilarating than any taped porn could ever be.

When the familiar three dots appear behind her name, I pause. She hasn't closed the chat. That means something.

NaughtyKitten: Okay, I found a mask.

A grin spreads on my lips.

I was waiting for her to say no. To tell me to go fuck myself. To quit the chat and never speak to me again. Yet she did the complete opposite.

Maybe I should've pulled the trigger. Pushed the button and stopped this conversation entirely before it got out of hand. Before I go in too deep and stay too curious to stop.

But I just can't bring myself to actually do it.

I want to find out how far she'll go … How far I'll take it.

And with this vixen, there's no telling how dirty it can get.

NaughtyKitten: Will I see you too?

"Not right now, Kitten," I reply, licking my lips.

I know she wants it badly … but I'm not about to reveal

my identity. Besides, I'm still at the office. I don't have any masks in here, and I'm definitely not going to go look for one either. Not when I'm horny as fuck and have her right where I want her.

No. We're going to do this my way.

"Now, are you going to please me?" I ask.

She begins to type.

NaughtyKitten: Turning on the camera.

When the notification pops up, I accept, and there she is in all her glory. Dark brown hair tucked into a tight ponytail. Thick, luscious lips. Half-naked body with a see-through top on, precisely the way I like it. The bombshell who has a knack for making cocks hard.

And better yet, she's got the camera on her phone switched on, and she's bringing it down between her naked legs. I can see the suction cup on the end of the dildo, and I watch as she pulls it out slowly. Slick wetness covers the length, making my mouth water.

Fuck, what I wouldn't give for a night of eating her out.

But I have to remain in control of my needs, in control of this situation, because it can't ever get out of hand. I could lose my career over this. Maybe that's why I find it so exhilarating. The thrill of getting caught is like a drug I can't get enough of.

She pulls it up toward the laptop screen, following along with the camera, and I lean forward in anticipation of what I'm about to see. My cock is already fully erect as I rub it through my pants. The strain is getting to be too much, so I unzip my pants and pull it out, jerking off to the image of her sticking the dildo to the screen.

"Suck it off, Kitten …" I say.

NaughtyKitten: One sec. I'll switch cameras. You'll see more.

The camera turns off for just a second, only to turn back on from a different view; her laptop. And I can see her up close.

I moan into the microphone. Her lips are wrapped around the tip of the cock, and from my view, it looks as though she's sucking me off instead.

Fuck.

"Show me how you'd suck me off," I murmur.

She giggles and types a few haphazard words while her eyes remain focused on the camera.

NaughtyKitten: Can't type. But I love your moan.

"Oh, do you now?" I say, grinning. "If you're a good girl, I'll let you listen to me come."

NaughtyKitten: Fuck yes.

She starts sucking on the dildo even harder, keeping her eyes on the camera. She probably knows I like to watch.

"Can you taste your pussy?" I ask. "If I were there, I'd lick you until you came."

My words only make her take it deeper, to the point where I can see she's having trouble. But she's not giving up despite nearly gagging. My type of girl. Never afraid of a challenge.

"Take it all the way," I say. "If you dare."

And she does exactly that … because I told her to.

I can't stop touching myself, lathering my pre-cum all over myself. Can't stop picturing her doing it to me with that filthy tongue of hers. Can't stop thinking about what it would be like to ram my cock down her throat and come while she fingers herself.

"Make yourself come while sucking it off," I growl, vigorously jerking off.

I want to see the look on her face as she falls apart with the dildo in her mouth as deep as possible.

"Think of me when you do it. Picture it's my dick forcing you to swallow."

And fuck, does she take it all the way to the base … until she coughs and heaves.

Her fingers are flicking back and forth between her legs. I can only see her hands, but it's enough to know she's thoroughly enjoying herself.

The saliva that covers the dildo drips from her mouth onto the keyboard, but she doesn't care. This filthy kitten keeps on sucking until I'm sated, and fuck me … do I want to come watching her do this.

Her eyes roll into the back of her head, and then she shudders. Goose bumps scatter on her skin, her nipples taut. There it is. That beautiful moment of destruction that leaves her utterly breathless.

And me … With a deafening roar, I come apart, shooting my seed against my own chest.

Fuck.

As I breathe like a beast undone, I stare at the screen in front of me. At the dirty kitten still licking the fake dick like it's a real one ... like it's me.

She's too sinful. Too compliant. Like a forbidden fruit I can't ever have ...

My first reaction is to close the laptop.

Before I know it, the conversation has ended. Just like that, it's done. Over.

No going back. No more. I can't allow myself another taste.

I have to call it quits tonight, so I don't get attached.

Because damn ... those lips and those sexy eyes hiding behind that mask took something from me ... a piece of my self-control I'm not willing to relinquish.

FIVE

Kat

As I lie in bed, I still can't stop thinking about D.

Jesus, what a man.

And that voice. It sounded like velvet. Like the frosting on a cupcake. Sweet and delicious but oh so bad for you.

I wanted to listen to it some more … and more. The entire day if I could.

But he cut me off so quickly.

It didn't even register for a couple of minutes until I'd already taken the dildo off the laptop and stared at a disconnected message. He really closed the chat without saying a word.

I wonder if I pissed him off somehow.

Though I don't know how that would've been possible, considering I did exactly what he asked.

Maybe that's just it. I gave him what he wanted, so what if he's had enough?

Was this all? Does it mean I'll never talk to him again?

I roll around on my pillow and close my eyes. Even though I always knew the end was coming, I never really thought about it. Or at least, I never want to when it comes to men like him.

Because you don't often find these men. The ones who easily make you go down on your knees and beg.

Still, I know he has every right to stop it at any moment. As I have every right, too, even if I don't want to. Not yet, anyway. I mean, I'm enjoying his requests thoroughly.

I can't help but wonder if this could ever be anything more … more than just *this*.

If I could ever meet him. Just once.

I sigh.

If only.

***

Ten hours later, I'm busy finishing up the article about the school lunches. It's part interview and part research conducted. That part was supposed to be Crystal's job, but I had to take it over partly. She was stuck at the doctor's office for whatever reason, and this article needed to be finished, so she begged me to help her.

Of course, I agreed because co-workers help each other out. It's what we're supposed to do. And I expect she'd help me out too if I ever needed it. Besides, we're both striving for the same thing. A better spot in the magazine means more work, but it also equals more pay.

Except, the longer I'm typing, the more I'm finding myself distracted.

Mostly because I want to think about things other than work … specifically D.

Every time I'm alone, I think of him. I can't get him out of my head, and it's getting annoying.

So I settle this distraction with just one look.

One peek at the images he sent me. I saved them on my phone too because I'm kind of addicted to the sight of his dick. Just looking at it gets my mouth watering again.

But the longer I gaze at it, the more I'm starting to notice something peculiar in the corner of one of the pictures. It looks like a window of an office and behind it is another building with a flag blowing in the wind. The snapshot caught the logo.

And it's familiar.

A well-known hotel here in town … Davies. It's on the square only a few blocks away from my office. And across from Davies are several other hotels.

My brows draw together.

Does this mean he works there?

A small part of me suddenly feels the urge to go out and investigate, but my morals immediately stop me from doing so. It would be ridiculous. I have no proof except for this picture. What if he just stayed there for a night? Besides, I'm not a stalker. I'm a decent human being.

Most likely, anyway. I try my best.

I swallow away the lump in my throat and tuck my phone into my purse, determined to stay focused.

I have to stop thinking about this. Stop thinking about if he really works there. Stop thinking about *him*.

But the longer I'm trying to ignore that nagging in my head, the more obnoxious it becomes. So bad that I eventually give in to temptation and go online via the laptop. He's not online. I'm not sure if I'm lucky or not. I should be working, but instead, I'm stalking this man I barely know.

Still, I can't stop myself from opening the chat box and leaving a message. I admit, I'm guilty of giving into my desires too easily, but this man … he's making it so hard to let go.

I don't know what it is about him that makes me this needy, but I want to know more about him. I want to know what he does, how he lives, what he likes, what he hates. I want to know what kind of body goes with that delicious voice.

I want to meet him. And I want him to fuck me into oblivion.

NaughtyKitten: Want to meet up at Hotel Davies?

No strings. One night.

Before I know it, I've already sent the message.

One click of the finger is all it takes to make sweat drip down my back.

I can't undo the message. Can't go back in time.

If he sees this, he might not ever speak to me again.

Fuck.

***

DECLAN

Another meeting. Another day.

I'm fiddling with my thumbs underneath the table, trying not to look bored, but I seriously have other things to do than report to the boss. I'd much rather work on the final preparations for the next event. But I guess he has to know where we're at.

"How far are you with the preparations?" my boss asks.

"I've got all the girls I need. Props are on their way. The room is being prepped."

"Good. Anything else I should be worried about?"

I check my notes. "Only a small issue with the sponsors."

"Can it be solved?" he asks.

"They're complaining because we're not using their

props, but if push comes to shove, I can always find a new sponsor. There are plenty lined up."

Suddenly, my phone buzzes, and I quickly take it from my pocket to check the messages.

I only meant to look for a second, but my eyes stay glued to the screen as I read the words over and over again.

She's asking to meet up … at the hotel right beside where I work.

A million things run through my mind right now.

Why did she pick that location? Does she know where I am?

And should I say yes?

"Okay. And the clients? Are they excited?"

I gaze up, but I'm momentarily dumbstruck, unable to form actual words.

Luckily, Sarah takes over for me. "From what I heard, very. We're fully booked for this event."

"Thanks," I mouth at her, and she winks in response.

I clear my throat. "We're pretty much ready to go. Just a few final preparations and that's it."

"Okay, great." My boss nods and then directs his attention toward Hans, who's in charge of staff. "Hans, see to it that Declan gets the additional part-timers where needed. Make sure to vet them properly. No press allowed."

"Right," Hans confirms as he glares at me. "I've got it covered."

"I'm good," I say, licking my lips. "I don't need any help."

Sometimes I do, but that's not the point. I don't want anyone else to do this job because it's mine. I won't ever give the impression I can't handle this job. Ever.

This hotel requires a certain kind of approach only someone as devious as me could provide. If any of them were ever to take over, I'm sure we'd lose customers, and they don't want that.

They like to think they could do what I do, and that's okay. I'll let them think that.

But I won't allow them, even for a second, to try to suggest that someone else could do this job the way I do it. And that I'd ever need help.

Because I'm not just aiming to stay an event coordinator and organizer. I want my boss to see how invested I am in this company ... so when the time comes, he'll see I'm the only reasonable choice for his successor.

All in due time.

For now, I'll stay in line and do whatever I can to make him happy. Including sitting through these arduous meetings.

"So that's it for today?" the boss asks.

Since no one else has anything to report, he closes his files and gets up from his chair. "Great. I'll speak to you all soon then. If you need anything, don't hesitate to ask. I'll be monitoring the guests during and after the event too."

After all the times we've done this, he's still worried.

I get it. The company means a lot to him. But it does to me too, and I intend to do more than just my best to make this an event our clients will remember. For the rest of their lives, even.

That's how confident I am in providing this service.

If you could call it that.

I smirk to myself and pack up my things as everyone leaves the room.

"Sorry if I stepped out of line there," Sarah suddenly mutters.

I frown. "What—"

"I filled in for you. With the bookings." She tucks a strand of hair behind her ear. "I saw you were distracted, so I figured I'd help you out. But I know you don't like that."

"No, no. It's fine," I say, smiling. "Thank you."

Sarah's about the only person in this room I can fully trust with at least part of my job.

Mostly because I'm pretty sure she'd never, ever want to take over for me.

Especially not the explicit parts.

No, she helps me out with the marketing here and there. Keeping the numbers straight. That's what she's good at. What she does best.

I'm more of a creative person, so I guess you could say we're opposites. In the good sense, of course. We can help each other out where necessary.

"You seem a little distracted lately. Are you okay?" she asks as she clutches her bag tight.

"Yeah," I say. But it's not true.

Ever since I started talking with NaughtyKitten, I've

found it incredibly hard to keep her off my mind during work. And now this … meeting up?

"Just a little tired," I lie, scratching the back of my head. "That's all."

"Okay. Well, you know what I said," she says. "I'm always willing to help if you need it." She adds a wink and then quickly disappears through the door.

I'm alone again, yet I can't relax.

The knot in my stomach grows thicker and thicker.

So instead of lounging back in my chair and fantasizing about possible upcoming events, I get up, grab my stuff, and march out the door.

I need to think about this. About *her*. Seeing NaughtyKitten in the building right next door.

Is it a coincidence that she picked that spot? Do we just happen to live in the same city?

Because I'm quite sure I didn't pick based on location … and neither did she.

And it's as if it's too good to be true. Like I somehow gave myself away …

Did I? No, that's impossible. I never showed my face. Never showed her my location, my job, anything personal. I keep it strictly hidden.

This has to be a stroke of random luck.

At least, that's what I tell myself as I drive down the interstate on the way home.

I keep thinking about her … all the way there. I can't stop wondering about what it would feel like to touch her in the flesh. To breathe her air. To smell her scent and have a taste.

My tongue dips out to wet my lips at the mere thought of claiming her.

The desire has been growing for days now.

Is it so wrong to give in? After all, it's only one night. One single meeting and then it's over. One can't hurt, can it?

It's within my rules, so why shouldn't I? Why should everyone else be allowed to live out their fantasies, but not me?

No. Fuck no. I'm not denying myself this because of fear. Fear is a weakness I despise. Something I don't need.

What I want is her.

Just one night of no-holds-barred sex. That's it.

I grin to myself as I park my car and walk up to my building. Guess I've already decided.

So I take out my cell phone and reply to her message.

D: Tomorrow. Be there at eight. Book under the name D's Kitten. Wear your mask.

When I press send, there's no going back.

I'll make sure I don't regret it.

SIX

Kat

My heart races as I go up the elevator. Soon I'll meet him for the first time.

Touch him ...

Taste him ...

My mouth waters at the thought.

God, I'm such a horny bitch, but I don't wanna stop either. This whole thing is so exciting, I could write a book about it. Or better yet, I could use it as inspiration for that piece I want to do for my boss. But I'll get to that when I can.

First, I need to fuck D. I just hope he wants to fuck me too. Because knowing him ... he wants to play with me just like he does when we're online.

My face is still flushed from having to tell the hotel staff which name I'd booked under.

D's Kitten.

I know it's not some random name just to be able to find each other.

He wants to humiliate me.

To sweat at the thought of people knowing what we're about to do. And to get giddy from the thought about being his for a night.

God, I wonder what he looks like. If he's as handsome as I imagined from those pictures.

If I'll be able to stop after this single night. Because if it's anything like the chats we've had, I'll have to detox hard. Side effects include overeating ice cream and bingeing on Netflix.

Not that I'll be able to forget about him, but still ... that's what we do this for, right? An experience we'll never forget.

That's what I keep in mind as I unlock the door to the room where it'll all go down.

I'm the first to get there, so I turn on the lights and check out the furniture, placing my bag next to the chair in the corner.

I take out the mask I brought and put it on in case he

comes early. Then I wash up in the bathroom, spritzing on extra perfume and applying body lotion. I want him to remember my scent.

The bed is nice and soft, and from bobbing up and down on it, I can tell it won't make too much noise. Good. I don't want the whole hotel to know what played out in here. Hell, I'm not sure I even want to know what's going to happen, but a small part of me is too curious to run. Oh, who am I kidding ... a big part of me is eager to find out.

I don't have to wait long.

Within seconds, the door handle clicks, and I hold my breath in anticipation.

A man in a black suit and a red tie steps in. The door shuts behind him.

My eyes glide over his body, and his glide over mine. His face is also hidden behind a mask.

He's tall, and his hair is thick and dark, just like his voice when he says, "Hello, Kitten ..."

I'm struck with awe at the sound of his voice. It's real. It's him.

That same shiver runs up and down my spine as he approaches me slowly.

In a split second, images of violence flash through my mind. All the possible things that could happen. All the things he could do to me.

We're alone, in a hotel room, and neither of us know each other by name.

He could do anything he wanted.

Take me. Use me. Lock me up.

Kill me.

And no one would ever know it was him.

The perfect setting for the perfect crime.

Yet I'm not afraid of him.

I'm only afraid of my own reaction to what's about to go down.

Meeting him was the only thing I wanted, and now that it's finally happening, I wonder if it'll be enough. If I can satiate my needs without crossing the line.

He comes even closer, but I don't move an inch. I don't know if it's because I'm scared, or if it's because my body feels as if it's made of rocks and ice.

I shudder when he stands across from the bed, leans against the dresser, and casually slides his eyes from the tips of my toes hidden in black heels all the way up to my high ponytail without any shame.

His tongue dips out to wet his lips, and for a second there, I wish he licked mine instead.

He cocks his head. "So this is what you want?"

I nod and part my lips to say something, but nothing springs to mind. Nothing important ... except for the fact I want him to fuck me raw.

Instinctively, my eyes draw to his pants and the package hiding underneath.

I swallow away the lump in my throat at the thought of finally touching him.

"Take off your coat," he says sternly.

It slides off my shoulders with ease, exposing my black, partially see-through lingerie.

"Now part your legs."

I await his next command with a buzzing feeling between my legs as they nudge aside, allowing him a full view.

A hint of a smile twitches his lips, but it disappears as quickly as it came.

"Take off your panties."

My heart beats like a drum as I push down the fabric and let it slip to the floor. He can see every inch of my pussy laid bare for him. And from the slight sparkle in his eyes, I can tell he likes it.

He sits down on the chair in the corner with broad legs and a swagger that tickles all my senses. With his elbow leaning on the armrest, he supports his face with two fingers, gazing at me like a hawk.

"Tell me, are you already wet?" he asks.

God, I could die for that voice.

Kill just to hear it again.

"Yes." My voice is soft, almost inaudible. As if my throat's shutting down because I'm nervous.

But the smirk spreading on his face makes me forget all that.

"Make it wetter. Touch yourself," he says.

I swallow and place my fingers right in the center of my slit, circling slowly, as I anticipate him coming toward me. But the longer I play with myself, the more he sits back and relaxes. He's watching me intently, checking out how I do it, and I wonder if it's because he wants to know how I like it so he can do it himself.

However, his hand draws my attention the moment it moves down.

Unzips his pants.

Pulls out his already hard cock.

My mouth salivates greedily.

He went commando. How appropriate.

"Go on … Show me how much you want this," he muses.

I do what he says, circling around my clit with two fingers to get myself all hot and bothered. I admit, it's hard to resist the pull, but I have to stay here on this bed. This is what he wants. This is what we agreed to when we started talking.

He's in control.

It's the one rule I know I shouldn't break if I want him to fuck me, so I'll do whatever he says.

Is it foolish? Maybe. But I'm enjoying myself enough not to walk away.

Not that I ever could with a dick like that staring right back at me. The exact same one I saw in the pictures and the video … so there's no mistaking now. It's really him, in the flesh, right across from me.

I wish I could taste him.

Fuck.

He's stroking it so nicely. Slowly, but with a tough grip,

as if he wants to do more but is holding back intentionally just to relish the view a little longer.

And I must admit … toying with myself like this right in front of him does make my face warm. As if he's caught me in the act and I'm still doing it because I can't stop. I don't want to stop.

He cocks his head and stares me right in the eyes. I don't notice right away because my eyes are glued to his cock.

"You want this?" he asks, his tongue briefly dipping out again. "Say it."

"I want it," I say.

Ripples of shame flow through me when I hear my own voice say that. It feels sinful. Wrong. But in a fucking good way.

"What?" he says, a devious grin spreading on his lips.

"I want your cock," I say, swallowing as I speak the words.

God, I feel so filthy. But I'm guessing that's exactly what he wants. To humiliate me.

"Show me then. Turn around on the bed."

As strange as his command sounds, I still do it.

"On your knees. Head down. Ass up."

When I'm in position, I'm staring at the blanket. I can't even see him anymore, and I'm not sure if I hate it or if I'm just so fucking thirsty for his cock.

"Spread your legs," he adds.

When I do what he says, my pussy is on full display.

Literally. All he can see is my ass … and all my openings wide.

While my face is smooshed into the bed, I don't even know what he's doing, but I bet I know what he's looking at.

Me. Spread like a fuck doll for him to use.

"Go on then … make yourself come," he says.

For a moment, I'm a dumbfounded. He wants me to play with myself … in this position? How?

"Do you want this or not?" he asks.

"Yes," I reply.

"Come for me then … and maybe I'll give it to you."

I lick my lips and bury my hand between my legs. My head sinks even farther into the fabric as my hand wriggles its way to my pussy. The position is tough and difficult to maintain. Exactly why he chose it.

He's testing my limits, I'm sure of it.

But what about the rest of this meeting? Is all this a test?

If I don't meet his demands, will he walk out on me?

Is this a way for him to see if I'm up for more?

If I'm good enough for his needs?

Questions flood my mind, but I push them aside and focus on the here and now. His gentle moans guide me as I flick my clit, knowing he's watching my every move.

The more I struggle, the more my legs begin to quiver, but I'm not giving up. His moans grow louder, the sound titillating me to the point that I'm getting wetter and wetter. Or maybe it's because I know someone's watching me fuck myself.

Because my fingers are dipping in right now, and I can't help but moan along.

"Yes, Kitten. Be a fucking slut for me."

His dirty words only turn me on even more.

I'm struggling to breathe as I dive deeper and deeper into a state of sexual consciousness. Where nothing else matters but my fingers and the anticipation of his dick thrusting into me.

And as the last of his groans roll off his tongue, I release myself from my lust.

Delicious orgasmic waves fill my body, and I moan out loud to let it out. I don't even give a fuck that he's listening to me coming undone. That I'm probably dripping on the bed right about now.

Suddenly, he grips my ass, his firm hands pulling me out of ecstasy and into the here and now. His tip rests at my entrance, condom and all. I didn't even hear him put it on.

"Spread those lips for me," he murmurs, grasping my ass cheeks and pushing them apart. I can practically feel his gaze on my naked skin.

That's when he pushes in.

Slowly … deeply … all the way to the base.

I suck in a breath and hold it as he sinks in and stays there, like he's making me his. Like he's marking me. Like he wants me to remember how I begged for his cock.

When he pulls out again, I almost want to start begging again.

One second passes when I can breathe, then he thrusts

into me once more, this time with a little bit more fervor. I bury my face in the sheets and bite down, delirious on lust. Each thrust of his cock brings me closer to bliss. And for a moment, I wish I could have this forever.

But I know once he's had his fill—once he walks out this door—it'll be the end of everything we've done together. And that makes me want to hold on, as sad as that sounds.

Because right now, I'm letting a stranger I met online fuck me. Someone I don't even know I can trust. Hell, he could be bad. My life could be in danger right now.

But none of that even matters to me.

All I can think about is him and me.

Together … at this moment … two strangers fucking each other into oblivion.

And when he slams into me with full force, I cry out with passion.

I don't want it to stop.

But as I unleash my moans, so does he. And his cock starts to pulse along with it, releasing its seed deep inside me.

When he pulls out, I wish I could get a redo.

Another try. Another time. A rain check for another fabulous night.

But as I roll onto my side and watch him stagger back, away from me, I realize that's not going to be an option. This was a one-night thing. One time only.

I was the one who asked for it. He agreed.

And asking for anything more wouldn't be right.

So I remain on the bed, breathing slowly as I try to come to terms with what happened. All while he chucks the condom into the bin, zips up again, and walks out the door.

Minutes pass. He's not coming back.

He never said goodbye. Didn't even say a word.

I suppose it's what I should have expected.

After all, he wasn't here for small talk. He was here to fuck.

It's what I wanted. What I asked for. What he agreed to.

I slide off the bed and gather my panties while looking around. The room is back to normal … or maybe it never changed.

My body is still vibrating, and the mask is barely intact. I take it off and look at myself in the mirror in the bathroom. My hair is half undone, and my face is red and puffy.

Apart from that, I don't look any different. Even though I feel completely new.

As if I've made a life-altering decision and took the path of no return.

I gleefully smile to myself.

I never wanna look back.

SEVEN

DECLAN

I sit down at my desk and open my laptop. Another day, another time to work.

My inbox is full of unanswered emails from yesterday. Clients with questions. Co-workers with last-minute changes to the décor or the props. My boss asking about the next event. And maybe a couple from Sarah too.

Nothing unusual.

Which is strange.

Because I feel unusual.

I sigh and sit back in my chair, staring at the laptop. I've been anxious to get back to work ever since I got home last night. Nothing's better to freshen up your memory than focusing on what's important in life.

If you can actually manage to reset your mind.

For some reason, I find that very hard to do. Because right now, she's the only thing I can think about. That girl and that amazing pussy I fucked in that hotel room last night.

It was as sinful as I imagined it to be. Two strangers fucking like there was no tomorrow even if there was.

I'm there now, and it still feels as though I'm floating on a cloud.

Why do I feel this way?

I've never actually had second thoughts about exiting right after getting some booty. But I almost feel guilty for leaving her there.

Why her? Why out of all people?

It doesn't make any sense.

I grasp a pencil and scribble down the rules again.

One: Never expose your real identity.
Two: Don't meet up more than once.
Three: Cut it off before she falls in love.

I stick it in front of me on my laptop to remind myself of what I'm not allowed to do. It's for a good cause, after all. No use in trying to become the boss if I'm hooked on a girl. And I'm not about to jeopardize my career over some silly

…

Fucking …

Kitten.

No. Not anymore.

I lick my lips and try to focus on the emails in front of me, but no matter how many times I try to finish at least one, I keep re-reading the lines. I don't even know what I'm reading or who's asking what. All I can think about is how beautiful she looked with her brown hair swooping down in a high ponytail, accompanied by that smirk. And that she did everything I asked.

It was perfect. Too perfect.

Out of nowhere, the pencil snaps.

For a second, I'm fazed. Then I pick up the pieces from my desk and chuck them in the trash, grumbling.

Goddammit. I have work to do. Instead, I'm wasting time thinking about a random girl I just fucked. But that's just it, isn't it? She isn't some random girl.

She's the first one to get under my skin like that.

And I don't like it one bit.

I open the browser and go to the chat website. When I find her, I immediately block her, then close the chat.

There. It's done. Now I won't be tempted to fuck her anymore. Or do anything else with her, for that matter. I'm not relationship material anyway.

It's for the best.

***

Kat

With an apple pie I bought at the supermarket, because I'm horrible at baking, I walk up to the house and ring the doorbell. Melvin opens the door almost immediately, greeting me with a smile. "Miss Mayer, what a delight. Come in," he says, opening the door farther. "Let me take your coat."

"Thanks, Melvin," I say. "Am I late?"

"Fashionably," he replies with a smile. "But don't worry, I told them your boss was keeping you at work." He winks. It's a total lie because I never called him or my parents, but I love it. He's always protected me; it doesn't matter that I'm not a little kid anymore.

I kiss him on the cheeks, and say, "Missed you."

We exchange smiles, and I go into the dining room where Mom and Dad are already sitting at the table. The moment I come into view, their faces go rigid and cold. *Here it comes.*

"Finally," Mom says.

"Sorry," I say, approaching her to give her a soft kiss on the cheeks. "Work."

I laugh it off as if it's no big deal even though it's not true. But admitting to her that Melvin lied for me would get him into trouble. Not to mention, she'll be twice as pissed off at me for going with it.

I take my seat as Melvin comes in to bring us some water and wine. "Dinner will be ready shortly," he says, pouring it into the glasses before leaving again.

It's awkwardly quiet at the table. Dad's staring at his phone while Mom's fiddling with the cutlery, adjusting them so they're aligned perfectly.

"So how are you?" I ask to break the ice.

She briefly looks up at me, smiles, then says, "Fine, fine."

"Dad?" I mutter, cocking my head to see if I can make him glance up from his phone.

"Yes, yes. Busy." He lets out a small laugh. "You know … work."

I nod, rubbing my lips together.

This is how it usually goes. Dad can't take his eyes off the business, and Mom's aloof as ever. It's as if they're purposely hiding from me, yet at the same time, they want to keep me under their thumb.

Melvin comes in with the dishes, placing them on the table one by one, and then excuses himself after a bon appetite. To this day, I keep having the urge to invite him to sit down, but my parents wouldn't accept it, I'm sure of it. They prefer the distance even though he's been with us— them—for more than twenty years. They'd say his hard work is rewarded with a lucrative salary, but I feel like they could show a little humility every now and then.

Not that it's something I could ever bring up with my parents without causing an argument, which is definitely not something I'm looking to do right now. I'd rather not end every visit with a fight.

"Well," Dad suddenly says, putting his phone down. "Let's eat."

I pick up my fork and knife and gladly cut into the meat, stuffing it into my mouth. God, I love Melvin's steak and beans. It's the perfect combination of salty and sweet.

"So … how's work?" Mom asks, putting extra emphasis on the word "work" as if it's some kind of fake job.

"Great," I reply.

She takes a small bite. "Earning enough?"

Here we go again. "Yes, actually. I'm very happy." I take another bite, trying to enjoy the taste instead.

"Really?" She looks up at me. "But you're still in that small house?"

"Yes," I say, wanting to roll my eyes. "I like small."

"Okay …" Mom takes a breath and bites down on her steak. "So you're not looking to upgrade?"

"Mom, I'm happy with my job."

"They caused you to be late."

"No, that was my fault."

She frowns. "So you forgot?"

"No, Mom. I'm sorry." I sigh. "I sometimes get a bit overenthusiastic. It happens. But I wouldn't want to miss dinner with you guys." I place a hand on her shoulder and smile. "I love you."

"We love you too, honey," Dad says as he stuffs the steak into his mouth.

"Fred." Mom raises her brow at him.

"What?"

"I told you." Now she turns toward me again. "Are you sure you like that job and house? Because there's an opening at Clayton's and—"

"I don't want to be a lawyer, Mom," I interject. I really don't wanna hear this right now.

"Why not? What's wrong with being a lawyer? You'd be helping people and get paid while doing it," Mom says, taking a sip of her wine. "I honestly don't understand why you stick with … that gossipy tabloid."

"It's more than gossip. We write articles about actual local news."

"But you answer the reader's questions too," she says.

"Yes, but I'm also working on getting my own column."

"Okay, but my point is, you can do so much better." She places a hand on my hand. "I want better for you. A better job. A bigger house." She shrugs, smiling. "Maybe even a great boyfriend."

I almost choke on my food. "What?"

"Well, I do know some handsome young men who are still single. They frequently visit the men's club your dad often goes to on the weekend."

Wow. I really did not need that information. At all.

She swirls the wine around in the glass. "So does that mean you're seeing someone?"

I can barely swallow the steak as I think about D and all the things we did. No way would I tell them. *No way.* Their sweet daughter doing all those raunchy things? They'd probably lose their minds. Or have a heart attack.

Besides, D isn't exactly boyfriend material. We only had sex once, and we don't even know each other's real name. I doubt it'll ever be more than that.

"I'm not seeing anyone right now," I answer.

"Well, then why not meet the boys? I know at least one of them has a job as a finance director at a pharmaceutical company. He works hard, and he's looking to settle. Maybe you'll end up liking him."

My eyes widen, and I immediately pull my hand back. "Mom ..."

"What? I'm just saying."

"Meredith," Dad interjects, gazing at her with intent. "Please ..."

She gives him a stern look. "I'm not the enemy here. I'm only trying to help."

"I know, but she needs to be happy on her own terms," Dad says.

I'm glad he's on my side with this one.

"No, that's just you trying to make up for something," she says, leaning back in the chair while putting down her fork and knife. "You don't *want* to get involved."

Now they're staring at each other, and I'm left in the middle, wondering what the hell is going on.

"Mom, I'm not looking for a job ... or a man." I gaze at

Dad now. "And thank you, but I'm fine. I don't need help."

"See?" Dad says, raising his brow at Mom.

Mom dabs her lips with the napkin and tosses it on her plate. "Fine."

I continue eating in silence, trying not to look at either of them because they're seething. I don't know what it is they're mad about, but this usually happens. Mom and Dad disagree a lot. Mostly over me.

"Meredith, please, stop," Dad begs. "Can't we just enjoy dinner, for once?"

"We could, if you'd allow me to help our daughter get a better job and maybe even finally settle down. Instead, our lives revolve around you trying to make it as easy as you can on yourself."

"Mom …" I put down my fork. "What is this about?"

"Nothing," she says, turning her head away. "Obviously, nothing."

I narrow my eyes and gaze at Dad, trying to let it sink in. Dad has always been … busy. It's what he does, what he's best at. During my entire life growing up in their home, I've experienced my mom mostly getting frustrated over me not being where I was supposed to be, not getting the grades I should've had, and going out with boys who weren't good enough in her eyes, but Dad? He was never involved enough to care.

Which begs the question … why?

He's always said he loved me. I believed it, and I still do, but I can't help but think Mom and Dad are keeping a secret just for the sake of me … and it's slowly ripping them apart.

"Please …" I say. "Tell me what's going on."

"Nothing," Dad reiterates. "Your mom and I just don't always agree on things that involve you."

"Why?"

His lips part but nothing comes out except a sigh. "Let's just all enjoy our meals, okay?"

"No." I lean back in my chair. "I want to know what this is about. Why Mom always keeps hammering on about me getting a better job while you try your best to avoid the subject."

Not just that, but he's avoiding looking at me too.

"I want you to be happy," he says.

"I am," I say. "I think."

"See?" Mom sputters, so I throw her a glance.

"The point is, she doesn't want you to hook her up," Dad says while glaring at Mom.

"I wouldn't need to if you'd just been—"

"Meredith," Dad interrupts. His face has gone rigid. "Don't. Not now. Please."

She gives him the look. *That* look. The one that speaks volumes, but I never know what it means.

"Never mind," I say, scooting back my chair. "I see this was a mistake."

"What? Honey, no." Mom tries to grab my hand. "Please, come sit with us."

"We're just trying to do our best," Dad says.

"No, can you both just be honest for once?" I ask,

grabbing my purse.

Neither of them speak. All they do is silently stare at their plates.

I wish I could say that I knew my parents. That I had a strong bond with them, and that they understood me. That they gave me everything I needed, all the love in the world. But all I know is strict rules, reprimands, and silence.

That's all they could ever do.

No explanations. No answers. Nothing.

Just as always, I'm left with disappointment.

I shake my head as tears well up in my eyes. "I have to go."

"Honey? Wait!" Mom says, clenching the table.

But I've already marched out the dining room.

Behind me, I can hear them argue about me. I don't listen anymore. I close my mind like I always did when I was living here with them.

And without saying goodbye to either of them, I leave the house.

Melvin chases after me, though. "Miss Mayer, please …"

I stop in my tracks and wait, letting out a breath. He should go inside. Give up. It's too late to mend this. Too late to fix what was broken long ago.

"Your parents mean well. They only want the best for you."

"It's hard to believe that when they're never interested in what I do or what I like. All they want to do is to push me in a direction I don't want to go."

"They're trying to protect you," he says, clearing his throat. "They always have."

Against what? The world? Each other?

At this point, I don't think I even wanna know.

"Right," I scoff. "Because I'm their only child."

"Because they love you," he says.

My eyes turn toward the pavement as I say, "Thanks for the food, Mel. It was delicious."

"You're welcome."

"Tell my parents I'm sorry," I add, before I continue walking.

I can't face him. Or them.

Not when I feel like this. Like I'm missing something without knowing what it is.

So I continue my stride until the house disappears from my view and out of my mind.

EIGHT

Kat

Work was a whirlwind of deadlines and meetings. Crystal was sick today, so I had to take over some of her tasks too.

By the time I finally get home, I'm left wondering if I even got anything done at all. After I throw my keys on the kitchen counter, I fix some nachos and dip to eat along with drinking some hard-earned wine while I settle behind my laptop. I need some downtime. Some fun. Something to take the edge off things.

So I open the browser and go to the familiar website, searching the chat for D. But he's not online. He wasn't online the evening I came home from my parents either. In fact, I haven't seen him online in days.

Is something going on in his life? Or is it something else?

I tap my fingers on the keyboard. What if he's done playing? What if he's done with me?

I'd hate for that to happen, but at the same time, I'd understand. After all, there comes a point when you just get too attached to a person. Something we should avoid at all costs when it comes to having sex with strangers we've met online.

Still … I can't help but wonder if he blocked me. Maybe he did. After all, I said it was a one-time meeting only. Sex in a hotel bedroom without ever seeing or hearing from each other again.

I gave him the choice. He made the decision. Yet … when I think about it, I'm not at all happy with the outcome. For some reason, I wanted more. More of what we had. More dirt. More play. More … of him.

He was so in tune with what I needed. What we both needed. It felt … special. Like something that shouldn't be waved aside and dumped, ready for the next anonymous fuck.

What if this is it? The end?

I take a large sip of my wine.

Fuck no.

I can't let it end here. Not when we were both just starting to enjoy it. And I could tell he definitely was.

I open the folder where I keep all my naughty pics and find his. When I open one of them, I keep staring at the window behind him, and at Hotel Davies, realizing I could pinpoint his exact location with this.

Whether he works there or stays there often, what's the chance he might be there again? And if he will be there at some point in time, could I possibly see him? Is it worth the risk?

Maybe not … but what's the worst that can happen? He might rat me out to the website and get me banned from there. Worst-case scenario, he thinks I'm a stalker, and things get ugly.

Best-case scenario? We fuck again … and again … and again.

A devious grin spreads on my lips. Nothing but my conscience is stopping me from going there, and right now, my conscience is on the losing end. Because the devil in me is winning by a long shot.

***

I'm right in front of the building. It's another hotel, one I don't recognize. Maybe I never really paid attention to this part of town. Or maybe I'm oblivious. And completely out of my mind.

My feet are already walking toward the doors before my

mind decides. I can't stop myself from going inside and marveling at the beautiful marble on the floors and walls, the vibrant colors of the big flower pots scattered across the hall, and the thick palm trees in every corner. The whole thing looks expensive as fuck. A place where I normally wouldn't even dream of booking a room.

People are walking around; mostly men donning suits with young girls on their arms, but a lot of staff too. It's very busy, like there's an event happening soon.

My eyes are instinctively drawn toward the large staircase in the back and the red velvety carpet that lies on top, welcoming guests. I wonder if D is up there. It sure looks magnificent.

Hotel O ... I wish I knew it existed. I would've come here sooner and tried to haggle off the price of a room.

They must be expensive. Far beyond my budget.

And D ... works here?

All kinds of questions run through my mind, but I'm distracted by a man clearing his throat to my right. The bellhop.

"Can I help you, ma'am?"

With parted lips, I stare at him, blinking a couple of times before I make my way over to his desk. "Uh ... yes." My face flushes because I feel caught. Like I'm not supposed to be here. "I'm looking for, uh ..."

Shit. I forgot, I don't even know his real name. What am I supposed to tell this man?

What the hell are you doing, Kat?

"Can I speak to the manager, please?" I say, making it up on the spot.

The man frowns, narrows his eyes, and stares at me for a few seconds. Sweat drops form on the back of my neck as I try not to panic. Please, just go and get him so I can run and pretend I never did this.

"We have several, ma'am. Which one are you referring to, or does it not matter?"

"Oh, uh … someone whose name starts with a D?" I say it like it's a question, but I'm just fishing for information now. I'm hoping D is part of his real name. If not, this may be the end of the line.

"May I ask what the reason is?" the man says.

Well, fuck. I don't know.

"My … uh …" I mumble. "No, in fact, that's for his ears to hear only," I say resolutely. "Now please, just get him. I have to speak with *him*." I don't even know why I'm pretending to be classy when I'm not, but if I can convince him I'm a disgruntled guest, he might step away for a moment so I can finally go.

However, as he turns around to pick up the phone on the desk next to him, a man walks past me wearing a familiar scent. It's the same cologne I smelled when I was in the hotel room … with D.

My head instinctively turns to take it in.

Thick, dark hair and a tight black suit.

It's him all right, and he's walking toward the stairs.

I gotta go after him.

Without thinking, I follow, and the bellhop yells at me, "Ma'am, where are you going?"

"I'll talk to the manager later," I say. "It can wait."

"Ma'am, please, can you wait?" he asks, but I'm long lost to the handsome stranger going up the stairs while I'm fighting my way through what feels like a crowd of people. He's right there, only a few steps away. If I could reach out, if I could only—

Suddenly, someone jerks my arm.

It's the bellhop.

Fuck.

"Ma'am ... do you have your card?" He sounds a lot stricter now.

I frown, confused. My head is spinning. "My what?"

He sighs. "Are you a guest at this hotel?"

I look up at the stairs, but I've lost sight of him. "Um ..."

"Come with me, please," he says, tugging my arm to pull me back down the stairs.

But I don't want to go. I was almost there. I almost had him. I could almost touch him.

And now he's gone again. Goddammit.

The bellhop tugs me along with him, forcing me back to the desk, where I know my search will end. I don't know why it's so important for them to keep me here, and why I'm not allowed to go up without some kind of card, but whatever.

At this rate, I'll be thrown out of the hotel if I resist, so I don't. Instead, I use my puppy dog eyes to persuade him to let me go anyway.

"Please, I need to speak to that man …" I say, trying to see if D's still there, but he's already gone.

"Who are you talking about?" the bellhop asks. "Can you show me your card, please?"

"The man in the suit with the dark hair," I say, totally ignoring his request. "He just went up the stairs."

The bellhop cocks his head, and says, "Wait … you're one of the girls!"

I frown, staring. "Wha—"

"We were expecting a replacement. Finally. I was starting to worry," he interrupts, grabbing a pencil and writing down something on a piece of paper. "You'll need to go to his office on the second floor."

He rips the paper off the stack and hands it to me. I stare at it, flabbergasted, unsure of what to do.

"Go on then. He's waiting for you," he says, pushing me in the direction of the stairs again.

I can't even protest. By the time I look up from staring at the paper, the bellhop is already talking to another guest.

The reason I'm so dumbstruck is because of the name written on the card.

Declan Porter. D. It has to be him.

A smug smile spreads on my lips.

I could turn around and tell the bellhop I'm not the girl he's looking for. Or I could press on and finally see D again.

My feet have already made the decision as I move up the

stairs to the second floor. My heart flutters in my chest as I approach the room number written on the paper. Thirty-five. All the way in the back of the hallway near a bunch of other offices.

I've never seen a hotel where the offices are on a lower floor, but maybe they do things differently here. I can't complain as long as I get to see him again.

I know he probably blocked me, but I want to know why. Because I'm damn sure he was enjoying himself just as much as I was. I need to know if a possibility for something more exists. *Something* ... whatever it is. I have to find out.

But as I knock on the door, sweat begins to roll down my back.

Anticipation is killing me as I await a response.

However, it never comes.

Frowning, I slowly push the door handle until it clicks, and the door opens. It's only a small peek to see if he's there.

My head tilts inside the room. "Hello?"

Like a curious butterfly, I wiggle into the room and look around.

Should I leave or wait for him?

A few seconds pass, and my eyes glide over the room. There's a drawing board filled with notes in the back along with a desk and a chair. To the side is a small bookcase with a bunch of books, and on the wall are several ... titillating paintings.

Declan is nowhere to be found. I should definitely not

be here right now.

Still, I can't help look around. Just a simple glance won't hurt, right?

My eyes immediately connect with the window on the other side of the desk. I step closer and gaze at the view outside. Across the street, the flag of Hotel Davies is blowing in the wind.

If I wasn't sure before, I am now … This is the place.

And the laptop resting on the desk has to be the one where he typed out all of those filthy messages to me.

I can't help but let my fingers glide along the desk and the leather chair. I pull it back and sit down, bouncing up and down on the soft cushion. It feels so luxurious. Definitely an office for a senior manager. Or something more.

I gaze at the laptop and touch the keypads with my fingertips, imagining him typing dirty words. I can see it in my mind … Him sitting here with his fly undone and his hand in his trousers while he bites his lip.

And me, on the other end of the connection, eagerly awaiting his next command.

God, what I wouldn't give for another round.

Suddenly, the door opens.

I scramble to get up from the seat, almost tumbling over on my feet.

A suited man with thick, dark hair, and those same full lips steps in. *Declan.*

NINE

DECLAN

When I returned from a talk with Sarah about the event, and how one of the girls had given us a notice that she was going to cancel the contract, I was expecting to have my office to myself so I could figure out a plan for the missing girl.

Instead, one of them is sitting in my chair right this very moment.

I never requested for anyone to come up. Why is she here?

When she spots me, she immediately jumps up from my seat and bumbles about the room, trying not to make a fool out of herself … even though she is. I cock my head as I watch her collect herself, wondering what in the ever-living shit is going on.

"Um … hi," she says, her voice giggly and a little agitated, but cute.

"Hello," I say, licking my lips.

"Sorry, I was just …" She doesn't seem at all certain of what she's saying, and I can't help but wonder if she's trying to make something up on the spot or if she's momentarily fazed.

"The bellhop sent me up," she says, smiling awkwardly.

I frown. The bellhop? Wait … could she be a replacement? Sarah said she'd already contacted one of the agencies with a last-minute request, but I didn't think they'd come up with a new girl this quickly. Especially not considering the amount of … discretion we require.

She stands near my bookshelf, still smiling, as if she's waiting for me to do something. So I stroll to my desk and sit down on the still warm seat. My fingers glide along the laptop, which she clearly touched, judging by the single strand of brown hair resting on the keys.

"So … you're the replacement girl, I suppose?" I muse.

"Replacement? Um, yes," she says, making me narrow my eyes.

She seems rather unsure of her answer. Maybe she wasn't briefed properly on her tasks. Or maybe the bellhop sent up the wrong girl. Only one way to find out.

"Okay then." Biting my lip, I grab the form and scoot it

toward the front of the desk along with a pen. "Read this and sign it, please."

She approaches the desk, hesitantly sitting down. She picks up the pen and glares at the document, but she can't help but throw glances at me every now and then. I wonder why. I don't think I've ever had a girl in my office who was this nervous about the job. Then again, she did show up rather unexpectedly, and it's thrown me off balance too. She looks rather familiar, but I can't put my finger on exactly why that is.

All I know is that she's hovering over first name without actually writing anything down.

"Is there a problem?"

Pausing, she looks up and parts her lips, but no words come out of her mouth. For a brief second, she sucks on the bottom of her lip, then continues filling out the rest of the form, skipping the name part.

I tap my fingers on the desk and mumble, "You know … you can enter a fake name if you're unsure of things. For now."

She looks up at me again with those questioning eyes that just push all my buttons. What is it about this girl that makes me want to adjust my collar? No idea, but I do it anyway.

It takes her ages to pen everything down. She's taking her sweet ass time as if she's stalling or something, and I don't like it one bit. When everything is finally done, the only thing missing is her signature.

"Here," I say, placing my finger on the lines.

"Before I sign …" she mutters. "Could you tell me what it is that you do?"

I frown and snort, but my amusement quickly dissipates when I see she's serious. Has her agency not informed her? What is she doing here then?

"Don't tell me you don't know," I say. "Why else would you come here?"

"Um …" She swallows, and her face is turning as red as a beet.

I snatch the paper and tuck it in my drawer before she does something she'll regret. But her eyes … damn, those big eyes immediately tug at me, forcing me to explain.

"I can't let you sign this if you aren't a hundred percent sure about it."

"Explain to me again what this job is about."

I'm getting more and more suspicious of this girl. Something doesn't add up.

"I don't have time for explanations, sorry." I clear my throat and get up from my chair, but so does she.

She places her hands on the desk and says, "I'm not here for you to just brush me off."

I raise a brow. "Excuse me?" Is she for real?

"Sorry, I just …" She sighs. "I'm excited about this … opportunity."

"Right …" I say, still not believing this whole charade.

So … she wants this, huh? Let's see how far she thinks she'll go then because I don't think she has any clue whatsoever. Smirking, I sit down on my chair again and casually lean back as I say, "Okay then … strip."

She stares at me and her brows draw together, like the words are still registering. "What?"

"Didn't hear me?" I reply. "Strip."

She sucks in a breath and takes a step back away from the desk. This is the point where I expect her to turn around and run. That or scream expletives at my face before throwing in the towel.

Except she doesn't.

Her bag drops to the floor. The buttons on her shirt slowly come undone.

I watch in silence, mesmerized by her sheer courage. Either she's really a stand-in who forgot what she came here to do, or she's completely insane. Either way, I like where this is going.

My attention is piqued the moment she reveals her strapless black bra and drops the shirt to the floor. She never takes her eyes off me while doing it, as if she's tempting me to come and do the rest myself.

But I'm not that easily persuaded. Especially not while at work.

This is what I do … and I like my job too much to spoil the fun.

I lick my top lip as her finger slides down her chest toward the zipper at the back of her black skirt, which she carefully peels down until that too drops to the floor. What's left is nothing short of beauty wrapped in sin.

And fuck me … do I want to give it a lick.

But that's not what she's here for, and she knows that.

This is a test. And right now, she's passing with flying colors.

Her hands move up along her back and clip off the bra.

When that too tumbles to the floor, my eyes focus on her nipples that tighten as I stare. Her face isn't red anymore like before. She looks confident and completely at ease. Like she's not at all afraid of what I'm going to say … as if she already knows I like what I see.

Not soon after, her panties follow, and I'm finding myself getting a hard-on just watching her stand still in the middle of my office, completely naked and ready to bend to my will.

But this girl isn't here for me; she's here for my clients.

At least … that's what she wants me to think. But I'm still not convinced.

"Turn," I say, twirling my finger in the air.

Her hips sway as she spins on her heels, her thick ass pushing all the right buttons. She'd be a great performer. Definitely.

But there is something about her. Something I can't let go.

Defiance. It seeps through everything she does. The way she walks, how she struts, and the way she looks at me with that intent gaze as if she's waiting for my reaction and it never comes.

Too tough to say no to … but I'm going to have to

make the call based on what I know my clients need right now. And this isn't it.

"Pass," I say.

She stays put, the look on her face rapidly changing from confusion to annoyance. "What?"

"It's a no from me," I say. "Put your clothes back on."

She parts her lips, but again, no words flow. Then she slams it shut again and silently picks up her things. No matter how many times I try to avert my eyes back to my laptop so I can continue working, I keep glancing at her as she puts her clothes back on. For some reason, I'm agitated, but I have no clue why. The whole room is oozing with an uncomfortable silence, and I don't like it one bit.

As she walks toward the door, I get up. Something compels me to say, "Wait."

What that something is eludes me, but I can't allow her to leave.

She stops in her tracks, still facing away from me, as if my voice was the only thing that made her stay.

I step away from my desk and approach her, narrowing my eyes to get a good look. There's something about her ... about her body, her voice, her eyes ... and I need to know ...

"Put your hair up," I command.

Her hand wraps around her brown hair and tugs it up into a ponytail.

I don't even need to see her face to know ...

It's *her*.

I place a hand on her shoulder and lean in. A grin spreads across my lips as a rumbling noise leaves my throat. "I know it's you … Kitten …"

TEN

Kat

Kitten.

The moment he says that, I suck in a breath.

How does he know?

I never said a word. Didn't mention our conversations, the chat, my name. Anything.

Yet he realized it's me.

Shit.

I didn't mean to lie to his face. I just didn't know how to tell him that it was me. Like, who does that? I know what I

98

did was wrong, and I feel so embarrassed right now. Fuck.

I try to turn around to face him, but he pushes me against the door and places a hand beside my head, trapping me in his arms. He's so close; I can feel his breath on my skin.

"You thought I wouldn't notice?" he asks, and I hear him sniff. "I can smell your perfume …"

My whole body erupts in goose bumps as he inhales.

I know it was wrong. I know. I just … couldn't fucking stop myself. God, I should've left when I still had the chance.

"I didn't mean to—" I mumble.

"Lie," he interrupts. "You had every intention to make me believe your little charade, whatever it is you were doing to get close. But it was too obvious when you didn't even know what you were doing."

"I'm sorry," I mutter, shaking my head, wishing I could take back what I just did.

Why did I even go along with his questionnaire? I should've just said it was me and stopped the whole thing. But I didn't because I didn't even know how without sounding like an idiot.

"Don't say that. We both know you aren't sorry you did it. You're just sorry you got caught," he says, laughing softly. "But I don't mind."

I gasp as he places a hand on my shoulder and spins me around on my feet, forcing me to look at him. Making me face the man who could make me fall to my knees and beg.

Without the mask, he's even more handsome than I could've imagined.

"How did you find me?" he asks.

"The window," I say in a single breath. "I saw it in the picture." His voice makes me do things. Makes me ... compliant. Makes me admit everything.

He turns his head and gazes at it before looking at me again. "Ahh ... the flag."

I nod, trying to hide my embarrassment behind my hair, but it's no use. I know he can see it ... and he's grinning too.

"You shouldn't have," he says. "I never said you could."

"I know. I just couldn't ..." I lower my head, ashamed of my actions.

I know it's stupid. Silly. Childish.

"You knew it was wrong, but you did it anyway." With the tip of his finger, he lifts my chin. "Without my permission."

"I'm sorry. I'm normally never like this."

He doesn't respond; he just keeps staring me down.

Fuck. I don't want him to be mad at me, but I know I royally screwed up. I need to make this right. "I'll do whatever you want me to do."

His lips twitch, and he narrows his eyes. "No ... you won't."

"You know why I'm here," I say, trying my best.

"This goes against all the rules," he scoffs.

"I don't care," I say. I just don't want this to end.

100

"Watch it." He raises a finger, placing it against my lips. "You don't want to go down that road."

I narrow my eyes. "Is that a threat?"

I wonder what he means by that.

"Maybe." His head tilts slightly. "Would it stop you from trying?"

I raise a brow, a smile spreading on my lips. "Maybe … or maybe not. Depends on what's going to happen."

Yep. I just couldn't stop my mind from going there.

He sighs and shakes his head, rubbing his forehead with his thumb and index finger. "This was a big mistake, Kitten."

"But you knew it was me. That has to mean something," I say, leaning forward and placing my hand on his chest. He recognized me. That means he kept an image of me in his mind. "Do you still think of me? Of that night?"

He makes a *tsk* sound but doesn't say another word. It's almost as if he's trying to deflect whatever it is that makes him feel this way.

I inch closer, but he shoves me back against the door and says, "You don't know what you've done. How dangerous this is."

"Why?" I ask, my tongue dipping out to wet my lips, which he obviously sees because he's following my every move. "Are you scared you're going to want me again?"

The electricity between us is undeniable. The sparks literally fly through the air. Why won't he acknowledge that? What is he so afraid of?

"I'm not scared of anything," he says through gritted teeth, but he's still holding me, still clenching, refusing to let go. In fact, his face is closer to me than it ever was. Almost close enough ... to kiss.

I know he wants to. I can see it in the way his lips part when mine do, how his eyes keep zooming in on every inch of my skin as though he wants to lick it.

"Remember how much fun we had?" I murmur, teasing him with a hum. The same noise I make when I come. Hard.

"Oh ... I remember all right," he says, his voice strenuous. As if he's trying his best to maintain his composure.

I lean in, pressing my body against his. "I'm yours if you want ... now ... whenever ... in whatever way you want," I whisper into his ear.

A few seconds pass, and his whole body tenses. Even between his legs.

"Leave."

I lean back. "You don't mean that, right?"

Even though his voice is calm and collected, the cold-hearted look on his face is too sharp, even for him. "Don't make me say it again," he sneers. "Before I do something we'll both regret."

"Do it then," I reply. I'm not afraid of him. "I dare you."

Suddenly, he grabs both my arms and pins me against the door so hard it almost hurts. Almost. But I like the pain.

I like when he gives me everything I shouldn't want. Everything I shouldn't crave. Maybe it's like that for him too.

"You don't know what you're asking. *Who* you're asking."

"Then tell me … Who are you?" I ask, not backing down. "Someone who makes girls strip in his office? A dirty hotel manager? Is that it?"

He snorts. "You've only just scratched the surface. And that's as far as it'll go."

"Why?" I'm genuinely interested. "I won't judge you. I actually liked where it was going."

"I could tell," he says, gloating. "But you don't know what you really want, or you wouldn't be here."

Really? "I know what I want. I want you to fuck me."

"No," he says, and suddenly he twists me around again, smashing me against the door until my face is flat against the wood and my ass presses against his dick.

He's fully hard.

I've never wanted anything more badly than this.

"This?" he murmurs. He grabs my ass, squeezing hard. "You think you want this?"

"Fuck … yes," I moan when he rubs me.

But then he smacks it hard and covers my mouth with his hand before I can squeal.

He pushes my skirt up and rips down my panties, shoving his fingers into my pussy without asking, without even thinking twice. I can feel him, everywhere, invading me, taking me, owning me.

My breathing is rapid, but so is his. His cock pokes my skin as I gasp for air, for a quick break, which he doesn't grant. He's merciless. Quick and completely uncivilized.

I'm not in control anymore. He is.

Panic bubbles up to the surface. Invades my very thoughts until my skin turns red and my eyes grow big.

And then suddenly, his fingers pull out again. Just like that. Disappearing as though it never happened.

"You're not ready for this," he mutters. A tear escapes my eye, and he swipes it across my cheek with his thumb. "I don't do dating. I don't do repeat fucks."

He releases me from his grasp, but I'm anything but stable. Swaying against the door, collecting my breath and my panties, I realize what just happened. What he just did. What I asked him to do.

I told him to do whatever he wanted, whenever, wherever. But I wasn't prepared for the outcome.

It's exactly what he wanted to prove to me.

That I'm not willing to throw myself into this. Into him. Because I'm afraid of what might happen. Just like he is.

I shake my head, shoving down my skirt to be presentable again. But nothing I do will take away the fact that I feel utterly humiliated … the exact thing that makes me want him so fucking badly.

He's played me.

"You hate me now," he says as I glance at him over my shoulder. "Good. Maybe you'll reconsider coming here again."

I make a face. "That was cruel."

"It was a lesson you needed to learn."

"I didn't ask you to teach me," I say.

"And I never asked you to come here, so now we're even."

Bitterness overcomes me. "Fuck you."

I open the door and walk out, slamming it shut behind me before he can say another word. I don't need this. I don't need him. And I definitely don't need the fucking wetness pooling between my legs right now.

Goddamn him and his fingers.

ELEVEN

Kat

The first thing I do when I get home is crack open a bottle of wine and chug it down. No glass. No nothing.

Then I grab my cell phone and call Flynn. I need a time-out, and I know he can give it to me just the way I need it.

"Hey, Flynn," I mumble when I hear his voice. "Got time?"

"Hey, Kat," he says. "What's up?"

I sink into my couch. "Nothing much. Wanna go out?"

He hums. "What, now? Don't you have to work

tomorrow?"

"Right now, I really don't care," I say, taking another sip of the wine.

"You're drinking alone again?" he says, but I don't like the tone of his voice. "Kat …"

"Who cares? I'm an adult. I can do whatever the fuck I want."

"We had a deal, though. We'd drink together or not at all."

"Exactly! So are you coming with me or not?" I ask, swaying the bottle.

He sighs out loud. "Where do you wanna go?"

"Downtown. To that raunchy-ass club at the end of that street … What's the name again?"

"The Factory," he says.

"Yeah, that one." I take another big gulp. "I need some distraction tonight."

"Bad day?" he asks.

"Don't ask," I reply. "Just tell me where I can pick you up."

"I'm just getting off work. I'll be home in like ten minutes."

"Perfect. I'll be there."

"As long as you let me drive," he says. "And don't you come here with your car or I'm taking your keys and you won't get them back for a week. Got it?"

God, I love this man, but sometimes, he needs to let me do my thing.

"Yeah, yeah," I reply. "I know how to take care of myself."

"Course you do. See you in a few."

"Bye, bitch," I say, snorting as I hang up the phone.

I take another sip and then put down the bottle, grab my keys, and march out the door again.

I walk all the way to his home. If I took a cab, I'd stand in front of a locked door anyway, so no use in getting there quick. Plus, I don't want him getting mad at me too. I need my partner in crime tonight. Need to relax and get this shit off my mind just for a few hours.

When I finally get there, the lights are already on, so I ring the doorbell.

He opens the door half naked, rubbing a towel across his chest. "Whoa. Put some clothes on," I mutter.

"Sorry, had to take a shower," he replies, sniggering.

I lean in and take a sniff. "You smell like old grannies perfume."

He raises his arm and smells his armpits. "Hmm, I don't smell it."

"Been hustling again?" I say, grinning.

"Like I'd tell you," he replies, winking. "Be right back."

"Put on a proper shirt, dude," I call after him as he walks away.

A few minutes later, we're both getting into his car, driving downtown to bust some moves and drink until we can no longer stand.

"So rough day, huh?" Flynn mutters as he parks the car.

"What happened?"

"Ugh, I don't wanna talk about it," I say as I open the door and get out. I want to put that bastard D out of my head.

Flynn gets out too and follows me inside. "Okay, well, as long as you're not gonna sulk while we're here."

The music immediately blasts our ears, making any proper conversation impossible. "Nah, I wanna party and get drunk tonight!" I yell, making a woohoo noise right after and diving into the crowd with him.

I grab his hands and drag him to the dance floor, immediately cracking some moves. I love the beat and the rhythm of the music. It allows me to lose my mind and let go. Especially when I have Flynn with me. He's my rock. The one who always picks me up after a bad day. A certified best friend without benefits.

I met him after my parents moved into that new fancy neighborhood and forced me to make friends with the neighbors. It wasn't so bad after all, considering Flynn lived there, and he was as raunchy and fucked up as I was, even at that age. We used to sneak out to go to secret parties and drink when we weren't supposed to. Good times.

I couldn't ever imagine my life without him, though our relationship is strictly platonic. Not because we decided it, but because we rolled into it.

I don't think I've ever thought of Flynn as anything else than my best friend, and that's okay. I need him just for that reason today.

I just wanna dance and cool off. And maybe score some good times while we're here. Both of us, in fact, because I've been watching these girls in the back constantly eyeing him. Guess tonight is his lucky night.

"Hey," I say, pulling him close, "see those chicks in the back?"

He follows my gaze. "What? Them? Nah, I'm not interested."

"Ah, c'mon, I can be your wingman-woman." I laugh.

"I'm here with you now," he says.

"Such a gentleman," I muse, raising a brow. "But I don't mind."

"Kat, I had enough chicks this week to last me a lifetime," he replies, winking.

"Course you have, playboy." I smack him on the butt. "Just keep busting some moves. I'll grab us some drinks."

"Kat …" He sighs, trying to grab me, but I avoid his grasp and stick out my tongue, which makes him roll his eyes.

Then I proceed to buy two Bacardi Sprites so we can have some fun. However, when I get back to the dance floor, Flynn's nowhere to be found.

After some searching, I find him sitting on a circular red couch in the back of the room, far away from the lights and music. "Here you go," I say, putting down his drink.

"Thanks," he replies, but he doesn't move to pick it up.

"You don't have to drive," I say. "We can get a cab and pick up your car tomorrow."

"Nah, I just wanna get us both home safe," he says, scooting the drink back to me. "That's all."

I shrug. "Fine, more alcohol for me then." I chug back the first glass and start on the next.

"Kat," Flynn says. "Take it easy."

"Why?" I take another sip.

"You're only trying to get drunk."

"So?"

"Tell me why." When I ignore him, he continues talking. "Was it a guy?"

I close my eyes and let out a breath.

He grabs my hand. "You can't lie to me."

Why does he see through me so easily? "Fine, yes. An asshole I don't wanna talk about."

"What happened?" The way he raises his brow reminds me of my mom when she's ready to scold me.

I roll my eyes. "I had this *thing* with a guy ... We met online."

"Oh ... boy," he says.

"Well, I tried to only make it a one-time thing. But it was just too good, you know?" I say. "The thing is ... we didn't know each other by name. Or looks."

Flynn makes a face. "What do you mean?"

"We had masks on," I explain.

"Okay ... sounds kinky." He grins, so I poke him in the side.

"The guy's an asshole, remember?"

"Right," he says. "Why exactly? If you had fun and all."

111

"Because I wanted to contact him afterward, but he wasn't online at all anymore, so I went to see him …"

"And then shit went down."

I lean back and nod, sipping my Bacardi. "Yup. He didn't know it was me, and I went about it the wrong way. Things went bad. And then it turns out he was a major douche."

"He told you off?"

"Not just that," I reply. "He shoved his fingers down my panties and into my hoo-ha."

"TMI, Kat," he says, raising his hand.

"What? You asked." I shrug, taking another sip. "Point is, after that blunder, I needed a drink."

"What you need is to find yourself an actual man. Not one of them oversexed bastards who are just out for a hump."

I snort. "Like you're the one to talk."

"Hey now, I treat ladies with respect."

"Right. But only before the fuck."

"And after," he adds, winking again. "And we're not talking about me right now. We're talking about your choice in men. It's bad."

"Thanks, dude," I say, slurping down the remainder of my Bacardi. "Think I'm gonna need another drink."

I get up before he can say more. I don't wanna hear it even though I know he's right. It's just that I don't want to think about it right now. So I go to the bar and order a tequila. I like trying out lots of different things while I'm partying. Makes for a fun evening, especially because you never know which drink is going to be the last. And the drink the bartender gives me makes my mouth water just by looking at it. Taking a sip, I grin from delight. God, I wish I could drown myself in alcohol tonight. Maybe it would make the memories of today disappear into the nether.

Except, the moment I turn my head, I come face to face with *him*. Mr. Rocket Fingers himself … Declan.

His face immediately darkens the moment he sets his eyes on me.

I really do not want to speak to him right now, so I quickly turn around.

"Well, hello there. What a coincidence. Out too?"

Crap. Just his voice makes me want to dissolve into a puddle. Guess he noticed me too. Too late to pretend I never saw him.

Mustering up the biggest resting bitch face I can, I glance over my shoulder and say, "Oh … didn't know you were here."

"Of course you did. I saw you looking," he replies, and he orders a rum and Coke from the bartender.

Great. Now I'm going to have to talk to him.

"If I'd known you would show up, I would've picked another place to hang," I sneer.

"Right," he scoffs as if he doesn't believe me.

I roll my eyes. "Whatever." I'm done with this.

As I walk off, he suddenly grabs my hand. "Wait …"

I pause and throw him a look. "What?"

His lips part, but it takes him a couple of seconds to gather his thoughts and put them into words. "Look. We had something fun. For a moment. That was it."

I frown. "Is that everything you want to say to me?"

"I just wanted to make sure you understand ..."

"Oh, I understand all right," I reply. "You're a dick, and I don't know why I'm still talking to you."

As I try to walk away, he tightens his grip on my wrist. "Hey, I get that I wasn't fair to you, but this was a mutual agreement. You knew that going into it."

"Why do you even care? Why are you still trying to tell me off? You don't want me, then let go of me." I try to jerk free, but he won't release me, and it's pissing me off.

He pulls me closer and whispers, "I care because I don't want you doing things you'll regret ..."

"Like what?" I hiss.

"My job is my life. Nothing jeopardizes that. *Nothing.*"

Really? After everything we did, that's what he's worried about? His job? That's why he was such an asshole to me?

"Are you threatening me?" I ask.

"No. I just want to make sure you understand my identity, the chatroom, the hotel, all of it is a private matter. It's important."

My lip twitches. "Oh, so what? You're afraid I'm going to tell people about your filthy kinks? About how you make girls strip in your office?" I have no pity for him. "Tough luck."

"Hey, don't think about telling anyone ..." he growls.

"Or what? You're going to force me to do more of your bidding on camera? Make me strip naked in front of all these people for your own pleasure? What else did I forget?"

His fingers are still firmly locked around my wrist. "Don't pretend as if you didn't like it. You begged me for more of my time. That's what you wanted, right? Why you came to my office because you wanted my cock filling your pussy. That desperate for more …"

Fuck no. I won't let him trample all over my dignity in public too. He might've gotten away with it in private, but not here, not now, not like this.

Without thinking, I chuck my entire glass of tequila at his face.

The shock causes him to release me, and I quickly walk off, vanishing into the crowd.

The music blares through the speakers, and I have trouble finding my bearings. My blood boils, but at the same time, I want to cry. I can't stop the tears from filling my eyes, but dammit, I won't let them fall.

Finally, I spot Flynn, who's dancing with a girl in the middle of the room. I don't want to disturb him, so I sit down at our table instead. Sighing out loud, I grab my cell phone and check the time. It's not even past ten yet, and I'm already done with this evening.

God, I wish I never saw Declan here. As if my night couldn't be any more ruined. It's as if he chose this place on purpose. Or maybe he followed me. But he wouldn't do that, right? He's the one who wanted to get rid of me, not the other way around.

And he was rude and insulted me too. Prick.

"Hey." Flynn suddenly appears from the crowd of people, this time without the girl. "Are you okay?" he asks when he sees my face.

I'm having trouble keeping myself together right now. I'm not sure if it's the alcohol or the thought of Declan that's making me want to sink into the floor and disappear forever.

"Kat?" his soft voice as he sits down beside me breaks me a little, and I can't stop a tear from flowing down my cheek.

"Shit, what happened?" he asks as he puts an arm around my shoulder.

"He's here," I say. "*That* guy."

"The one you fucked? The asshole?"

I nod.

"Did he come up to you?" he asks.

I don't even dare reply. I don't want him to get upset too.

"If he hurt you, tell me, Kat, or I swear to God, I'm going to find that son of a bitch and punch him in the face right now," he says through gritted teeth.

"No, no, don't. Please," I say, grabbing his arm so he won't get up. "Just don't, okay? Promise me."

"Fine, I promise," he growls.

"Thank you," I say. "I don't want to make a scene. I just want to forget about it all and pretend he doesn't exist."

"Okay." He makes a face and sighs. "Fuck ... did he follow you here or what?"

"I don't know. I don't think he did. It's just ..." I don't even know how to finish my sentence. All I wanna do is go home and drink the night away behind my little TV. Alone and miserable.

"Aw, c'mon," Flynn says. "Let's go." He pulls me up from the couch and drags me along with him.

"Wait," I say, stopping in my tracks. "What about that girl you were dancing with?"

"I got her number," he says, winking as he pulls me along. "Don't worry about me. Let's just get you home."

I let him lead me outside. I'm way too tipsy and annoyed to even care to stay. Besides, there's a nice breeze that keeps me wide-awake.

Flynn helps me into the passenger seat of his car, and then he jumps behind the wheel. He still seems fresh as a bird while I'm sinking into the chair like a badly baked soufflé. I'm so glad he didn't accept my drink. I'd have to feel this way but with a fucking cabby listening to all my gripes and moans.

God, he really is the best friend I could ever wish for.

"Thanks, Flynn," I say as I buckle up.

"That's what friends are for," he says, winking.

I smile. "You're the best. Sorry about that chick you had to leave there."

"Aw, stop worrying about that," he says, waving it off.

"I'm sure you can get a boatload of other girls with a

snap of your finger," I joke.

"That's true." He wriggles his brows.

"Soon, you'll be drowning in pussy. And then you'll have no more time for a little pick-me-up with this girl," I say. "But that's okay. I'll just have to stop relying on you to hold my head above water while I navigate this ... fucking ocean of assholes."

"Kat, you know you'll always have a special place in my heart," he says, grinning at me like a stupid fucker. "And yeah ... you really do need to stop fucking assholes."

I laugh. "If only I could find one as chivalrous and hot as you."

God, I'm too intoxicated to even realize what I'm saying.

"Thanks, babe," he says, grinning. "I like you a lot when you're drunk."

"I know you do ..." I giggle, wrapping my arm around his shoulder.

Right before we leave the parking lot, the car stops for a moment and Flynn looks my way.

"Kat ..."

"What?" I mumble, feeling the sudden urge to kiss him.

"What are you doing?"

"I don't know."

Actually, I do. I'm hanging onto him. Literally, physically. I wonder how it would feel ...

"Have we ever ... kissed?" I ask.

He frowns, then laughs. "What, you think you actually

want that?"

I only wonder because I don't think I've ever thought of him that way before. I've never seen him in that light—as dateable material—even though he totally is.

And he's right. I should go for better men, and he definitely is a good man.

"I don't know. Have we ever even tried?"

He raises a brow. "No. Do you want to?"

"Sure … I guess." I giggle, totally out of it.

I pucker my lips and lean in, and so does he. But when I get close enough to see his face, I burst out into laughter … just like he does.

"I'm sorry, I just can't take it seriously," he says.

I can't even breathe; that's how much I'm laughing right now. "Sorry, I knew it would be a failure. I can't even think about kissing you," I say, feeling disgusted already. "You're like my brother."

I guess it wasn't meant to be. I just wanted it to be him because he's so perfect, but I'm just not into it. At all. In fact, this whole thing makes me want to go rinse my mouth and brush my teeth.

"Phew," he says, letting out a breath. "I was starting to worry there."

"Nah …" I playfully punch him in the shoulder. "I just had to be sure. That's all."

He's right, though. We don't need this. We're perfect as we are right now. No reason to ruin a good friendship.

"And the verdict is …"

"Hot but totally not for me," I say, and we both laugh again.

"Thanks for the vote of confidence, babe," he says, hitting the gas. "Now let's go take you home."

TWELVE

DECLAN

The event went down as expected this weekend. Though we were one girl short, the clients didn't seem to notice. They were enjoying themselves thoroughly with the girls present, and we had an amazing lineup of games that got them excited. Many of the clients came to me at the end to tell me how much they liked the décor and how much fun they had doing whatever their filthy minds could conjure up.

Now that the pressure is off, I can finally focus on relaxing again. Though I have to keep in mind we'll have another event soon, I still need some time off like everyone else, and today's finally that day. At home, there's no worry about being disturbed, so I find myself starting up my laptop for another bout of personal gratification.

However, the moment I start the chat, my eyes immediately hover over that name...

NaughtyKitten.

She's still there even though I blocked her. I can see her name on the list of people online.

I wonder if she's still looking. If she already found a new guy to play with. If he's giving her as much pleasure as I did.

I sigh. I shouldn't even think about her.

Her showing up at my office never should've happened.

I should've been more careful. Should've checked the picture I sent her before it was too late.

Smart girl.

But it was foolish. And, not to mention, dangerous.

She knows who I am and where I work. What if she tells someone what I do? What happens to this hotel when people find out what it is that we deliver here?

I can't let it happen, which is why I'm so frustrated right now.

It's the sole reason I kicked her out. Not because I don't like her. I do. Or I did. I just can't deal with the fact that I broke my only rules. Never meet up with a girl twice. Never expose your identity. Two of them broken now.

Goddamn that girl and her fantastic tits ... not to mention that ass. So tight and squeezable. I can still feel it in my hands when I picture her in front of me. It was hard to stop the boner from growing when she stripped in my office.

Even then, I already knew something was up.

The shape of her body and the look in her eyes were too familiar, though I just couldn't put a finger on it because we'd both worn masks when we first saw each other.

But her fragrant perfume gave it away ... and then the ponytail sealed the deal.

I can't help but stare at her name, which is still blocked. I lean back in my chair and sigh.

For some reason, I can't get this girl out of my mind. Despite there being so many other girls I could contact, so many others willing to play a filthy game, she was the only one who accepted everything I made her do. She was open to it all—every dirty thought and game—which is why it's so hard to detach.

She gave me what I needed, and now that I no longer have it, I'm disappointed. Like I already know none of the other girls will live up to my expectations now that I've fucked her.

I groan and rub my face. Why does this have to be so hard?

Can't I just put her aside and focus on someone else? Something new?

Maybe I should go look at porn. Another one of those videos where a girl just screams her lungs out and pretends to like it even when she doesn't.

Nah. That isn't real. It isn't sexy. I need raw, uncensored, unfiltered.

Someone real and tangible. Someone like *NaughtyKitten*.

Except it can't be her. It can't ever be her again.

That was one of my rules ... though they were already broken the moment she stepped into my office pretending to be someone she's not.

What was she thinking? That I wouldn't find out? Was she going to give me a fake name?

I'm sure that's why she hesitated to fill out the contract. But why go through the trouble of seeing me then?

She probably thought I would see past my rules and fuck her again. I have to admit, I was so fucking close to actually doing it ...

Especially when I shoved my fingers up her pussy and felt her get wet.

God, how badly I wanted to throw her over my desk and fuck that pussy raw there and then.

Just thinking about it gets me hard.

Not that I'll ever get a chance again. I fucked that up pretty good by kicking her out like that.

Maybe I shouldn't have been so harsh to her. Denying her was one thing, but I treated her like trash. I was just so angry about the whole thing, and I acted rash to get rid of a problem that I created myself.

It wasn't her fault I was careless.

And it's definitely not her fault that I saw her again at the club that night.

Fuck.

I was only there to cool down after what happened, and

then I run into her there. What are the chances? It's as if fate wanted me to face my own mistakes. It pissed me off so much, and I lashed out at her.

I was terrified of the consequences of meeting her. Of her knowing who I am and where I work. The risk my job involves.

So I took it out on her.

Only after she'd disappeared through the crowd did I realize what a giant douche I'd been.

I should've gone after her to apologize, but I didn't see her again that night. Maybe I never will.

God, I really do make a mess of things sometimes.

But this is a mess I might be able to fix.

I open my drawer and sift through my papers until I find the one I'm looking for. The contract she almost signed. I brought it home with me so no one would ever find out what happened. I was going to burn it, but now I figure I may be able to use it for something good … because her address is written on the document.

***

Kat

At work, I take a pill to fix my hangover. Even though I went out with Flynn two days ago, my head is still roaring. I don't think I'll get any work done, but I'll do my very best. I should've stopped drinking, but instead, I finished the bottle of wine I had left at home. I don't even remember what happened afterward.

Only when I woke up did I remember that I'd almost kissed Flynn.

God, what an embarrassment I was. I still haven't gathered the courage to speak to him, but I should. He supported me when I needed it. Especially when that prick Declan showed up at the club. I still can't believe he was there. What a way to ruin an evening.

Sighing, I grab my cell phone and dial Flynn's number. "Hey."

"Hey, babe," he says. "What's up? Feeling better yet?"

"Yeah, much. I just wanted to say thanks. For bringing me home safely, you know?" A small laugh escapes my mouth.

"Don't mention it."

I wonder if he remembers what I tried to do. He probably does. "Sorry about that awkward ..."

"Ah, forget about it. You were drunk. I can't take anything you do seriously then," he replies, laughing.

"Fuck, please don't. I mean, I really don't want to kiss you," I say.

"Thanks," he says sarcastically.

"Not that you aren't attractive," I add. "But you're my best friend."

"Right."

"I just hope it didn't ruin things between us," I say.

"It didn't," he says, and I can hear him smile. "Relax. It's fine."

"Okay … phew." I breathe out a sigh of relief.

"Oh, now that I've got you on the phone, a package was delivered to my home today. But it had your name on it."

I frown. "Huh? How's that even possible?"

"I don't know, but I sent it to your office, so if you haven't received it yet, it should be there any moment now."

I frown. I didn't order anything, and if I did, I wouldn't have it shipped to Flynn's home address.

"Okay … that's odd," I say. "Well, thanks anyway. I'll see what it is when it gets here."

"No probs. Hey, aren't you supposed to working right now?" he asks.

Well, shit. I'd hoped he wouldn't notice that I'm slacking. "Yeah, I just wanted to make sure we were okay."

"We are, Kat. Stop worrying and go get your ass to work."

I laugh. "Okay, okay. Thanks, dude."

"I got you."

We hang up, and I put my cell phone back in my bag and open my browser again so I can get back to my emails. However, the moment I do, Crystal bursts into my office without warning.

"Kat! Look," she says, prancing into my space with a huge bouquet of roses.

"Nice," I say. I'm sure she's proud, trying to show them off. "Who'd you get them from?"

"They're not for me … They're for you." She puts them down on my desk like I'm supposed to do something with them, but all I can do is stare.

"Go on then … who're they from?" she asks, bouncing up and down as she glances at the card stuck between the flowers.

I gently pick it up and open it, reading the text written inside.

From the dick who went too far. Please forgive my indiscretions. I apologize for making you feel the way I did. I hope we can meet again. My office, seven p.m. tomorrow? Yours, D.

I read the words over and over again, but they don't seem to register in my brain.

Declan wants to meet up again? With me? Is this for real?

"And?" Crystal asks. I nearly forgot she was here.

"It's from … a friend," I reply, lying through my teeth. But she doesn't need to know. My private life is none of her concern.

"Oh, right." She winks. "Well, I'll go back to my desk then. If you need something, let me know."

She sashays back out the door, and I lean up to sniff the roses. They smell so nice … I wonder if he handpicked them.

But how the hell did he find out about Flynn? And why send them there?

Then it hits me. That's the address I put on that contract of his. In case I needed to protect my identity … which I apparently did.

I laugh to myself. Poor Flynn. I should apologize for using his home address as a scapegoat for my adventures. I just didn't want Declan to know where I lived because it'd be too easy to find out my name and more details about my life I didn't want him to be privy to.

I'm not even sure I'll ever share those details with anyone from a chat room.

I mean, a girl has to do everything she can to stay safe.

And with people like Declan, you never know.

The question is, though, whether I want to see him again.

He's been such a douchebag. Although, if I think about it, I can understand why.

He wanted to protect his business. His identity. And I

busted into his office like it was nothing. I didn't explain who I was, and he never had the time to adjust. He probably felt like I was a threat even though I wouldn't tell a soul about what we did.

He probably assumed I would, which is what made me so angry with him.

But he did apologize. And the roses do smell lovely. They're so nice that I sniff them again.

Maybe meeting him again wouldn't do any harm. Besides, I went to his office for a reason, and that desire never changed. I wanted something more, something exciting, and now that he's willing to make amends … maybe I should take him up on his offer.

THIRTEEN

DECLAN

When the sun is low in the sky, shining brightly through my window, a knock on my door alerts me. *She's here.*

A devilish grin spreads across my face.

For a few minutes there, I was almost starting to worry she wouldn't show up. After all, I'd made myself out to be the bad guy. I chased her away with threats and anger.

But I changed my mind along the way, and now I want to see whether she'll accept that. I'm not sure yet if I want to go any further than we already have, but I just couldn't leave it alone. I couldn't stop thinking about her even after she practically broke into my office.

I was too careless, and I do think it's partly my own fault that she's so greedy for more.

Maybe there is something more to all of this ...

More that I could take ... and give.

At least once or twice wouldn't hurt. Right?

When she enters my office, I take a deep breath and stand from my seat. She's as beautiful as she was the last time I saw her. This time, she's wearing long white pants and a black crop top with thick stilettos underneath. Too sexy not to lick my lips to.

"So ... you've come," I say, casually tucking my hands into my pockets.

She wears a clear smirk as she closes the door behind her and remains near the edge of the room. "So I have."

When our eyes lock, it feels as though lightning sparks through the air.

She drops her bag on the floor but remains silent. I smile at the sight of her mischievous gaze. "Did you like the flowers?"

She cocks her head and folds her arms. "They were nice ... unlike you."

"I apologize for my anger at the club," I reply. I don't want her to be upset, but I don't want to linger on it either. The past is the past. What was said and done remains there. I'd much rather focus on the here and now. On her ... in the living flesh.

"I'd be able to accept them if you were honest about what you wanted."

"Right now? You," I say.

There's not a single ounce of doubt in my voice. Today, I know I want to see more of where this could go. What comes after is a mystery. And that's fine, as long as she accepts that.

"Tell me why I should believe you?" she asks, shrugging. "You change your mind every time."

"Because I was hasty, and I regret that," I say.

"You feared I was going to tell people about you. Maybe you shouldn't assume I'm that kind of girl?"

She's humoring me. But that's okay … I can take it. "I'm not the only one who's hiding in plain sight …"

A small, lopsided grin briefly forms on her lips before disappearing again. She knows what I'm talking about. "You used the contract to send me flowers," she says.

Clever girl. "But it wasn't your address," I fill in.

"How did you find out?" she asks.

"The company that delivers them for me told me the guy who accepted them said he lived there alone."

"Right …" There's a hint of amusement on her face. I'm not quite sure whether to love it or hate it or both.

"Whose address was it?" I ask.

"A friend's," she replies.

Cautious. I like that. She's not going to make the same mistake twice. Trust is hard to give to someone who doesn't give it in return, so I understand.

I walk up to the front of my desk and lean against it, casually crossing my arms.

"So ... Kitten ... you never left your name on the form."

"Nope," she says. "And I wouldn't have written down my real one either."

"Figured," I muse, licking my lips.

She's so protective of her identity. We have more in common than I thought.

"But since you know my name, it's only fair I know yours, don't you agree?" My blatant request grabs her attention. I can tell from the way she shifts her position. It's just an inch, but it's enough to notice.

A few seconds pass. "Call me Kat."

"Kat ..." I don't know if it's her real name or not, but it sounds good. Rolls off the tongue easily. And it explains her choice of nickname on the site, so this must be the truth. After all, I'm sure she feels a bit guilty for knowing my real name and the location of my office. She doesn't look like the type to continue a lie without feeling the need to level the playing field.

And she's certainly playing the game right.

"I like your name," I say.

"Thanks," she says. "I like yours too, Declan."

The teasing glint in her eyes is almost too much to take.

It makes me want to grab her, throw her over my lap, and spank her ass until it's bright red.

But that wouldn't be appropriate right now, would it?

Or maybe it's exactly what she needs ... What we both need.

She smiles. "So are you going to tell me what that contract was for?"

"Nope," I reply. "Not happening."

She should be happy I let her go after seeing it. This hotel requires sensitive things like that to stay top secret.

"Figured," she mumbles. "It's not why I came here anyway."

"So then ... why *did* you come?" I ask.

She swallows as if she's actively engaging with my words, picturing me saying something else. Maybe I did. She's not the only one who likes to tease.

"Because, like you, I don't enjoy giving up," she says.

"I'm not something to keep either," I reply.

I grab the visitor's chair in front of my desk and twist it, holding the armrest to see where her eyes go. I want to witness her reaction, but she remains steadfast, holding my gaze as if it means the world to her that I'm looking.

But no matter how badly she may try to distract me with her beauty and wits, I don't intend to avert my eyes.

"No, but I'd like to see where things could go," she says.

"*Things*? You assume there's more to this than just once."

"We already passed once."

Touché. She's got me there.

"Lock the door," I say.

I watch her do exactly what I ask. It's entertaining to see how easily she responds to my commands. As if she was born to listen, but only to me.

I smirk and then sit down on the chair right in front of her, watching her reaction, her every move. With one finger, I beckon her to come forward. No words. No sound. Just the tip of my finger commanding her to walk.

And she does.

When she's right in front of me, I say, "Take off your pants."

She narrows her eyes. "And what makes you think I'd do that?"

My lip twitches. "Why else would you come here?"

It wasn't a request or a demand. She can grab her bag and leave if she wants to. I'm not stopping her. I'm not even thinking about it. The only thing going through my mind right now is making her rethink her own desires. Seeing how far I can push her until she finally realizes there's nothing more to me than just sex. Until she turns, runs, and never comes back.

But she doesn't. Instead, her fingers gently curl around the fabric of her tight pants and roll them down. She finishes removing them by stepping out of them. Like she's getting rid of her inhibitions, layer by layer. It's amazing to watch.

"Panties too," I say.

My tongue dips out when she gazes down at me, her eyes questioning. As if she's waiting for me to do something to her—take off her clothes, ravage her, kiss her, anything. But I'm not going to give in to her that easily. I want to see how far she'll go to get this … to get *all* of me.

136

When she's stripped bare, I have to physically restrain myself from grabbing her and pressing my mouth between her legs. Patience is a virtue. First, she needs to be aware of the consequences of me fucking her twice.

I'm breaking all my rules for her ... and I *want* her to know.

So I pat my lap while staring at her, and say, "Lie down on my lap. Face down."

She swallows again as if she's holding back the words. Fighting the need to speak up.

She doesn't want me the way I really am ... yet she can't stop herself from needing more.

This is why we started chatting in the first place. Why we met up.

Her need for humiliation brings her to levels of shame she can't cope with.

But in my world, shame isn't a bad thing. It's something to cherish. Something to revel in. Something to bask in and feed your soul with.

Shame is sin, and sinning ... feels so fucking good.

And nothing beats the feel of her across my lap with that juicy ass on display.

As she lies down, her head faces toward me, but I'm not touching her. Not until she turns away and accepts whatever comes next. And after a few seconds of staring, she finally does.

FOURTEEN

Kat

When his hand touches my skin, my butt cheeks clench. His hand is so warm and cold at the same time. Rugged but soft. Like he knows he means business ... but wants to take it slow.

Then out of nowhere, he smacks my ass.

Pain ripples through my body, my legs ... my pussy.

I squeal from the sudden onset but remain positioned where I am just from his hand resting on my ass. He gently strokes it, causing delicious sensations to dart everywhere.

Another smack has me in complete bliss.

I don't know what it is about being handled like this, but I can't say no. I don't want him to stop, despite my feeling humiliated.

His smacks are hard and sharp and not at all sweet. It's as if he wants me to feel punished. Like he intends on making me feel bad for what I did. For tracking him down, coming into his office without invitation, and for everything that happened between us.

Maybe that's why he wanted me to lie on his lap … So he could make me feel just how much of a dirty girl I really am. And how badly I want this.

My cheeks grow warmer with every strike, and I can feel the sizzle. And with every slap of his hand coming down, he inches closer and closer to my pussy, which is already wet and buzzing.

"So … do you like this?" he asks. "Do you enjoy my hand owning your ass?"

I moan in response. "Fuck … yes."

There's no point in lying. I know he can tell just from my sounds. And I'm sure it won't be long until he discovers just how wet I already am.

"You don't even know what you're saying …" he growls, and he smacks me again for good measures.

I'm still turned on, still convinced this is what I want.

I want him to take everything. To do every forbidden thing and more. To take me where I'm not supposed to go.

He keeps alternating which cheek to spank, and I catch

myself moaning to his hits more and more. I'm not sure whether it's the sounds I'm making or the mere contact of his hands on my body causing it, but he's groaning slightly too. But I know for sure he's as excited as I am when his cock grows against my belly.

Everything about this feels wrong, yet I want nothing more than his fingers diving between my legs.

As I lose myself more and more in ecstasy, his fingers slowly travel down toward my pussy, leaving delicious trails of hot flashing pain wherever he strikes. When his fingers touch my bare lips, I almost explode right there and then.

He pauses. I tense.

His dick bounces in his pants when his thumb pushes inside.

I bite my lip to stop myself from going over the edge.

I moan out loud when he thrusts into me.

"Hmm ... wet already," he murmurs, and a chuckle follows. "What a surprise."

Is that supposed to be a snappy remark? Honestly, I don't even care right now as long as he continues doing what he's doing to me.

Because fuck me ... does he do it good.

He touches me in all the right places with just the right amount of pressure.

Cupping my pussy, he takes me with two fingers, claiming me like I've never belonged to anyone else. As if he's my first. Even though I'm not a virgin anymore, he makes me feel like I am.

His fingers expertly dart in and out, casually circling my clit to get me panting until I can't stop moaning out loud. His dick responds to the sounds I make, bumping me in the belly to remind me of its presence. Right now, I'd do anything to take it, use it, fuck it, lick it. Anything, I'd do it as long as he makes me come.

God, I'm shameless.

Especially for a man like him …

So fucking cocky and a dick at the same time, he makes me want to jump his bones.

I'm a sucker for pain and humiliation. Always have been.

And he gives just the right amount of both to satisfy my every need.

"How does it feel to have my fingers inside you, Kitten?" he asks, his voice dark and heavy, full of lust.

God, I don't think I'll ever get used to him calling me Kitten.

"Damn … so good."

"Better than last time?" he muses.

Fuck, I hate that memory. But he wants it there. Plants it there on purpose just to mess with my mind.

But even though I'll let him fuck my body, I won't let him play with my emotions.

"I'll take whatever you'll give me," I say, not giving a shit about what that means.

He could get even rougher, even harsher; the pain could be so bad I could scream. But I don't care. Right now, all I want is for him to use me however he wants. Even if I hate every second of it, I'll still love it in the end.

Because that's who I am ... a masochist at heart.

And the way he smacks my ass and then continues rubbing my clit as if he never stopped tells me he's enjoying himself just as much ...

Fucking sadist.

He smacks my ass again. "Anything?"

"Yes," I reply.

"Good ... I'll hold you to that."

I don't have to look at him to know he's grinning. I can hear it.

His fingers drive me wild as he says, "Come. All over my hand."

And fuck me, do I come hard.

My legs are literally shaking, my whole body covered in goose bumps and sweat as I fall apart on his lap. I feel like a marionette whose wires have been cut. All I can do is lie on his lap and take deep breaths while my body floods with endorphins.

A sudden spanking pulls me back into the here and now, forcing my body to jolt up and down. "On your knees," he growls.

I do what he says, crawling off his lap as if I'm some kind of pet. A real kitten, sitting right there between his firm, muscular legs while he stares down at me with content in his eyes.

That ... and a hint of hunger sparkling in his pupils.

I could stare at those eyes all day long.

Fuck, what is wrong with me?

I've only seen him a couple of times, and most of the time, he was an asshole. I can't fall head over heels with someone like him. Can't let this be more than a game. Even if it's a fucking delicious sexual game at that.

And I do like where it's going when he brings his fingers to his mouth and takes a lick.

"Hmm …"

My whole body electrifies at the sound of his hum and his approval of my taste.

My eyes follow his hand as it trails down his shirt, where I wish he'd pull open the buttons so I could have a peek at those rippling muscles. Instead, he brings it down to his pants … and the rock-hard dick underneath.

He unzips and pulls it out.

My mouth salivates at the sight of his length. Delicious and right in front of me, it's ready for the taking.

I lean forward, my mouth opening to take him in, but he holds it steady with his hand and says, "Don't be greedy."

I pause and inch back. "But I want to—"

He silences me with a finger on his lips and a soft, "Shh," adding, "It's my turn now."

As our eyes lock, he starts rubbing himself. From the base to the tip, and all the way back until he's even stiffer and longer than before. And he keeps going even though I'm literally licking my lips at the anticipation of having him in my mouth.

But he never tells me to lick him or suck him off.

Instead, he gleefully watches my reaction as he continues to jerk himself off. Not even pre-cum rolling down his shaft stops him from doing what he does best, and I know he wants me to watch. He wants me to witness what he can do to me just by making me look.

Just by using the thing I want most—to touch him—and then not giving it to me.

Fuck him. And fuck me for wanting this so badly.

After a while, he gets up and kicks back the chair, then stands right in front of me. He never stops rubbing himself, never stops looking at me with that intent gaze. Like he thinks he owns the world … like he wants to own me.

"Open your mouth," he growls. His cock looks so damn tasty I find it hard to keep my tongue inside.

"Tongue out."

Well, I guess that makes it easier.

I sit up straight but leave my legs parted a bit so he can peek, and when he does, a spark of enthusiasm bolts through my veins again. The look in his eyes is intense. He's completely focused on us. I'm finding it hard to look away even though I can see him jerk off from the corner of my eyes.

And boy, does it look good. I wish he would let me have a taste.

But that's probably the exact reason he's not giving it to me.

Because I want it so badly, and he's not here to give me what I want.

This is solely for him. His pleasure. My punishment.

I was greedy when I came to his office, and this is the price I pay.

But even as I realize this, I still can't bring myself to do anything but stay on my knees in front of him with my mouth wide open, ready to accept him.

"How badly do you want it?" he asks, his voice heady. "Show me."

I lean in with mouth open even wider than before. "Give it to me."

"Give you what?" he groans.

"Your cock."

"No," he growls, still furiously jerking himself off.

So that wasn't the answer he was looking for. What else? I can only think of one other thing. "Give me your cum."

"And what do we say?" he murmurs.

"Please?" I add.

A devilish smile forms on his lips. "Good Kitty …"

He lathers his pre-cum all over his length, his veins bulging out of his skin. I can't stop staring, can't stop salivating, can't stop wanting to inch closer, but he won't let me.

With his thumb, he tips up my chin as I hold out my tongue.

A guttural sound emanates from his throat. A spray of cum hits my tongue and the back of my throat, covering me. I try not to gag, but it's hard when it keeps coming. Within seconds, his spunk has covered my entire face. He finishes it with a few swipes of his tip along my cheeks.

Then his thumb pushes up, forcing me to close my mouth. "Swallow."

Instinctively, I do what he says. The taste is salty. Delicious.

But the way he did it is what stays in my mind.

He deposited it inside me like I'm some kind of sperm bank. Like he wants me to know I'm nothing more than a cumslut. His Kitty to use as he pleases and humiliate at his discretion.

"Now smile," he says.

In shock, I stare at him.

"What's the matter?" He cocks his head. "Cat got your tongue?"

It's not funny. But he's not doing it to be funny. He wants me to hate him. To regret all this.

So instead of answering him, I smile. Widely. Despite knowing he did all of this only to dissuade me from ever wanting him again.

But it hasn't. My infatuation has only worsened.

He tucks his cock back into his pants and bends his knees just a bit. "You wanted this, remember?"

I nod. "I did."

"Still think it's what you want?"

"Yes," I reply.

No hesitation. No regret.

He frowns, clearly confused. "Why?"

"Because ..." I look down at the wetness pooling

146

between my legs, dripping on the floor. Only when I've seen him follow my gaze do I open my mouth again. "I like what you give me."

***

DECLAN

I'm stunned. That was … unexpected.

I frown, staring at her for a while. Nothing about her has changed. Not her demeanor. Not her facial expression.

Well … except for all the jizz covering it right now.

My cum. Consumed by lust, I sprayed it all over her. It felt so goddamn good to fucking humiliate her like that. To give her exactly what she wanted, what she begged me for.

Yet I expected her to be upset. Angry. Hell, I expected her spit it right back at me.

Instead, she swallowed it down.

And she's still happy. Despite me using her like some fuck doll, she's still smiling.

That wasn't supposed to happen.

"So what now?" she asks.

I sigh and grab the box of tissues off my desk. "Here." I hand her a couple.

"Phew," she says.

"What?"

"For a second there, I thought you were going to make me walk home like this," she says, snorting right after.

I narrow my eyes. "Maybe I was."

She glares at me for a second before rubbing the cum off her face. Now that's the kind of gaze I like to see. The one full of contempt. The one I know and trust. The one where they all run and never come back.

I hope she doesn't, for her sake.

She chucks the dirty tissues into the trash and puts on her panties and the sexy black pants, patting it down until it appears as though nothing happened. But I'm sure she won't forget this encounter ... The only question is will I?

She tucks a strand of hair behind her ear and licks her lips. "Well, that was fun," she says. "Again another time?"

The mere suggestion sets me off. "What? No."

"Why not?" She shrugs, raising a brow. "We both enjoyed it."

"You know why," I say.

"Oh, right ... Secrets," she jests, tapping her finger against her cheek. "You like keeping them."

"Exactly." Why do I get the feeling she likes figuring them out?

"Well ..." She approaches me and starts fondling my tie, readjusting it in a very intimate way. "I promise I won't tell anyone what happened here."

She'd better not.

She leans in, and whispers, "It'll be our little secret."

The grin that follows makes my cock semi-hard.

Fuck.

She turns and flips her hair as if she owns the place. "See you again ... Maybe online?" she taunts.

"Don't count on it," I say.

I don't want to be harsh, but I have to be. For both our sakes.

She shrugs. "Suit yourself."

Then she struts out the door with her head held high.

The moment the door closes, I sink down on the chair and scratch my chin.

Good God ... this woman. She's going to be the end of me.

FIFTEEN

DECLAN

No matter how many hours and days have passed, I still can't stop thinking about that damn girl.

KittyKat ... she's stuck in my mind like glue to paper, and I don't know why.

It was just sex. Casual ... dirty ... raunchy sex.

I fucking loved it, but that doesn't mean I can do repeats.

I only gave it to her in the hopes that she'd keep my secret. That she wouldn't talk to anyone about us meeting and leave it at that.

But now I'm the one questioning everything.

Fuck. Why does this have to happen?

I sigh and close the browser even though I still have several emails to answer.

The next event is looming, and I need to prepare, but my mind's not set to working right now. It's constantly distracted by the image of her naked body doing anything I want that got seared into my mind.

She was the perfect girl to subject to all my kinky needs … but at what cost?

Am I infatuated with the idea of having more freedom to explore my own sexual desires?

Or am I infatuated with her?

I don't even know, which is why I'm so confused.

I've only seen her a few times. I can't already be head over heels.

But maybe she's already gotten me addicted to the curves of her body, and the way they felt under my hand.

God, every time I think about the way I spanked her and made her come, my dick grows hard.

It's as if I haven't had sex in ages even though I have. I'm normally never this horny, but just thinking about banging her again already has me going. She tasted so damn good; my mouth salivates just thinking about it. And honestly, when I think about it, I can't even fathom not ever tasting that again.

So fuck this. I can't call it quits.

Not when I'm like this. And definitely not when I know

she'll probably continue to pursue me.

But when will it stop? And how?

Should I ignore her when she comes into the Hotel again? Risk exposure? Or should I give in and see where this could head?

I open the browser again and instinctively press the tab that goes directly to the chat site. I'm not even thinking about it. And instead of stopping myself before I do something I'll probably regret, I actually unblock her name.

***

Kat

I'm at work when the chat bubble to Declan's name suddenly turns green again.

"Well, hello there," I mumble to myself.

I'm not surprised. Not even a little bit.

When I left his office the other day, I could see the lust pouring out of him. Even after all that filthy shit we did, he still needed more, and I didn't blame him. I'm in the same boat, constantly thinking about all the things he did that got me hot and bothered. It still makes me salivate. And worse, I'm not even mad at him for raging at me and being an asshole at the club.

I've forgiven him. Partially. Mostly because of my needy pussy.

What can I say? I'm an addict.

I'm not going to stay mad at him or myself. I know what I want and giving in is easier than fighting it.

Him on the other hand … I'm not so sure what he wants. He may want me, but he doesn't want the danger that comes with it.

He thinks he needs to protect his business, and I get it. But I also know neither of us can resist the pull. It was only a matter of time.

And now he's finally back online, waiting for me to message him.

NaughtyKitten: I thought you said I shouldn't count on it?

D: You shouldn't. Do you want me to block you again?

NaughtyKitten: No. But would you really?

D: Try me and find out.

NaughtyKitten: So angry.

D: No, just tired of playing games.

I grin to myself. I'm not. I love these games. Especially when they're filled with raunchy sex.

NaughtyKitten: I'm not. I know what I want. I think we've established that.

D: And what is it that you think you want?

NaughtyKitten: For now? You.

D: But you don't know me.

He's asking tough questions, but I won't let him corner me that easily.

NaughtyKitten: I know what you can do. That's enough for me.

D: How do you know that?

NaughtyKitten: I just do.

Boy, he's really making this hard.

NaughtyKitten: Why are you even online if you don't believe it?

He doesn't answer. At least, not as quickly as I would've liked.

D: Don't ask questions you already know the answer to.

NaughtyKitten: Right. Because you want me just as much.

D: Sexually. Physically. Not emotionally.

NaughtyKitten: Right ...

Why do I get the sense he's trying to convince himself more than me?

D: For now, online is good.

I frown, confused.

NaughtyKitten: You don't want to meet anymore? I don't get it. Why go back?

D: Because it's dangerous.

NaughtyKitten: Because you're hiding something.

D: Retract your claws, KittyKat.

I narrow my eyes.

NaughtyKitten: It's true, though.

D: This is for pleasure only.

NaughtyKitten: Oh, I know. And I find it pleasurable for you to fuck me.

D: You shouldn't. I'm only in it for me. I'm selfish and greedy.

NaughtyKitten: I don't mind.

D: Why? Why is everything so easy with you?

I pause. I'm not sure whether I should take that comment as an insult or a compliment. I'll go for the more positive outlook.

NaughtyKitten: Because I don't mind being used.

D: Explain.

NaughtyKitten: It makes me feel … free.

D: So we're both using each other then.

NaughtyKitten: In a way, yes.

I guess we're not as far apart as he thinks.

D: Well, thank you for being so honest.

NaughtyKitten: You're welcome. Your turn.

D: I never said I was going to spill.

NaughtyKitten: But you want to keep things going with me, right?

I know I'm taunting him, but I have nothing else to lose either. He already blocked me once. Who's to say he won't do it again?

D: Don't make me choose.

NaughtyKitten: I just want to know why you wanted to make me sign that contract. What the bellhop meant by 'girls.' Why you made me strip when you didn't even know it was me.

It's quiet for some time, and for a second there, I wonder if I've chased him off.

D: What if I told you that knowing that might scare you off?

Wait. Is he actually admitting he'd rather not see me gone? I smile. He's actually afraid I might not want him anymore.

NaughtyKitten: Try me.

Maybe there's more to this than what he wants to admit.

D: No.

NaughtyKitten: Aw, c'mon.

D: It'll jeopardize my job.

NaughtyKitten: I promise I won't tell anyone.

D: Promises don't mean anything.

I'm feeling a little hurt by that comment, but I get it. Without the relationship factor, there's little holding me back from spreading the news. No matter what I tell him, he can't believe it because there's no risk in it for me.

Except losing him.

That's a big risk right now. But I doubt he's aware.

D: It's not because I don't want to.

Oh … now we're getting somewhere.

NaughtyKitten: No, I know. I just … wonder why you make girls strip. Is it because you offer explicit services to the hotel guests?

D: Perhaps.

Aha! Admission.

NaughtyKitten: What kind? Can I see?

D: No.

NaughtyKitten: Aw.

D: It wouldn't be for you.

NaughtyKitten: You don't know that.

D: I do, and it's dangerous. If my boss finds out, I might get fired.

NaughtyKitten: He doesn't have to find out about us.

D: I get that you're excited, but being fucked by me should be enough for you.

NaughtyKitten: Fine ...

I just want to know what he does for a living. And why this hotel offers such strange services. It must skirt the law, right? Maybe that's why he's so iffy about sharing details.

Still, I'm curious to know what it is that they offer exactly. Fun nights out for the guests? Strippers who dance on a stage? Or is it more like an escort service? It could be any of those ... or none, and my curiosity is piqued.

D: I don't have time for this.

Is he backpedaling? Must be because of all my questions. It's probably getting too hot under his feet.

NaughtyKitten: Sorry, but why did you come online then? Do you want to arrange another hookup?

D: I didn't say that.

NaughtyKitten: Then what? Just to chat? About what? Work?

D: *Never mind.*

Suddenly, he logs off.

Goddammit. I guess that's what I get for being sassy and nosy. I can't help myself. It's in my veins to find out more. It's why I do what I do, why I work here at this magazine, writing articles as if my life depends on it.

I live for the juicy details. And he's got plenty of them. So many, I could fill an entire magazine with my thoughts and experiences.

I smile to myself. Maybe I should. I mean, I always wanted to write a big hit. And this ... this seems like a topic that could go viral. How anonymous sex with a stranger uncovered the biggest kept secret of a hotel. It sounds perfect on paper.

I just need more information. More things to go on. More ... of him.

I can't let him push me out like this. He's not won this argument yet. And besides, if we're both so addicted to each other's bodies, we might as well try to make an effort, right? Who knows what this could become.

I close the website and Google the hotel's site. It's about time I did a bit of sleuthing.

And boy ... what I find makes me want to giggle.

An event is coming up this weekend. Saturday, nine p.m. VIP pass holders only. But I don't need a pass to get in ...

After all, I have a young, energetic body and a smart mouth.

Why not put them to good use?

SIXTEEN

Kat

When it's finally Saturday, I put on my sexiest dress. A bombshell red elastic dress that fits tightly around my curves, along with some sky-high pumps. Add red lipstick and some thick eyeliner to the mix and you've got the perfect hooker outfit.

Not that I'm fishing for men ... or making them pay.

I just want to find out what the hell Declan's hiding ... and how disturbingly fucked up it can be.

I mean, there must be a reason he's keeping it a secret,

and I can't wait to find out. I wonder if it's as juicy as I think it is. A bunch of strippers dancing for some rich dudes. If I show up like this, they'll surely think I belong there.

The bellhop already thought I was one of the girls, so it wouldn't surprise me if he makes the same mistake twice.

I grab a few of my masks and put on the most sparkly one, smiling when I look at myself in the mirror. Perfect.

I don't know if a mask is needed, but I better bring one to be sure. After all, we don't want anyone unnecessarily finding out who I am.

After grabbing my purse, I rush out the door and lock it behind me. There's no time to waste; it's almost nine, and I want to be on time for whatever's about to happen.

I wonder if Declan will be there. Though, if I go by my own deductions of his profession, he probably will. He makes girls strip in his office, so there's a high likelihood he's the one organizing the explicit events and whatever they entail.

And as an organizer, I'd expect him to keep track of the event itself to make sure it's going well. So I'm assuming I'll be able to catch a glimpse of him there. I just have to make sure he doesn't see me.

He made it clear that he doesn't want me there, but I'm too nosy to stop. I wanna know what he's up to. Besides, he doesn't even have to know. What's the harm? In and out in a jiffy. He won't even notice I'm there in the first place. And I might have the memories of a lifetime.

I only wish I could've asked him more about this before

he cut me off again. We've had little to no contact since the last time we spoke via chat. Once or twice, he asked me to come to his office, but when I asked him if he'd tell me more about his job, he cut it off, so I said no.

We played that game for a while. But it became tedious, and I'm not in the mood for playing games.

He might not want me to delve deeper, but that doesn't mean I can't try. What's a girl got to lose? It's not as if he wants a relationship with me. I just want to know what it is that hotel does. And the name has to mean *something*.

I take a cab to the hotel because you never know what might happen in terms of drugs or alcohol, so I like to be prepared. My car will be safe at home, and I've brought enough cash to get a ride back home. I told the driver to ask for me at the desk around twelve p.m., so they'll know where to look for me should something happen. You never know, right? Not that I'm expecting anything bad to happen, but it's better to be prepared.

As I walk up the stairs, I'm passed by several men in suits, all adorning masks and accompanied by beautiful girls. I wonder if they're part of the show or just visiting guests.

There's also a whole truckload of guards standing beside the doors, checking people's cards and whatnot. I don't know what they want, but I don't have it. I just hope I can pass through unnoticed.

Swallowing away the lump in my throat, I gaze through the crowd until I find a man without a girl, and I quickly shuffle to his side and wrap my arm around his.

"Hey there," I say.

"Um …" he mumbles.

"Oh, I'm one of the girls," I say with a flirtatious voice.

"But I don't have anyone accompanying me tonight …" he says, sounding confused.

"Oh, no worries." I smile my way through my lie. "I'm just here for the introductions!"

The guard stops us. "Card, please."

The man seems befuddled, but then fishes out his card from his chest pocket and hands it to the guard. "Welcome, Sir," the man says, and we're quickly walked inside by the push of the crowd.

When I'm safe, I unlock arms with the unknown man and say, "Thanks!"

He looks a bit confused, but I manage to slip away through the hoard of people and into a nearby hallway where he hopefully won't come look for me.

I didn't give him anything. Not my name nor my face. The only way he could recognize me is by my dress. However, even that option fades the moment I spot some girls walk by in velvety red dresses. I grin. Good luck identifying me now.

When I've watched the man go upstairs, I follow behind the mass, traipsing up the stairs and through the hallways, not knowing where the hell I'm going.

Suddenly, I'm pulled aside.

I almost squeal but manage to keep it together when I notice it isn't the unknown man or Declan. It's an older woman I've never seen before.

"What are you doing?" she asks.

"Following everyone into the event room?" I say, laughing it off like it's no big deal.

Fuck. Have I been caught?

"But you're one of the girls, right? The preparations room is this way," she says, dragging me along.

I'm completely distracted, but I'll go with the flow. "Oh, okay."

"Why don't you know this? It was on the papers you received," she scolds.

"Sorry, I forgot," I lie. "It's my first time."

The woman frowns. "That's strange. Declan normally never invites newbies to these ones."

"He said I was special," I add. God, I'm such a bad liar.

"Hmm …" Her lip curls up. "And what's your name?"

"Uh … Kitty," I make up on the spot.

"Where's your sticker?" she asks.

"I … I …" Damn, why does she have so many questions that I don't have any answers to? I'm running out of excuses.

"Doesn't matter," she adds, rummaging in her pocket to take out a booklet of stickers and a pen. She quickly scribbles down my name along with a number, then tears it off and hands it to me. "Put this on your chest after you're done dressing."

"Dressing?" I mutter.

But she's already dragging me along again. "Come with

me."

She pulls me through a bunch of doors and into an elevator. As the doors close, I feel like I can barely breathe. Sweat drops roll down my back as I try to maintain my composure. I have no clue where we're going. I would've much preferred to go about this alone, but now that she's here, I can't suddenly disappear on her. She looks like an important person. She'd probably call the guards on me and get me kicked out.

I have to avoid that at all cost. Better lie my way through it so I can get in and out as quickly as possible. I'm here for the show anyway. Might as well stick around and pretend I'm one of the girls, right?

As long as I keep my eyes peeled, I'll be able to find an escape route. That, or I'll ride it out and see what kind of kinky shit they do around here. Who knows? Maybe I'll like it.

I follow the lady into a dressing room where a bunch of other girls are all taking off their clothes.

I'm momentarily stunned, wondering what I'm supposed to do.

"Go on then. Put on one of the outfits," the woman says. "No time to waste."

"Right," I mumble, trying to find something, but everything seems to have holes in it. Not torn, but ... meant this way. Precisely above the crotch and chest area.

I swallow away the lump in my throat when the woman keeps looking at me as if she's waiting for me to move.

"I'll expect you all down in the ballroom in a minute. You all picked your own expertise, so you know where to go. Any questions, you can come find me in the back of the room. Left corner, staff section. Good luck." Before I can ask her any more questions, the woman has already disappeared, and I'm left with all the other girls.

There are five of us, but luckily, they're not paying attention to me. They're busy doing their makeup and checking their masks to see if they're on correctly. One of them is even pushing up her boob and spraying her vagina with something.

I wonder what the fuck is going to happen. Still, curiosity has got the better of me, so I grasp an outfit from the stack and casually put it on after taking off my dress, which I lay by the window so I know where it is. I'll come back for it later.

I peel off the sticker and push it against my skin. Surprisingly, it sticks. Number fifty-one, Kitty. That's me.

When the girls start to walk, I follow suit, out of the door and into the hallways. We pass a few doors and go down a staircase where a few women are waiting in the middle of a grand hallway.

"Welcome, ladies," two of them say, and they open the doors into a gigantic ballroom.

While the girls step inside, my heart begins to race.

The moment they step aside, each going into their own corner of the room to meet with fellow guests, my brain struggles to comprehend what I'm witnessing.

Everywhere I look, I see men fucking half-naked or partially naked women—on chairs, couches, tables, and even the floor. Several contraptions are set up in each section of the big ballroom. Like a cross with a woman strapped to it. She's being whipped with a spiky leather strap that leaves red welts all over her body. Her screams fill the room, but no one seems bothered by it. Most are too busy themselves, and others are enjoying the sight.

With my lips parted and my breath faltering, I stroll through the crowds slowly, watching the spectacle of debauchery all around me.

Two men fucking one girl on a sofa while another girl alternates between two men's dicks in her mouth. Another girl casually plays with herself on a stool, spreading herself for all to see.

Another one is strapped to a wooden chair, her legs and hands bound while men use her mouth and hands to pleasure themselves. Another one is tied to something metallic hanging from the ceiling, her body floating in the air tied down with ropes in a very uncomfortable but beautiful looking position.

In the middle of the room, twenty or more men are fucking three girls. Each rotate position after a few minutes have passed. The middle one is on her belly with her ass high up in the air and covered in lube. In fact, everyone in this room seems slippery and wet, with the exception of the men still wearing their suits. But nothing can hide their obvious hard-ons, protruding through their pants as they watch the show in front of them.

"Beautiful, isn't it?"

I turn my head. Someone's behind me, but I have no clue who it is. I don't recognize the voice. All I see is a man in a black suit, just like all the others, only this one has his hair tucked up into a bun.

"Yes," I mutter, not even sure how to respond. "Everyone is so … relaxed."

It's as if everyone here is already used to this. Like they were expecting this to happen.

Everyone … but me.

"Yes, the ultimate satisfaction."

"An orgy," I reply, stunned and mildly confused by my own excitement at seeing the girls grin so gleefully at how they are being used.

"Do you see it?" the man whispers, pointing at one of the girls in the middle of the room. "The happiness on their faces?"

I nod, still breathless.

"They're doing this out of their own free will," he says.

If that's true … wow.

All these people together in one room, coming together just for the sake of having wild, kinky sex. It's almost like I just jumped into a movie, but it's playing out in real life, right in front of me. And here I thought I was depraved …

Still, I wonder why all these people would sign up for this. Is it only because they're interested, or is there more at play? How would they gather so many people willing to give their bodies to one another?

"They're getting paid, right?" I ask.

"Yes … but I'd wager at least one of them would do it for free," he replies, then he looks at me questioningly. "Would you?"

"Me?" I stammer, my cheeks flushing with heat.

"You're one of them, aren't you?" he asks as if it's the most natural thing. His eyes casually dip down and gaze at my tits.

Only then do I remember the clothes I'm wearing. Or more specifically, the lack thereof. Because my tits are in full frontal view with this mesh top, and my pussy too.

I struggle not to cover up.

So many people are here. All of them can see me.

A pang of guilt and shame hits me right in the guts.

That's when his hand touches the back of my neck. "Don't be shy. All of us are here for pleasure. Nothing more."

When he attempts to kiss me, I move back.

"Sorry, I'm just getting my bearings, okay?" I mutter. "I have to find … my client." I clear my throat even though it feels completely clamped up.

He pauses, and for a second there, I fear he might attempt to grasp me, but then he smiles sweetly. "I didn't know you were already taken. Well, have fun then. I'll be off to find another girl."

"Good luck," I reply, laughing it off as if it's no big deal.

Even though it is. This whole thing is … beyond a big

deal. It's like nothing I've ever witnessed. Bigger than anything I've ever known to exist. An event like this? No wonder Declan kept it a secret.

Speaking of, I haven't seen or found him yet. I wonder if he's here and where I can find him. Would he stand in the back or in the shadows, watching his clients to check whether they're content? Or would he actually participate to show them how it's done?

I walk a bit more, looking around to see if I can find him, but there are so many people here that it's hard to filter anything recognizable. All I see are masks, suits, nudity. The only bit that makes people stand out is the way they style their hair … and maybe their height and weight … and the size of their dick. Still, it's not enough to find Declan. Not in this sea of people.

Still, I can't help but be amazed at the spectacle, the music, and the scent of perfume filling the room. The mixture makes me feel strangely relaxed, my body floating through the room as I stare at all the scenes.

Both women and men cry out in pure lust, bodies entangling, stacked on top of each other, people grasping one another, sucking in the air, moaning out loud. Not an ounce of shame is visible. Not in any one of them.

I admire their willingness to give in … the power that it holds over them as they sink deeper into what looks like sexual nirvana.

And for a second, I wish I could join them.

Suddenly, a voice behind me pulls me from my

thoughts. "Fifty-one. Come with me."

It's a woman. The same woman who pushed me into the changing room. She grabs my hand and pulls me along, this time gently, into the middle of the ballroom to the big table where the three girls are being fucked.

"Time to switch," the woman whispers to the girl on the left.

She immediately leans up and crawls off the table, her body covered in lube and cum.

"Lie down," the woman tells me.

I do what she says.

I don't even think about it.

My brain is on complete survival mode. Completely shut off from reality.

When my body hits the cold table, I go into a trance. My breathing slow and soft, my muscles letting go. With my eyes wide open, I stare at the man propping himself in front of me. His hands grasp my face, tilting my head back over the table until everything is upside down.

The only thing I see is his hard dick bouncing up and down as it comes closer to my face.

Two hands suddenly grip my thighs, fingers digging into my skin.

"Wait."

A burst of panic flows through me. I break free of the stranger's grasp around my throat and lift my head. When our eyes meet, my heart stops beating.

Declan.

170

SEVENTEEN

DECLAN

It's her.

I knew it the moment I laid eyes on her when she first appeared through the crowd of people coming into the ballroom. She had that same walk, that same long ponytail, that same devious smile on her face. It had to be her.

I was hesitant to approach at first because I didn't want to make a scene and upset the customers. But the moment Greta called her out to come forward, I knew I had to put a stop to it.

And holy shit, the moment our eyes connect, an ungodly amount of rage fills me to the brim.

Why is she here? How did she pull this off?

Goddammit, so many questions with no answers because I can't ask her right now.

She's on that table, about to get fucked by a client.

No, not just one ... twenty or more.

They were all going to have their way with her, coming on her body, her hands, her face ... inside her.

And the mere thought of that angers me so much that I squeeze her skin and don't let go.

"Hold on, one second," I say to the man, trying not to sound like a growling animal even though I feel like one.

I lean in and grab her hand, slowly pulling her up, keeping an eye out for the clients who are still fucking the other girls. I don't want them to stop. The event must continue, no matter what.

So I lean in and softly whisper into her ear, "Follow me."

She nods, staring at me as if she's seeing a ghost.

She looks completely out of it. The perfume, music, and atmosphere have done their jobs well, it seems. But it wasn't supposed to happen to her. She wasn't supposed to be one of the girls. She wasn't ever supposed to see any of this.

And now she has.

I snap my fingers at Greta, who immediately pulls another girl from the crowd and puts her on the table as a replacement. I turn my head to her and say, "Take over for a while."

She nods and eases the clients back into the event. I

don't want them to pay any attention to me. In fact, I don't even want them to notice I'm gone.

Nor do I want them to know they ever saw *her*.

Kat … what the hell is she thinking?

With her wrist firmly in my grasp, I pull her outside the ballroom and instruct the staff not to let anyone in unless they can show a card. Then I proceed through the hallways.

"My clothes …" she says as I pull her down the stairs.

But I don't give a shit about her clothes right now. If she has the balls to dress up as one of the women hired for this event, then she can walk naked through the lobby too.

"Wait!" she says, trying to pull away, but I won't let her.

I push her against the wall and hiss, "You loved the shame, remember?"

Then I tear off her mask and throw it on the floor, exposing her face.

I'm not mistaken. It's really her. And it doesn't even fucking surprise me.

She seems shocked. Scared, even. I almost feel guilty, but then I remember why I'm so angry.

"You put this on. You made that choice," I growl. "Now c'mon."

I drag her along down more stairs and into the hallway until we finally reach my office. I push her inside and slam the door shut behind me.

***

Kat

For every step he takes, I take one back until my butt leans against the desk. I search around to try to find anything to defend myself with, but all I find is a pen. It's enough ... no, it's not nearly enough, but it's something.

I don't even know why I think I need something to protect myself with.

But damn ... that look in his eyes ... it's murderous. And I think I understand why. A grin spreads across my lips, and the fear fades by the second. Now I know his secret. And boy oh boy ... how juicy it is.

Neither of us dare to speak despite our mouths being unhinged. I know whatever words come from my mouth have to be good or he won't believe them. But the same goes for him. I need explanations. A reason for this madness. And I definitely need to know more.

"What the hell are you doing here?" he asks through gritted teeth.

I casually lean back and place my hands on his desk. "Enjoying the show."

"That's *not* what I asked," he growls, marching toward me.

"Actually, it is." I know I'm being snarky, but I can't

174

help myself when he gives me that look.

"Don't. Lie. To. Me." He's practically in my face right now. But I'm not scared.

"It's not a lie," I reply.

His lip twitches, and I wonder what he's thinking. If he has as many questions as I do. If he feels caught in the act.

"Bullshit," he says. "You came here to spy on me. Why?"

"Spy?" I say, narrowing my eyes.

He grabs my arms. "What are you hiding?"

"Nothing," I say, frowning.

"Who do you work for?"

He seems out of his mind.

"It's none of your business," I reply.

His grip grows tighter as every second passes. "The moment you walked into my hotel, you made it *my* business."

"So it's *your* hotel now?"

"Don't play semantics with me," he growls. "You knew what you were getting yourself into when you walked through that door."

"Why would I come in the first place if I knew what kind of sex show you guys were putting on?"

"Oh … oh-ho-ho." He laughs. Hard. And loud. "Don't pretend you don't love the kink."

"I didn't—"

"Stop lying," he says, pushing me further against the desk. "I'm done with your games."

"Let go of me," I say.

"No, not until you tell me who sent you."

"What?" I make a face. Has he lost his mind? "No one sent me."

"Lies. Who was it ... Davies from across the street? The national gossip paper? The cops?"

"No one," I repeat. I don't know what he wants me to tell him. "I came here because I wanted to know what you were doing."

"Right ... and you know *everything* now," he sneers.

"Because you wouldn't tell me," I say.

"No ... of course not. Look at what happened," he says.

"Nothing would've happened if you'd just explained what you do here at this hotel."

He narrows his eyes. "Oh, and you think I'm just going to tell you? Do you think I'm stupid?"

"No, I think you find it hard to trust people. And that's okay," I reply.

There's a momentary pause, a silence that thickens in the air, causing us both to choke up.

"Can I even trust you?" he asks, his lip curling up.

I nod. I don't think I can gather the words. It's hard. So hard ...

Because all I want to do right now is go back home, sit down behind my laptop, and write that motherfucking story like my life depends on it. But I can't. At least, not right now with him breathing down my neck like a certified dragon.

He's pissed off, and rightfully so, but I can't turn back

time. I made this choice for a reason.

He sighs and shakes his head, releasing my arm. Instead, he places his hand on the desk behind me. "You play a dangerous game, Kat."

"I guess it's what I like." I lean forward, using my boobs as leverage.

I know it's wrong, but I also know I don't want to get into trouble. Especially not with him. I'd rather keep him on my good side. Whatever that means right now.

"What were you thinking?" he says. His voice still sounds strained, but less than before.

"I just wanted to see. That's all."

"You were curious. I get it. But you should've come to me," he says.

"I did. Several times. You ignored me," I reply.

"For good reasons. This company lives and survives on discretion."

"I can be discreet," I say.

"Right," he scoffs.

I eye him up and down. "What?"

"Like this?" He grabs the bottom piece of the short outfit I'm wearing and waves it around as though it's a bunch of leaves. It's truly whimsical, but it makes sense in the setting.

But I am well aware of how it looks … and how naked I feel right now.

"Your people made me wear this," I reply, feeling my face warm just from the thought of him seeing all of me.

And when his eyes actually roll down, my whole body tingles.

"These are for the girls we hire," he says. "And you aren't one of them. How did you get in?"

"Easy." I shrug. "I followed the crowd, pretended I belonged to one of your customers, and presto."

He frowns. "I'll need to have a tough conversation with my guards."

I smirk. "Sounds like it."

"Don't think I'm letting you off the hook," he says. "What you did was wrong."

"*Oh* … are you going to have me arrested?" I jest, jokingly poking him, but he doesn't even flinch.

"I should." His voice is so serious I don't even know whether he's for real. Yikes.

"Sorry," I say. "I just couldn't stop. I had to see for myself."

"And?" He cocks his head, lifting a brow.

"I …" God, I don't think it's ever been this difficult to find the right words.

Suddenly, he lifts my chin. "Tell me what you saw."

"People … naked … fucking …"

"And?"

"A woman was screaming while she was being hit."

"And how did that make you feel?" he asks.

"Strange …"

"In a good way or a bad way?"

I lick my lips and think about it for a second. "I don't

know. I don't know why she did it."

"Some people like pain. Others like giving it," he says. "But they're all there because they want to be."

"Okay." I frown, letting out a sigh.

"What you saw is strictly confidential. Do you understand?" His sudden shift in tone has me on edge.

"You want me to give you my word," I fill in for him. "But even that won't be enough."

He pauses for a moment before answering. "You're right."

I fold my arms. "You don't trust me."

"You haven't exactly given me any reason to."

"Likewise," I retort. "But I *am* trying."

"Maybe you should've come to me first before attempting to break into an event."

"Like I said, I already tried. You blocked me. *Again.*" My emphasis on the last word makes his lip twitch.

"Because I was busy organizing the event, and I didn't want you snooping around."

"So do you pay these people or what?" I ask. Now that we're back to square one.

"Yes. Some. Not everyone," he admits.

"The clients pay you for the joy of fucking women. Got it."

"Women aren't the only ones subjecting themselves to this. There's ladies' nights too."

"Great," I say.

"And gay nights. We organize pretty much anything our

clients request."

"Okay. But is it legal?"

"Of course, it is. Our hotel wouldn't be operating if it wasn't," he retorts.

"Then why are you so upset about me finding out?"

His face darkens, and his mouth shuts. I guess I got him there.

"Why are you so into me?"

The question hits me like a truck. Like he just bulldozed over me.

"Why do you have to ask that question?"

The look in his eyes has changed from rage and confusion ... to utter defeat.

"I've been a dick to you. A straight and utter asshole. I've done nothing but be unkind to you. I've been pushing you away so hard," he says, his head tilting down to look me in the eyes. "Why do you keep hanging on?"

"Because I feel like there could be more between us," I whisper, barely able to breathe with him this close to me.

His lips are so close I could almost taste them. And fuck, do I want to ... so badly. Even after all this. All this rage, all this pushing and shoving, all this filth.

I still want him so badly that I swear my heart would stop if he said yes.

But he doesn't.

No matter how much I lean in with my lips parted and my chest pushing up against his, he doesn't make the plunge.

180

Suddenly, the door opens, and the moment is gone.

"Declan?"

He steps back, clearing his throat, pretending we weren't even close enough to touch.

"Sorry, am I interrupting?" the woman says.

"Maybe," he answers. Not quite a yes … Dammit.

"Sorry, but Greta called me to ask if I could come and get you. It's important. Something about a girl wanting out."

"Fuck," he growls, running his fingers through his hair. "Why now?"

As he pulls away, my flimsy outfit is exposed, and the woman stares at me. I immediately attempt to cover up using my hands, but it's not enough to hide my shame that's probably turning my face red right now.

"She said it was urgent. The client's objecting. We need you."

"I'm coming," he says. "Just … give me a minute to sort out this mess."

Mess. Right. That's what I am. A mess.

To him. To my parents. To myself. And everyone else.

"Of course," the woman says, and she closes the door behind her.

Declan turns around to face me again. "I think we'd better get you home."

I nod, having lost the energy to fight him on this. For now anyway.

He grabs a long coat from the coat hanger and holds it out to me. "Put this on."

I do what he says. I don't protest.

"I'll call a cab."

"It's fine," I say. "I already had one on call."

It's not fine, but right now, I don't want to make things any more awkward than they already are.

"Are you sure?" he asks. His voice strains as though he wants to say more but is holding back.

"Yes," I say.

I don't know why he suddenly cares so much. Maybe he still wants to keep tabs on me.

I smile as he frowns. The room feels as if it's on fire right now. Like we're both avoiding responsibility for what happened here.

It feels so bad that I don't even say goodbye before walking out the door and running out of the hotel. Out of sight, out of mind. At least for now.

Because I'm sure as hell not going to sleep tonight. And I don't think he will either.

EIGHTEEN

DECLAN

When I finally get home after a difficult day, I immediately jump under the shower. But it doesn't cool me down, not by a long shot. Today was such a racket, and I can't even wrap my head around it. Nothing I do can pull that image from my mind.

Kat ... lying there on that table ... almost being fucked by another man.

My fist balls as I step out from under the shower. I have to stop thinking about her, but it seems an impossible task, especially after what she did today. I'm still amazed at how she managed to sneak in. Now I have to reprimand all my guards or hire new ones just to make up for this mishap. I can't believe she actually got past them. They definitely need a schooling.

And that's not even the worst of my problems. What if my boss finds out? I'd be fucked.

I'm lucky no one noticed anything off when I intervened. Greta simply went on with her task and never asked me about the girl I dragged out. And Sarah wasn't even fazed that I had a one-on-one with one of the girls. Apparently, she thought I was scolding her for doing a poor job, which is technically true. But it wasn't for the reasons she thought.

Still, all I can do is hope they keep their mouth shut about what happened.

Let alone Kat herself. If any of this gets out to the press, we're screwed. *I'm* screwed.

I can pack up my things and leave. And worse ... the hotel will probably be ruined. No one will want to stay here anymore for fear of exposure.

Everything rests on our ability to stay under the radar. Our client's privacy is the priciest commodity there is. Nothing can ever pay for that. They give us their hard-earned trust, and now, because of what Kat did, it almost shattered.

Or rather ... because of what I did.

Because Kat only went there to search for me. To find the answers to the questions she had because I wouldn't give them to her.

God, I never should've even gone to meet her.

I slam my fridge shut and take a much-needed sip straight from the bottle of wine. I'll have to ship her clothes back to her, I guess. That, or invite her back to my office to personally hand them to her, which is the stupidest idea ever, considering the way I've been following my cock lately.

Why do I have to be such a horny bastard all the time? If I could've kept my dick in my pants, none of this would've ever happened. But guess what? It did, and now I have to deal with it.

I sink down on the couch and groan. Fuck. I'm sounding like a whiny old bitch.

Another sip.

The heat going down my throat doesn't erase the image of her in that outfit. No matter how many gulps I take. In fact, the more I down the alcohol, the more her image becomes brighter.

Her face lighting up at the sight of me. Her lips curling up when she catches me off guard. Her nipples peeking through her top. Her wet pussy waiting for me to claim it.

Fuck.

I don't know what about her has me so infatuated, but I'm hooked.

I slam the bottle down on the table and grab my cell phone, opening the browser. I immediately go to the site and click her name.

I'm typing the message I know is the bad choice, but I can't stop my fingers from doing it anyway.

D: Let's meet up. Tomorrow evening. My office.

***

Kat

When I see his message, my heart practically jumps out of my chest. Is he actually pursuing me? After claiming again and again he didn't want to take it any further?

I mull it over for a few seconds. Should I go?

I mean, after his blatant attempts to get me to fuck off, this seems to come out of nowhere. Although I am interested in seeing where things could go with him. After all, they say you should find a partner who matches your sexual energy ... and he definitely fits all the criteria.

But is it even healthy? Starting things this way with a guy like him?

I don't want to get my heart stomped on.

If I could only tell myself not to let emotions get involved, it would be easy. A quick and easy bang evening, and then I slip away again as if I was never there in the first place.

But can I really tell myself that when I already feel my heart flutter every time I speak to him?

I sigh and grumble to myself. The only solution to my problem would be to cut things off now. Completely stop speaking to him.

But who am I kidding? As if I'd ever be able to do that.

I'm so easily persuaded to do things because my body wants it.

So before I change my mind, I quickly type in the chat.

NaughtyKitten: Changed your mind?

D: We should talk more about the other night.

NaughtyKitten: Right ... if you say so.

D: Yes or no?

NaughtyKitten: Yes, sir!

D: Good Kitten. Sleep well. Don't be too naughty.

NaughtyKitten: I'll think of you before I rub one out.

D: Take some pictures if you do. Bring them with you tomorrow.

NaughtyKitten: Will do, if I take them.

D: Good. And one last thing ... what's your number?

I pause, staring at the screen for a second. I thought he was against giving out personal details, and a telephone number is definitely personal. Then again, this might mean he's up for something more. Maybe I should trust him. After all, I already did everything I wasn't supposed to, so maybe this is a great way to extend an olive branch.

So I send him my phone number and wait for his reply.

D: Thanks.

NaughtyKitten: *You're not going to give me yours?*
D: *You'll get it when I give it.*

The chat ends, and he goes offline.

Well, fuck me ... that was quick.

Why would he not give me his number? Is he afraid I'm going to use it for something bad? Or maybe he wants to take things slow ...

Well, one thing's for sure, the moment he texts me, I'll know his number.

I grin as I close the chat site and curl up with my phone in my hand.

Fuck me. I'm really losing my shit to this man.

***

The next day, I march into the hotel without shame. Without the mask, no one will recognize me anyway. The bellhop immediately walks toward me when he spots me, and for a second there, I fear he might remember me from that day I lied to his face.

"Hello, ma'am. Can I ask you what your room number is, please?"

"No room. I'm here for an appointment with Mr. D. Porter," I reply.

He frowns and says, "Oh ... do you mind if I check this with him?"

Well, well. I guess they upped their security. Declan probably reprimanded them because of me.

"Sure, go ahead," I say with a smirk. This time, I don't come uninvited.

"One second," the bellhop says, and he leans over the desk and calls a number using the phone there. "What's your name?" he asks.

"Kat," I say, smiling.

There's a quick conversation back and forth, but I'm not listening. I'd much rather look at the guests, trying to find one I recognize from that night. I wish I could pinpoint them just by their hairstyles, but it's proving much more difficult than I thought. I guess the masks did provide ample protection for the guests.

I wonder if all events are like that. Secretive. Exclusive. Sensual.

What would the women's nights look like? Or the gay nights? I hope there are mixed nights too. There probably are, knowing people and their sexual needs.

I wish I could see all the events, but I'm pretty sure Declan won't let me. And now that he's caught me red-handed, I doubt I'd ever be able to sneak into the other events.

I guess I should be lucky I even got into one of them. And what a memory it is.

At first, I wasn't sure whether I liked it because I was struck in awe at what I was seeing right in front of me. But after letting it sink in, I realized that was only the initial shock, which I got over pretty quickly.

So quickly, I knew the next day I'd do it again in a

heartbeat if I could.

A door has opened wide for me, and I don't think I want to shut it.

"Okay, you're good to go," the bellhop says as he puts the phone back on the desk. "He's waiting upstairs for you, ma'am."

"Thank you," I say, winking as I walk off.

That was surprisingly easy. Then again, I have nothing to hide this time.

I make my way up to his office and knock on his door. It takes him a while to answer.

"Come in." His voice already makes the goose bumps scatter on my skin even though he didn't say anything sexually charged. My body is so used to following his commands that it gets excited at the slightest amount he gives.

When I open the door and step inside, he's already waiting in front of his desk, casually dipping his hands into his pocket.

"Glad you came," he says.

Immediately, the image of me coming on his lap flashes into my mind.

From the look on his face, I think he knows exactly what I'm thinking.

Goddamn him and his constant innuendos.

"Wouldn't miss it," I reply.

His eyes slowly pan down my body, taking his sweet time. "Nice dress."

"Thanks. I quite like it." It's banana yellow and has folds at the bottom that make it flowy. It's also perfect for a quick romp on a desk. Not that I was thinking about that when I put it on.

"So tell me ... what did you think of the event?"

"Now you're interested?" I narrow my eyes.

"I wasn't ever *not* interested. I'm just worried ..." he admits.

"That I'm going to tell someone," I fill in.

"Exactly." He crosses his arms.

"I won't," I say, smiling as I walk toward him.

Now he's smirking too, but it's not the kind that makes you happy ... more the kind that makes you incredibly mischievous.

"Did you bring the pictures?"

Of course, he'd ask.

I printed them out especially for him since my face doesn't appear on them, of course.

I reach into my purse and take them out, placing them on his desk. Then I place my purse on his chair and look out the window. It's so peaceful and quiet out there today. A typical Sunday.

But my Sunday's anything except typical when it involves him.

I can hear him shuffle through them. He's probably enjoying himself thoroughly right now, smirking at the sight of my fingers inside me, and my nipples hard and on full display.

"Did you enjoy yourself?" he asks.

I'm not going to lie. I loved making them. And I love that he's now feeling that same excitement flow through his body. "Yes."

Suddenly, he's behind me. His hand snakes around my belly, his mouth dangerously close to my ear. "Did you think of me while pleasuring yourself?"

I grin. "Maybe."

"Don't play coy with me," he teases.

"The answer depends on what this whole thing is about …"

"I wanted to see you. That's it."

"Really?" I find it hard to believe. "Then why send me away every time we meet?"

I know I'm asking tough questions, but I just wanna know. I'm tired of playing silly games. I'm into adult games only.

"You know why … the rules …" he whispers.

"Fuck the rules."

"They're there to protect us. Like my rules protect me from exposing this company and losing my job."

I snort. "How's that working out for you?"

"That's exactly my problem. It's not."

"And it's my fault?" I reply.

Suddenly, his lips are on my skin. So soft … yet so erotic that my legs feel as though they're going to collapse underneath my body. And the moment he drags them along my ear, my eyes practically roll into the back of my head.

192

"Don't talk back to me, Kitten. It makes me mad, and you don't like me when I'm mad."

"Maybe I do," I taunt, biting my lip when he sinks his teeth into my skin to nibble gently.

"You wouldn't say that if you knew all the things I want to do to your body …" he groans, his fingers digging into my skin as he holds on tight.

"Show me. I'd love to find out," I murmur, closing my eyes so I can enjoy his touch.

I don't think he's ever been this close with me. Or that we've ever kissed.

"First, Kat Bronson … you need to tell me where you work."

What?

Before I can turn around, he's already spun me. He grabs my arms tight, and says, "Yeah … I searched your number."

Fuck. Why did I give it to him? Of course, he'd do that.

"Surprisingly, all it returned was a few old forum posts of yours, but no social media."

"I don't use them," I lie.

"Of course, you don't," he says with a stupid grin on his face. "You just use a sex chat site …"

"Right," I reply, as my entire face heats up.

He's still so close that I can feel his breath on my skin, and it tingles like crazy.

"So Kitten … what's it going to be?" he hums, leaning his forehead against mine.

"I don't care. I don't mind. I just want you …"

"Are you sure about that, Kitten?" he murmurs, his lips so close I can almost taste them. "You haven't told me everything yet."

"Neither have you," I murmur with a ragged breath.

The smirk on his face is seriously sexy. "Is that why I'm so attracted to you? The secrets?"

"Maybe," I reply, grinning too.

Suddenly, his mouth latches onto mine. Without even being able to finish my sentence. The one I can't remember anyway because oh my God, he's actually kissing me.

And I fucking love it.

His lips … are everything.

Addictive. All-consuming. Hot. Needy.

His tongue dips out to lick my lips, groans coming out as he takes what he wants. His body presses against mine, smashing me into the window as I wrap my arms around his neck and pull him in for more.

Just one kiss and I'm already done for.

And the moment his mouth unlatches from mine, it feels like I went through a whirlwind of emotions, a roller coaster I don't want to get off from.

"So are you going to tell me why I can't find anything about you?"

"No," I reply. "I don't like being searchable online."

Why can't we just go back to kissing? I lean in, attempting to do so, but he leans back.

"Or you have a second number that you didn't give

me."

"Wha—"

"Don't pretend you don't know what I'm asking. It's as if you don't exist online. The only possibility is that you gave me a number you rarely use."

I swallow away the lump in my throat.

"That's it, isn't it? Tell me. Do you have a second phone?"

"Yes. I have a personal phone and a phone for work. So what? A lot of people do."

"No, just those with a profession that needs privacy. Like mine. Or you know … law enforcement, journalists … people who want to protect whatever it is they're hiding."

I lean back away from him, but there's nowhere to go.

I'm stuck between him and the window with a heart that's going a million miles an hour.

"I'm not hiding anything," I repeat.

"Yes, you are," he says through gritted teeth. His grip on my arms grows firmer. Then he spins me around again, shoving me face first against the glass pane.

"You wanted to be fucked? You wanted to be mine?" he growls. "I'll give it to you … my way."

NINETEEN

Kat

His hand snakes down my body, all the way to my ass, and squeezes tight. I suck in a breath as he pushes up my dress and claims ownership of my ass.

"Still want it?" he growls. Then he smacks it so hard I squeal.

"Fuck!" I can't hold it in. My skin is glowing, and it sizzles everywhere.

"That's what you get for being dishonest," he says.

He slaps the other cheek, making the pain reverberate all

over my body. I can even feel it in my pussy, making it thump. *Fuck.*

"I'm not lying," I say, but he smacks my ass again when I do.

He rips off my panties, throwing them in the corner. "Stop denying it," he growls.

Another smack has me moaning out loud. I'm not sure whether it's from pain or pleasure. The sensations are all over the place. The palm of his hand is against my back as he spanks my ass with his other hand again and again until my skin is hot and my legs begin to quiver.

"Are you going to tell me who you work for?" he asks, his voice dark and heavy.

But that's just the thing. I don't want to tell him. If I do, I'll probably never get into the hotel again. And despite him being such a raging bastard, I do fucking love it when he humiliates me like this.

The curtains aren't even closed, and it's broad daylight, so anyone could see us. Anyone could see me. Naked, in front of the window, for everyone to see. And I can't even tell him to stop.

His hand gently caresses my ass and then it dips between my legs, claiming what's left of my dignity.

"Already wet, huh? Are you such a dirty little slut that you can't keep it together?"

Fuck. I have a love-hate relationship with the way he talks to me. It makes me want to snap back, but at the same time, I want nothing more than for him to take me hard.

His hand cups me, and then he pushes two fingers inside. I gasp, bracing myself against the window as he thrusts in and out of me. "Still determined to keep your little secret?" he asks.

I don't respond. Anything I say can and will be used against me. Not in the court of law, but definitely when it comes to his fingers and cock. And I seriously don't want to miss out on that.

As much as I hate to admit it, I'd do anything for him to continue. Anything. Even moan when he smacks my ass while his fingers are still inside me.

When he pulls them out, I feel delirious. Overcome with need.

I can hear him suck and moan. "Delicious."

His voice is far less harsh, but much darker ... like rich, creamy chocolate I wanna eat all day long.

"So are you going to tell me your little secret?" he murmurs.

"I don't have—"

"Yes, you do," he says. "Are you working for the competition? Is that it? Trying to steal our ideas?"

"No," I reply, glancing over my shoulder.

"Okay then ..." A wicked grin spreads on his lips. "Guess I'll have to fuck it out of you then."

His zipper is pulled down, and a packet is ripped open. Three seconds later, his tip is right at my entrance, and he pushes inside. Firm thrusts fill me, causing me to tiptoe around as I struggle to maintain my balance.

He's so deep inside me that I feel as though I'm about to burst.

Every push and pull has me struggling to breathe.

Suddenly, he tears down the back zipper of my dress and yanks it off my shoulders, exposing my tits. And that's not even the end of it because it drops down to the floor, leaving me bare naked. Right in front of the window. For the world to see.

"Fuck! What are you doing?" I try to cover myself, but it's impossible with only two hands.

"Enjoying what belongs to me," he growls, thrusting right back into my pussy again.

No hesitation. Only rabid lust filling this room as he fucks me raw.

"No limits. That's what we agreed on, no?" he asks.

"But everyone can see," I say, trying not to panic even though my body feels like it's about to succumb to the pleasure. Because let's face it … even though it's a scary thought to know people could be watching—and so fucking wrong—I'm still letting him do this.

I'm willingly letting him fuck me against the window for the whole world to see without pushing him away.

"We're high enough not to be lewd in public," he muses. "But I'm sure someone will see your thirsty pussy."

"Fuck!" I moan as he slams into me with fervor.

"You had no limits, remember?" he says. "Or do you want to quit?"

This is a taunt. It has to be.

And no fucking way am I going to answer that question.

"Just say the word, and I'll stop," he growls.

He's unrelenting. Like he's fucking me out of rage. Fucking me to get me to talk.

But I won't budge. Not yet.

"You love this, admit it," he groans.

We're banging like animals. As if I'm merely a fuck doll to him. And I don't even mind. All I crave is the fix he gives me. I'm literally addicted to the way he treats me. How he degrades me. Uses me. Humiliates me. Turns me upside down. Makes me remember his name, his touch, his cock, his claim on my body.

Everything. I want it … and more.

The pressure is building, and I'm on the verge of coming when he pulls out and smacks my ass so hard that I squeal out loud.

"Not yet, Kitten. Wait until I say you can," he says, sliding his finger along my slit to make me aware of how badly I've caved to his will.

He leans to the side and grabs something off his desk. I can't see what it is, but it's definitely a bottle because a liquid is squirted onto my ass.

"Now the real fun begins …"

***

DECLAN

First, I insert one finger. Slowly but not gently. I want her to feel every inch. Every nook and cranny of her body … that I own. Every piece of her that she wants to give to me.

I want her to know she gave it to me willingly … but I intend to take it without remorse.

I'm not the type to ever desire a girl more than once or twice, but this girl is begging for it. Her struggled moans make it so much more fun, especially when I add another finger.

She gasps and tries to look over her shoulder to see what I'm going to do, but I shove her right back against the window.

"No peeking," I say. "Just enjoy."

"It feels so tight!"

"It'll only get tighter …" I groan from the thought of claiming her ass. God, I can't fucking wait. But first, I need to prepare her for my size.

I grab more lube and spread it all across, making sure my fingers are nicely oiled before I push them in farther.

"Have you ever been fucked in your ass, Kitten?" I ask.

"No …"

"Toys?"

"Maybe once or twice … Okay, a few more times. But

no dick." She gulps, her body shivering as I go deep and start to thrust. "Oh God …"

"Don't fight it. Relax and take it deep …" I whisper into her ear, filling her completely.

As her head tilts back to rest on my shoulder, I add another finger.

A high-pitched noise escapes her mouth, so I cover it with my free hand. "Shh … don't want anyone to hear now, do we?"

She shakes her head softly, then nods, sending mixed signals.

I grin. "Confused about what you should be feeling?"

The look in her eyes is enough. It tells me everything I need to know. All the ways in which she'll submit to my every desire. She's perfect … so perfect I can't fucking get enough of her.

When I'm done sizing her up, I take out my fingers and push my cock into her ass instead.

She's caught by surprise, her mouth forming an o-shape as I slowly enter her ass.

"You wanted it filthy?" I moan, going deeper and deeper. "Then take it like a good girl and moan for me."

When I take my hand away from her mouth, she makes a sound that pushes all my buttons. And I bury myself inside her to the base. The more noise she makes, the more turned on I get even though that's not at all what's supposed to happen.

I'm fucking her to get information out of her, yet she

and that delicious body of hers have gotten me to the point that I just want to ravage her, end of.

The tighter she feels, the harder I get, and the greedier I become. I grab her wrists and use them as reins to fuck her even harder. Every crevice of her body is exposed. Anyone could spot us right now, and the mere thought makes my cock pulse and my balls tighten.

But I have to keep the goal in mind.

"Are you finally ready to tell me what you're up to?" I growl, slamming into her with every word.

"Fuck …"

That's all she manages to pronounce, and I don't blame her. It's hard to talk with a dick up your ass.

So I start fingering her while I keep fucking her, amplifying the sensations and driving her wild with lust. She gyrates against my fingers as I toy with her clit and push them into her pussy. Her body seems to sing and dance to every single one of my tunes. Like it was made solely for me.

But right before she reaches her climax, I stop touching her entirely, and I pull out.

She sucks in a breath, and mumbles, "What … why did you stop?"

I slide my length across her ass, making her acutely aware of just how much her body is under my control. "Because you're still not being truthful …"

"Please …" she mumbles.

"Oh, so you want more of this?" I ask, prodding her back entrance with just the tip. "Beg me for it."

"Please ... give it to me." Her voice is unsteady—weak—as if she's given up the fight.

Good. "Where, Kitten? What hole belongs to me?"

"All of them," she responds.

A devious grin spreads across my face. "And which hole do I want right now?"

"My ass ... fuck my ass, please."

God, I love it when she says those dirty words. I don't think she's ever said them to anyone else before.

"Good ... you're finally learning," I growl, and I shove my dick back inside. "You're my little slut, and you do as I say."

"Fuck!" she mewls as I bang her hard and fast.

Even though I let go of her wrists to play with her, I don't let her adjust positions as I pound away. I want her to know she belongs to me now. Whether she likes it or not, she gave herself to me willingly, and this is what happens when you prance around in front of me. Tease me and you're going to get royally fucked.

And even though I still don't have an answer to my question, I keep taking her ass because I'm already too engulfed in lust to stop. Her nipples push against the cold glass, peaking hard, and in the reflection, I watch myself fuck her. I keep flicking her clit, feeling it swell underneath my fingers. And right before I come, I tell her to come.

When she does, her ass contracts around my dick, making it even tighter, and it sends me over the edge.

I pull out, rip off the condom, and squirt all over her

ass, covering it with cum. Then I lather it all over her with my shaft, making sure it's nice and glossy for me to enjoy.

Then I grab my phone from my desk and take a picture of her.

"What's that for?" she asks, still panting, still dripping wet.

I smile, cocking my head when she gazes at me over her shoulder. "Insurance."

Her face turns sour. "For what?"

"That you'll keep me and this business a secret."

The infuriated look on her face means I'm right about that.

"What?" she gasps, turning around to face me. Her eyes shift down toward the phone. "Show me."

I lift it up but hold it far away, showing her the picture that clearly shows her face and ass. "Should you talk about my work … This will have me covered."

"You wouldn't," she says through gritted teeth.

"Try me," I reply.

I barely manage to tuck my phone into my pocket before she tries to snag it away from me. "Ah, ah." I lift a finger and sway it from side to side. "Mine."

"That's *not* fair."

"Life's not fair," I say, raising a brow.

"Really?" she scoffs, cringing. "What does that have to do with you keeping pictures of me?"

"I like to be prepared for the worst." I tuck my cock back into my pants and zip up, then pick up the condom and throw it in the trash.

Still enraged, she snags some tissues from my desk to rub her ass dry. "You're only assuming I'm a bad girl who works for some evil company. I'm not."

"Well, since you won't tell me, I don't know that for sure, now do I?"

She rubs her lips together, clearly holding something back. I know it's because she's frustrated that I don't believe her. But what else can I do? Why else would she have two phone numbers?

"You're an asshole," she grumbles, pulling up her dress and zipping it.

My lip twitches. I hate it when she calls me that. All I'm trying to do is protect this hotel. She should understand its importance.

"I'm doing what I think is best," I reply.

"For you, yeah," she says, clearly pissed off. "But I'm not the one with a compromising picture of you saved on my phone. Are you trying to blackmail me?"

"No. It's just for safekeeping. That's it."

She crosses her arms. "Right, so I'm supposed to trust you, but not vice versa? Got it."

"Trust? You wanna talk about trust when you're the one stalking my ass?" I growl back.

"You know what? Never mind. I don't even know why I came here in the first place." She turns around, marches toward the door, unlocks it, and throws it open.

I follow her as she walks out on me. She doesn't know

206

what she came here for? Bullshit. She knew from the get-go … Fucking. That's it. None of this emotional bullshit. None.

"You came here to be fucked!" I yell at her as she bolts down the hallway.

But she doesn't turn around. All she does is stick her middle finger in the air before disappearing from view. And for some reason, it pisses me off more than anything.

Only when she's gone do I notice all the people staring at me, co-workers and guests. I quickly turn around, grunting, and slam the door shut behind me. Some fucking peace and quiet—that's what I need. *Fuck.*

Fuck that fucking Kitty Kat messing with my head.

Messing with my … feelings.

Why do I even have them? Why am I so fucking angry?

I march to my desk to get back to work and forget about it all, but something stops me in my tracks. Something I see lying on the floor on the way there.

Her ripped apart panties.

A stark reminder of how badly I fucked up.

TWENTY

Kat

Who does he think he is? Fucking asshole, prying into my private life, trying to find out where I work and who I am. He actually tried to track me down online—like an actual stalker—and then had the nerve to reprimand me for doing the exact same thing. How is that not hypocritical?

I make a "tsk" sound even though no one here in my tiny little house can hear it. But I don't care. I need to vent and cool down, and right now, this glass of wine just isn't doing enough for me.

So I call up my best buddy, Flynn.

"Flynn? Where are you?" I ask the moment he picks up.

"I'm at work, Kat," he responds.

"Right now? It's night," I say.

"Yeah. I don't work regular hours."

I groan out loud. "Fuck. I really need you."

"What's wrong?"

"Oh … a certain asshole did something pretty shitty today."

"That same asshole?" he says with a sarcastic voice.

"Yep."

"Kat …" He sighs. "You're better than this."

"I know, but I can't quit him. It's like coffee, you know? No matter how many times you tell yourself it's gonna be your last cup and you're gonna go cold turkey … it always fails."

"Only you can put coffee and sex on the same scale."

"What? They're both just as addictive," I say, snorting.

"Then try a different blend."

"A what?" I frown, confused.

"A different man. C'mon, Kat. You're not stuck with him. There are plenty more fish in the sea."

"Oh, I know, but this fucker has my picture now. What if he spreads it all over the internet? It'd ruin me."

"What?" His voice gets louder. "What picture?"

I don't like admitting this, but I know I have to. "Um … dirty ones."

"How dirty?" he asks.

I close my eyes while speaking. "Naked … ass crack … and my face."

"Kat …" There he goes again. "Really?"

"What? I didn't know he was going to do that!" I grab a pillow and shove it in my face, groaning into it so Flynn doesn't hear. When I move it away, I say, "I know I fucked up."

"Big time," he adds. "And you can't get him to delete them?"

"No, I don't think so. He's keeping them in case I talk about him."

"That's messed up, babe," he replies.

"That's what I told him, but he wouldn't budge!"

"Tell me where he lives or works. I'll bust him up for you."

I laugh. "Seriously?"

"Yeah, I'm serious all right," he says. "No one messes with my Kat."

"Aww …" I sit up again and take another sip from my wine. "That's sweet of you. But don't."

"Why not? The bastard deserves it."

"No, it wouldn't be right. We'd be stooping to his level."

"Fine," he grumbles. "But not because I couldn't because I definitely would. Fuckers like that always take advantage of beautiful girls."

"Aww …" Now I'm blushing from the compliment. "Thanks, dude. I needed that."

"Don't worry about it. If you need a little pick-me-up,

we can go out tomorrow. I have to work tonight, unfortunately."

"Sure, that'd be fun," I reply.

"Before I go, if you could just give me his name, then I can at least try to find out more about him," he asks.

"Why?"

"In case someone mentions his name, I'll know where to go when we need to get that picture back."

"You honestly think that'll work?" I grin. I don't know about that, but I like how persistent Flynn is.

"Maybe. Doesn't hurt to at least try. Now c'mon … what is it?"

"Promise me you won't do anything stupid," I say.

"Fine." He sighs again.

"Okay. I trust you. Just don't do anything rash," I add. "His name is Declan Porter."

No reply. Not for a whole minute.

"Flynn?" I mumble.

He's still not responding.

Suddenly, the line cuts off, and I stare at my phone as if that's going to fix it. Did he just end the call, or did something happen?

***

DECLAN

I'm working on the next event when an employee comes busting into my office.

"*You're* the one fucking *her*?" Flynn, one of the part-time male workers, marches toward my desk.

I look up from my laptop, completely befuddled, and close it immediately when I notice he's right in front of my face.

"Kat," he growls.

"What?" My eyes widen. "How do you—"

"I'm her friend," he interrupts. "She just told me Declan Porter is the asshole who's been using her all this time."

I raise a brow, leaning back in my chair. "Asshole? That's funny, considering she willingly participated."

Flynn slams his fist on the desk. "This is not a joke."

"Be careful there, dude," I say.

Is he just a friend or a boyfriend? I'm starting to wonder.

"I don't care," he yells. "You hurt her."

"No, she got hurt because she was looking for it," I reply, tapping my fingers on the desk.

"By trusting you with her feelings, yeah!" he yells.

I'm momentarily taken aback. Feelings? No way. We had an agreement that it would be a physical thing only.

"And you took pictures?" he growls.

"She gave several to me willingly," I say. I can back it up if I need to, but this is getting embarrassing.

"Not with her face showing!" He's turning temperamental on me now, and I don't like it one bit. "You should be ashamed of yourself."

"What I do in my free time is none of your business," I say, cutting it off as short as I can. I don't want to fuel the fire any further.

"If I'd known she was seeing you, I would've told her not to get involved," he snaps.

I narrow my eyes. "Do you really think I'm that bad for her?"

"Yes! Goddammit!" His face is red, and he can barely keep his anger in check.

But I doubt he'll come at me. I'm his boss, after all, and that would mean he'd get fired.

"I swear to God, if you weren't my boss … I'd … I'd …"

"You'd what?" I dare him to answer that.

He growls out loud. "Just stay the fuck away from her."

Before I can say another word, he's already turned his back to me and rushed off, slamming the door shut behind him.

So … Flynn's friends with Kat, and he hates me now because she told him everything, apparently. Should I fire him for busting in like that and screaming his lungs out? Maybe. It was inappropriate and bad. But then again, I get that he's upset. If the roles were reversed, I'd probably do the same.

Plus, if I fire him now, there's no way in hell Kat would ever forgive me. And one way or another, she will find out that he works for me, whether it be through him or through me.

And she's probably not going to like it.

Do I care? Maybe. Maybe a little too much.

Especially considering he might be more than just a "friend." Fuck. I don't want anyone else to touch her. Although I don't even know why I'm this possessive over her.

I don't want to admit it, but she is on my mind for at least half the day, if not more. Every time she leaves, I think about when I'm going to see her again. That alone makes me question what it is that makes me so infatuated with her ... and why I can't seem to stop thinking about her.

One thing's for sure, though. It's too late to turn back now.

Flynn may want me to quit her, but I definitely don't.

TWENTY-ONE

Kat

A few days later, I've begun typing out my story from beginning to end while at work. Everything about where I met the mystery man, to when I sneak into his office, to the sex event, and even the hookups between. Nothing's left unmentioned except for the actual location and names.

I don't want to name and shame anyone. For now.

I just know this story has to be out there. And for that to happen, I need to type out something interesting to read. Juicy and gossipy but not too damaging.

Though, as I'm nearing the middle, I realize I don't really have an end to write.

At least not one remotely interesting.

Should I make something up or stick with facts?

There's no way anyone can verify what I write. I don't want to show any literal records or proof. For now, anyway.

But something about lying makes me all itchy. I can't do it. No matter how hard I try.

So I sigh, lean back, and stare at my story, wondering how the hell I should continue it.

I was hoping this one would be the big one for the magazine, but I know my boss would never accept a half-finished story. Let alone an erotically charged one.

I need to let this simmer for a while. So I close the page and check the time. Not yet quitting time. Then I remember today's also the day I get paid … and a smile immediately forms on my lips.

Not because I'm happy to get some cash. It just means I get to do something I can only do once every month.

I go to the site that has a list of all the charities looking for donations, and I pick one that I haven't sent anything to before. Then I go to the donate form, fill in all my info, and pay directly.

No ifs, no buts. I give them all I can spare right now. Without it, I can still live, pay rent, buy food, etcetera. It's the minimal amount I need to survive, and that's enough.

These people need it more than I do. And giving it away means they get to do something good with it, which makes me happy. It makes me feel good about myself, so what more could you want?

Besides, I've had my fair share of living the rich lifestyle when I lived with my mom and dad. It wasn't exactly as picture perfect as it's often portrayed. I'd honestly rather live how I live right now than spend one more minute in that toxic environment where the only thing that seems to matter is how others view you.

I don't care about what other people think of me. I don't need money, or a husband, or a big house to feel like I have something worth giving. To feel like my life matters.

This—giving my salary away so these people can do something good with it—is what matters.

Suddenly, my phone rings.

It's not the one I use for work … or anything else important.

It's the one Declan has the number for.

Without picking it up, I stare at the screen, frowning. Should I take the call? He was such an asshole last time. How much worse can it get? Then again, he has my picture. Maybe he wants to negotiate.

However, Dad always said never to negotiate with people who are only out to make you crumple. I shouldn't even attempt to talk to him as long as he still has them. At least, that's what I think my dad would say. I'd never actually go to him for advice on these things. No way. I'd rather die than have him know about all my failed attempts at romance and sex.

No, I have to decide this on my own. And without Declan providing me with proof that he's not keeping the one that shows my face, it's not worth going any further. I can't risk him exposing me publicly like that.

So I ignore the call and turn off that phone, hoping he won't try again.

I need some time away from him so I can think about what to do next, and talking to him isn't going to make that any easier.

My phone rings again, and for a second there, I almost get pissed off before I realize it's the other one that's ringing now. It's Mom, so I pick it up.

"Kat, where are you?" she asks.

"At work."

"Did you forget we had an appointment today?"

Appointment? What is she …?

"Fuck!"

"Kat!" She always hates it when I swear out loud. Oops.

"Sorry!" I say, checking my calendar, which indeed shows I penned down that my mom was coming over to dinner early today. "I completely forgot."

"Should I go back home?" she asks.

"No, no," I say, quickly packing up my things. "I'm coming."

"How long is it going to take?"

"I'll be there in a minute, I promise," I say.

"Okay … don't make me wait too long," she says, before hanging up the phone.

Great. Just what I needed. Forgetting an actual dinner date with my mom at my place because I was so obsessed with work … and someone else.

Oh well, better get there quick before she loses her temper and calls my dad. I don't want to give them another reason to fight.

As I hurry out the door, I bump into Crystal, who immediately opens her mouth. "Kat, I was just looking for you. Do you—"

"Sorry, can't!" I yell back to her as I run through the hallway. "Forgot my dinner date with Mom!"

"Oh, okay," she replies. "Have fun!"

"Thanks." I quickly run out before she asks me anything else.

I really do not have the time right now to worry about what article she's working on or the advice she usually asks me for. I quickly run to my car, drive home, and rummage in my pocket, looking for the keys to my house so I can get in and call Mom to ask if she's still in the neighborhood. Because she's definitely not here anymore. Knowing her, she's probably already had her driver take her back home, and I don't blame her. I would've done the same if someone stood me up like that. God, I'm such an idiot for not keeping track of my schedule.

After I've finally pried the door open, I throw my purse on the floor and take off my coat, then immediately fish my phone from my pocket.

"Hey, honey!"

My mom's sudden voice makes me drop my phone.

"Mom?"

She walks out of the kitchen. "Oh, did I scare you?" she asks.

"Just a little," I reply, laughing awkwardly.

"Sorry, I just let myself in. Figured I'd make some teas since you weren't here yet."

She still has a key? Crap. Why did I give that to her again? I completely forgot about that too.

When she attempts to hug me, she inches back and winces. "What's that smell? Ugh."

I sniff my armpits. A bit of sweat but nothing extreme. "I'll go shower," I say.

"Good," she says, making me roll my eyes.

"Don't burn down the house while I'm in the bathroom," I retort.

"Why would I do that?" she yells as I close the door behind me and snort.

"Just don't start cooking, please," I say. Knowing her, she'll attempt it anyway, regardless of what I say or ask her. She'll never fully admit she can't actually cook.

"I'll just go sit here on the couch then," she says while I take off my clothes.

"Feel free to turn on the TV," I reply as I turn on the shower and step under it.

I let out a sigh of relief as the warm water rolls down my skin. The solitude that comes with the heat feels amazing. It allows me to think about what's been happening in my life recently and how I'm going to deal with things from now on.

I should be more careful with who I choose to trust. Who I want to spend my time with. Because you never know when your heart will decide to slowly fall for the wrong person. And there's nothing you can do about it.

Suddenly, I hear my phone ring, and I turn my head only to realize I left it in my purse. Well, shit. Guess I'm not going to pick it up then. No way am I going to rush out the bathroom naked with my mom sitting on the couch.

So I shrug it off and wait for the noise to stop. It's hard to tell with all this water rushing into my ears, though. Instead, I focus on lathering my body with soap, and then washing my hair, making sure I'm squeaky clean before turning off the shower and grabbing a towel to dry off with.

I wrap it around my body and walk out of the bathroom while my mom's still sitting on the couch. She's constantly flipping through the channels like she doesn't find any of them remotely interesting.

"So how's Dad?" I ask, trying to casually stir up a conversation.

"Fine, I guess," she snaps.

Well, this is going great.

"Still not slowing down with all the work?" I ask.

"No, and I don't want him to."

I slam my lips shut. Right. Okay. Awkward.

"Fred and I haven't actually spoken in days."

"Really?" I say as I go into my bedroom and put on a

comfy light blue shirt along with a pair of white sweatpants. "Not even during dinner?"

"He's never home for dinner!" she squawks. "Let alone the rest of the day. I don't know what it is that he's doing at work, but I'm getting sick and tired of it, and I've had enough."

I suck in a breath and brush my hair out while thinking of what to say. I was hoping this would be a casual dinner date, nice and quiet, but I don't think Mom's doing so great right now.

"Have you talked to him about it?" I ask as I tuck my hair into a bun.

"Like he's ever available," she says, taking a sip of her tea. "With whatever it is he's doing." She makes a "tsk" sound with her lips.

Why would she not know what he's doing? Is Dad really that secretive? Or does Mom just not care about the business?

"I don't even wanna know at this point," she adds. "I just want him to be there, you know?"

"I get it," I say, smiling. "Maybe I could ask him …?"

"No, that's all right," she says, giving me that fake smile again that she always gives me when she doesn't want me to see any weakness. In that light, we're the same. Small moments of shared feelings and traits are where I find solace with her, so I have to treasure it. And I need to pull her out of that negativity right now. So I sit down on the couch beside her and place my hand on her knee.

"So what would you like to eat?" I ask, trying to shift the conversation.

She puts down the tea she made herself. "Oh, well, I've already taken care of that."

I frown. "What do you mean?"

"Oh, this nice gentleman on the phone who said he was your friend wanted to bring takeout, so I gave him your address."

My eyes widen, and I immediately jump up from the couch. "You did what?"

"Well, you weren't going to still cook for us, were you? He sounded so nice, and he wanted to stop by. Why not?" she says.

But I'm already panicking, pacing back and forth while sweating profusely.

"No, Mom, what was his name?" I ask.

"I don't know, something with a D ... Daniel ... no that wasn't it," she mumbles.

"Declan! It was him, wasn't it?" I say.

"Yes, that's it," she replies.

"No!"

"Why are you yelling at me?" She grabs her tea and takes a sip.

"You invited someone into my home!" And not to mention *who*. Oh my God, Declan. He's coming over, and I am *not* prepared.

"So?"

"It's my house!" I say, groaning. "Fuck." Of course,

he'd ask her for my address. I should've known he'd apply some shady tactics to find out where I live.

"Kat, really? Language, please," Mom huffs, making me sigh out loud.

Now I have to solve this shit again. Why the hell would she give him my address? Goddammit, she's so gullible sometimes. Always trusting the wrong people … just like me.

I quickly sift through my purse, looking for the phone, but it's not here.

"Where is it?" I ask her.

"What?"

"The phone!"

I know I'm yelling, but I need to call him before he gets here.

"It's on the kitchen counter," she replies.

I run like my ass is on fire, grabbing the thing to immediately dial his number.

But it's too late … because my doorbell rings at the same time the telephone is beeping.

"Fuck," I mutter.

"Oh, food's here!" Mom casually says, getting up from the couch with a smile on her face. "About time."

I'm stunned. Completely in shock as the doorbell rings again and my mom walks over to it like she owns the place. "You grab the plates, honey," she says. "I'll let him in."

"No, don't!" I say in a last-ditch effort.

But it's too late. She's already opened the door.

224

Declan's standing right there with two bags in one hand and his phone pressed against his ear in the other. And when he opens his mouth to speak, I can hear it on the other end of the line, echoing through my own phone.

"Hi, KittyKat."

Fuck.

TWENTY-TWO

DECLAN

I slowly lower the phone in my hand when she does too, tucking it into my pocket. The twitching on her face makes me grin like a motherfucker. I'd say she's angry, but that's probably an understatement.

"Hi there," I say to her mother to defuse the situation. "You must be her sister, right?"

Her mom chuckles as her cheeks glow rosy. "Oh, nonsense. You know I'm her mother." We shake hands. "I'm Meredith."

"Nice to meet you, Meredith. Name's Declan Porter."

Meanwhile, Kat looks like she's about to turn into an

exploding volcano.

So I hold up the bag filled with Chinese takeout as a peace offering. "Hungry?"

"Mom, close the door," Kat says through gritted teeth.

"Why would I do that?" her mom says. "He brought us food. That's more than you've done today."

I snort, trying to hide the laughter in my sleeve. Why do I have the feeling they don't get along very well?

Kat winces as she marches toward me. "Mom, let me talk with him, please."

As her mom steps aside, she clutches the door and holds it tight. "What are you doing here?"

"Bringing food to hungry people, what else?" I muse, shoving one of the bags into her hand. "And your clothes."

She blinks a couple of times. "What—"

"The ones you left at the hotel. From the event," I interrupt. I wink, which makes her eyes twitch in annoyance.

"Stop. Just stop," she says, throwing the clothing bag in a corner of the room. "All this?" She points at me and the bags. "I see right through this."

"Great. Do you like what you see, or should I have bought some more stir-fry?" I jest while holding up the Chinese. It's hard not to when she's looking at me with those vulture eyes. It makes me want to push her buttons to see how far she'd let me go before she explodes.

"You know what I mean," she hisses. "You think you're clever? Figuring out where I live by calling my place and having my mom pick up?"

"Hey, that's not my fault," I say, raising my hands. "I only passed on the message."

"No, you lied," she whispers.

"Did I?" I show her the bag again. "I have food, just as promised."

"What are you even trying to do?" she asks, putting her hand against her side.

"Nothing. I'm just here to make peace," I say, licking my lips. She definitely reacts to that because her eyes follow my tongue.

Fuck, I love it when she does that.

"For what?" she asks. "You were pretty clear last time."

"Because I know I was an ass," I say, shrugging. "I admit it."

"You're always an ass," she retorts.

"Kat!" her mother shouts from the living room. "I heard that."

"I deserve that," I reply.

"Just let the gentleman in already. He's your ... *friend*, right?"

The way her mom says the word friend like it's some special status only important men get makes me snort, and Kat immediately retaliates by slapping my arm. "Stop doing that!"

"Stop what?"

"Stop pretending we're some kind of happy couple or some shit for my mother. We're not," she mutters under her breath.

"I never said we were," I say. "I'm just here to bring food. That's it."

"Great, then can we eat already?" her mom hollers.

"Gladly. If you'll let me in," I say, gazing directly into Kat's eyes.

She rubs her lips together a few times, mulling it over while staring at me intently.

"Food's getting cold," I whisper.

She sighs out loud, on purpose, probably to let me know how badly I fucked up again, but this time, I did it on purpose. I knew there was no other way to get her to talk to me than to find out where she lived and just come over.

At first, I was going to track her down online using the number, but when I called and her mom picked up, it was the perfect excuse to find out more.

Am I a stalker? Maybe. But so is she, considering all the things she did to find me, so I call this an eye for an eye. Besides, I'm not here to act like an asshole again. I've learned that doesn't get me far with her.

And I don't want to give her up just yet.

"So are you going to let me in?" I ask, cocking my head while holding the bag up.

"Ugh, fine." She opens the door wide. "But"—she places a finger on my chest, stopping me halfway through the door—"don't tell my mom anything about any of the shit we've done."

"All right," I say. "Wasn't even contemplating it."

"And take off your shoes," she says, gazing down at

them.

It takes me three seconds to kick them off. "Anything else, milady?"

"*Don't* call me that," she hisses, almost like a real kitty. I'm amused.

"Got it, KittyKat," I say as I pass her, ignoring her obvious growl. I place the food on the table and say, "Nice place you've got."

"Thanks," she replies, closing the door loudly.

"He's never been over?" her mom asks.

"No, Mom. He's a friend from ... work."

I turn my head so she can see my obvious confusion at what she means with work, but she doesn't seem to care.

"From the office?" Meredith asks.

"Yeah, from the office, Kat?" I ask, raising a brow while I go through her kitchen in search of plates.

"No, different ... work. Please, don't ask, Mom," Kat says, as she sits down at the table while trying to pretend I'm not here.

"Okay." Her mom makes a difficult face.

"It's complicated," I say, winking at them as I place the plates and cutlery down.

"Ooh ..." Her mom chuckles.

Kat takes a sip from her glass of water and rolls her eyes.

Meredith gasps. "So you're her boyfriend?"

Kat almost chokes on her water. "No, no!" she repeats. "Not boyfriend."

230

"Then what?" Her mom unpacks the food while I sit down too.

"An acquaintance," I fill in to make it easier.

"Oh ... Well, I must say, I'm happy for you to join us," Meredith says, smiling.

"Glad to be of service with some tasty food."

"Hmm ... Tell me about it," Meredith mumbles, taking a sniff. "It smells lovely."

Kat can't stop rolling her eyes. She's probably wishing tonight was already over, but I'm not going anywhere right now. Not until we've had a chance to talk in private. And until then, I'll continue to play my part.

"Kat, would you like some crunchy wontons?" I ask, grinning as I hold them out to her.

She doesn't even seem remotely happy about it as I place them on her plate, but I know she wants them. Her stomach is growling, and I'm sure her mouth is watering by now.

"What would you have done if I hadn't come?" I ask.

"Ordered takeout myself," she growls.

Her mom laughs. "We had a dinner date, and she forgot."

"Ouch," I say. "Can't forget about your mom, Kat."

"Shut up," she says.

"Kat, be nice," her mom interjects.

"It's just food," I add, giving her the sweetest smile I can muster, but all I get back are death stares, which only makes me want to laugh more. I don't know why I love it so much when she's upset. Why it makes me hunger for the time when her mother leaves and I'm alone with her … so I can strip her naked and lick her skin.

But first … dinner.

***

Kat

When everyone's full, Declan brings the plates to the kitchen and starts washing them off while I help Mom out.

"Let me know if you need any help with Dad, okay?" I say.

"It's fine, honey. I can handle him myself," she says with a smile. "Besides, you have other … business to take care of." She gives Declan the side-eye. Kissing me on the cheeks, she turns toward him, saying, "Lovely to meet you, Declan!"

"It was great meeting you too, Meredith," he replies with a big smile, making me wanna vomit. But that would be a waste of the good food.

"Such a sweet young man," she says, nudging me in the side with her elbow while winking.

Declan snorts, but when he sees me glare, he

immediately turns his head toward the sink and continues washing the dishes.

I'm not finished with him. Not by a long shot.

As I march over to him and tap him on the shoulder, he puts down the fragile plates and glances at me over his shoulder. "Enjoy the food?"

I fold my arms. "Really? That's what you're going to ask?"

"What else?" He shrugs, casually avoiding the actual problem, which he knows damn well.

"Why are you even here?" I ask, licking my lips.

"You didn't answer my calls, so I figured I'd stop by with some food. You were hungry, no?"

"That's not the point," I say even though I did eat my fair share. "You used my mother to get to me."

"I didn't, really. Like I said, it's not my fault she picked up the phone," he jests.

"Seriously?" I lean against the counter beside him, waiting until he finally stops doing the dishes to look at me. "Last time we spoke, you were a complete asshole. Just like all the times before."

"I know. That's why I'm here," he replies, glancing at me with those sexy eyes of his again.

Goddamn, I can't even stop thinking about him that way, despite wanting to so badly.

"No, you said you didn't want a relationship. Why all this wooing?" I ask.

"Who says I'm wooing anyone?" he says, smirking like

233

he always does. And fuck, it actually makes me want to kiss him. But I shouldn't. Fuck him and his fucked-up sense of judgment.

"Listen, dude," I say, clearing my throat. "I don't like getting fucked."

"You sure about that?"

The way he says it immediately makes my heart drop, and I know I'm turning red, but I don't care. "I mean the emotional way, not the literal."

"*Oh ...*"

God, he's really getting under my skin now, and it's making me grind my teeth.

"The point is, you've been stalking my ass, and I don't like it one bit," I say.

"Likewise," he retorts, throwing in another smirk that makes me want to punch him ... or kiss him. I'm not sure yet which one is more accurate.

"I wasn't stalking you," I say. "You sent me that picture. Wasn't my fault I found out where you work."

He stops washing the dishes and steps closer, placing his hands on the counter right beside me. "I didn't ask you for your address. Wasn't my fault your mom picked up to tell me anyway."

The grin that follows makes my heart flutter ... and my fist tighten.

Well, fucking touché to him.

He inches closer again, this time placing his hands right beside my body so I can't escape. "As a matter of fact, I still don't know if Kat Bronson is really your name, considering you have two cell phones and all," he muses. "Are you ever going to tell me?"

"Maybe," I say, cocking my head. "Or maybe not."

"Hmm … secretive …" he murmurs. "Which is strange, coming from a slutty kitten like you."

I gasp, and my immediate reaction is to dunk my hand in the water and throw it at him. By the time I realize I actually did it, half his shirt and face are soaked.

I put my hand in front of my mouth as I notice his white shirt has become see-through, partially revealing his thick pecs and ripped abs. Lord, give me strength.

When he opens his eyes again, he seems mildly pissed off.

"Sorry, I didn't mean to ruin—"

Out of nowhere, water splashes all over my face and shirt.

I sputter it out. "Really?"

"You started it," he says.

Jesus, we're like a bunch of kids.

"I like the view, though," he murmurs in a low voice.

Only when I look down do I remember I was wearing a light blue shirt … with no bra underneath … and my nipples are poking through right now.

"Likewise …" I reply, raising a brow. "But my eyes are up here."

"Oh, I know," he says, still not averting his eyes.

He's not even ashamed of blatantly staring, and it's

making me blush like crazy.

Fuck. How do I stop this?

Suddenly, he lifts his face and presses his lips onto mine, catching me by surprise.

I don't even know what's happening right now. Only that he's kissing me, and that it feels so, so fucking good. And that, for some reason, I'm kissing him back too.

Crap.

I nudge him away. "Wait, this isn't supposed to happen."

"It shouldn't ... but it did," he replies. Always so smooth, like his voice and hair, and just about everything else about him, goddammit.

"And I don't regret it," he says.

Immediately, he lunges in for a second taste, but I stop him right before his lips touch mine.

"I can't do this."

"You've been trying to screw me ever since you met me, and now you're suddenly having second thoughts?" he says.

"I am, considering our history. You said it yourself ... This is all about the sex. No relationship."

"Exactly," he says, licking his lips.

"Then why are you kissing me?" I ask, frowning, confused.

He pauses, cocking his head ever so slightly. "Because I like doing it."

"That's it?" I make a face.

"Yeah." He shrugs.

Well, that was simple. So simple that I don't even get it.

"No, no, there has to be more to this," I say, laughing a little. "You're trying to fool me into doing something, aren't you?"

"No," he says. "Unless you count sex as fooling you. Then yes."

I narrow my eyes. "Just sex …"

"Yes," he says.

"What about the other time—"

He places a finger on my lips. "I don't want to talk about last time. Or any time before that. I just want to enjoy this for what it is at the moment. Understand?"

I nod softly, but I'm not even sure what I'm agreeing to.

When he takes his finger off my lips, he murmurs, "I don't want to make this any more difficult than it already is …"

He's still so close I can taste his breath on my tongue.

But I have to remind myself what type of guy he is, and what's at risk. He doesn't know where I work, what I do for a living, and I want to keep it that way … for now.

"I'm not going to tell you anything if that's what you're after," I reply, trying to hold my ground. "And I want to see what else you do in that hotel of yours."

"Oh, so you're demanding things now?" he asks, biting his lip.

"I'm not demanding things. I'm just saying that it's a perfect way for you to make up to me."

"Really …?" He makes a funny, scrunched-up face, and

it's hard for me not to laugh, but I do my best.

"Yes, really. I want to see what else there is. Beyond the events," I say. "I don't want to go any further unless you trust me."

That was a bold move, but I need to know more about him and what he does before I let him kiss me again. Before I let these feelings get to my head.

He leans away, sighing, his face darkening. "Are you sure you want to? There's no going back. I don't know if you can handle seeing it all."

"Yes, I'm ready for more," I say. No question. I want to experience it all. "Can I participate?"

His eyes widen. "Participate? With others?"

"Why not? I almost did it before, if it wasn't for—"

"That was different," he interrupts, his tone suddenly shifting. "That was before ..."

"Before what?" I ask.

He takes a deep breath as he turns his head toward the floor and sighs. "Never mind," he says, before looking up at me again. "The point is this hotel is my job. My life. If what we do comes out ..."

"I'm only there for the experience," I say. "Nothing more."

It's a lie, and I know it. I just don't want to admit it, neither to him nor myself.

My curiosity is just too big to stop myself from wanting to know more. Is that so wrong?

"Okay ..." he says. "My office. Tuesday evening. Eleven

sharp. Bring a sexy outfit and a mask."

I grin, that's how giddy I am. "Done."

"You'll need to get a clean bill of health."

"I can make an appointment with my doctor," I say.

"Good. And bring a suitcase with whatever else you need," he adds. "You'll be staying the night."

"Great," I say with a smile. I don't even mind that he's ordering me around, telling me what's going to happen. I love it when he's like that toward me. Makes me feel excited.

He shakes his head. "You don't even know what you just agreed to."

"I don't care," I say.

"Hmm …" he hums, rubbing his lips together. "We'll see once you get there."

TWENTY-THREE

DECLAN

When she steps into my office, I'm surprised.

I was hoping she might change her mind. That she might reconsider, but she hasn't. And here she is.

"Well, well, well …" I say, folding my hands behind my head.

"I'm here," she says, placing her bag in the corner of the room.

"Yes, you are." I bite my lip at the sight of her short pink skirt and black crop top. I like it.

"So what now?" she asks, crossing her arms as she swivels her hips sideways.

Damn, I like the view a lot from here.

Still, I'm worried about her. She's far too serious, too headstrong, and she has no idea what's about to happen to her.

"Now," I say as I pull out a paper and place it down on the desk. "You sign this."

"What is it?" she asks.

"A form to make sure you don't sue us when you don't like what happens," I reply.

She stares at me for a few seconds, and judging from the look she's giving me, she isn't sure whether I'm serious. But I'm dead serious.

After a few seconds have passed, she walks to the desk, picks up the pen, and casually scribbles her signature at the bottom of the document along with her name.

"Done," she says, pushing it back toward me.

"You decide quickly," I say.

"It's a shorter document than last time," she replies.

A smirk forms on my lips. "That one was an application form. This one is what comes after it."

"Oh," she muses. "So I don't even have to apply. Are you playing favorites?"

"I like to cut to the chase," I say, winking. Then I pick up the document and briefly scan over it. "So is this your real last name?"

Her eyes widen and her lips part, but it takes her a while to respond. "Why would you ask that?"

"Because you have two phone numbers. Figured you

probably wouldn't give me your real last name either."

She doesn't say a word. Caught in the act, huh?

"It's okay," I say. "You don't trust me. I understand."

"I never said—"

"You don't have to say anything," I interrupt. "I know."

I'm tired of the anger, the fear. If I want her to trust me, I should start by trusting her myself.

I clear my throat, and ask, "Did you bring the doctor's bill of health?"

She produces it from her pocket. "I blacked out my name," she says. "But it's mine. You can see the address."

"I know," I say, quickly looking it over. "On the pill?"

"Yes," she says.

"Good." I put both documents in a drawer and pull out another one. "Here's my clean bill of health."

She briefly looks over the document for a second before sliding it back. "And now?" she asks.

I tuck the paper away and get up from the chair. "Let's go."

"Where?" she asks, still trying to pull herself together after I've clearly caught her in a lie.

"Follow me," I say, nodding at her before opening the door.

She grabs her bag and walks behind me as I take the lead. Stepping into the elevator, I use my card to take us to the VIP floor. Once she steps inside, the doors close. The silence is … deafening. The closer we get, the more my heart begins to race. Not only because she's so very near, and I'm actually fantasizing about kissing her right now … but also because of what's about to happen next.

I wonder if she'll be happy. Excited. Upset. Or maybe even mad.

She's the only girl who's ever gone up here without knowing what her purpose is. Every client who's up here knows exactly why they're here, along with every other staff member.

Except her.

She's not a part of this hotel nor a part of its clientele.

She's something … different. Something … special. Like a secret no one else knows about. Something that belongs to me and me alone. And now I'm about to share it.

***

Kat

We walk through a corridor of endless doors, one after the other. I wonder what's happening behind each one of them. If these are just exclusive hotel rooms or if they're used for something else.

I haven't stopped being excited since last night. I couldn't even sleep; that's how much I was looking forward to seeing all the other things that go down in Hotel O. Kinky shit, I'm sure. And I can't wait to find out.

He stops in front of a door and steps aside, beckoning me to come closer. "Look."

I frown, stepping closer, unsure of what he wants.

"Go on," he says, nodding toward the door. "Have a look."

I stand in front of it, but there's nothing to see. Just a dark, wooden door with a red circle right underneath the handle that says occupied.

Declan positions himself right behind me, moving his hand up to a metallic slider at the top.

Just one push reveals a hidden looking glass.

And a man and a woman in the room beyond … fucking.

Or more specifically, she is giving him a blowjob in front of a mirror while he watches himself and her. All while she's sitting on what looks like a vibrating machine.

And the sight makes me … horny.

"Can you hear it?" Declan whispers in my ear. "The vibrations?"

I struggle to breathe. Wantonness fills every fiber of my being.

That's when the man's eyes settle on me.

He's not even wearing a mask.

In shock, I look away.

Declan immediately grabs my chin. "Look," he says, forcing me to. "Don't turn away."

"But he can see us."

"That's what he wants," Declan whispers, his tongue so close to my ear I can almost feel it dipping out to touch my skin. Almost. And for a few seconds, I wish he did.

"They like being watched," he murmurs. "So enjoy."

I gasp as the man grabs a rod and whacks the woman's ass as she's giving him head. Apart from the soft moan, she doesn't even seem fazed. In fact, the more he does it, the more she wiggles around on the vibrator, and the harder she sucks.

"Can you see how much they're enjoying themselves?" Declan asks.

I nod, amazed at how naturally it comes to them. Like being watched gives them more pleasure. In fact, my own pussy thumps in response to them.

As if he could sense it, Declan's hand finds its way down my body, along my legs, and up my skirt, leaving a trail of goose bumps as he slowly inches up toward my pussy. When he touches me, I have to physically stop myself from quaking. Luckily, the door keeps me from falling.

He's touching me in public in a very private way, and all I can do is widen my legs and let him feel how wet I am. Jesus. I really am a slut.

"Does it turn you on to watch them fuck?" Declan asks, his fingers gently circling my clit.

He's not the slightest bit ashamed of doing this in the hallway … and neither am I.

Is this what this hotel offers? The chance to experience

uninhibited pleasure without social pressure or any form of guilt? If so, it resembles nirvana.

"Don't fight it," he whispers into my ear, then he places a soft kiss right below it, making my body tingle with need.

Still, I want to know how a thing like this could exist. How people would know of it, and why they'd come here. What's in it for the girls doing it? If she's, in fact, the one being hired. I don't even know.

"Who is the client, and who's getting paid?" I ask.

"Does it matter?" he asks. "Both of them signed a contract to remain silent out of their own free will."

"I suppose it doesn't," I reply.

"What happens at Hotel O stays at Hotel O," he murmurs, planting another kiss right on top of my shoulder, that tiny spot that makes me want to moan.

But what if they could hear? Would they mind? Is that what they're here for?

So many questions. It's like this hotel means that you'll never stop searching for the answers. Never stop searching for that next big thing. The next hit to bring you closer to ecstasy.

"C'mon," Declan says as he stops touching me and instead places a hand on my arm and pulls me along to the next door.

Again, he pulls the slide at the top to reveal another couple. This time, it's two women; one of them is face down on a bed, chained to the bedposts, while the other dribbles her with wax. When she spots us watching, she puts down the candle and grabs a toy instead, shoving it up her ass.

I'm completely engrossed in what they're doing, but Declan keeps closing the sliders and pulling me along. One room after the other. All of them we check. Women and men everywhere. Men on men, women on women. Sometimes three, four, up to ten—I don't know. I can't keep count.

But all of them are having sex in the most fucked-up ways ... and I love it.

I love every little thing they're doing, and the more I see, the more I'm beginning to realize ...

I want this too.

I wanna do it all.

It doesn't matter what it is. The pain. The voyeurism. The exhibitionism. The dirty, raunchy sex. I want to see how much I can handle, how far I can take it before I finally reach my limit.

My entire life was nothing but limits until I finally moved out of my parents' house and lived out on my own. And since then, I've only ever wanted to experience true freedom.

This is it. It's right here in front of me.

"Is this what you want?" Declan asks as we watch five people having an orgy with cum and moans flying everywhere. It's like he can read my mind.

I don't even have to think about it before I answer. "Yes."

I can hear him grin near my ear. "Just say the magic

word."

"Please," I utter.

I've never wanted to beg for anything this badly.

Declan grabs my hand, entwining his fingers through mine as he pulls me along the corridor and into a room with a green dot under the handle and a metal slide at the top. He closes the door behind him but doesn't turn the lock.

He rummages in his pocket and takes out a small black mask, which he uses to cover his eyes while never breaking contact with mine.

"Take off your panties," he commands.

I do what he asks, slipping them down my legs while keeping the skirt on.

"Put on your mask," he adds.

I pull open my purse, take out the golden feathery mask I brought, and put it on.

Then he slowly starts to strip. Just the top part of his suit, but one look at his gorgeous body makes me salivate. He throws down his shirt in a corner and stays put in the middle of the room, almost like a challenge.

I can't stop staring. Can't stop myself from touching him. My hand on his chest, sliding down his abs, every inch of rippling skin. I love how his chest rises and falls with each breath, getting a little more erratic as my hand goes lower and lower.

Until he tells me otherwise, I continue. I feel like he's giving me permission while still watching me like a hawk.

I zip him down and lower his pants until his dick

bounces up from the elastic band. Its firmness makes me want to lick it.

So I do.

I lower myself to my knees on the floor in front of him and open my mouth.

Taking him into my mouth, I swirl my tongue around his length. It bobs up and down, and a groan escapes his mouth.

Salty pre-cum drips onto my tongue.

Still, the door is not locked.

Anyone could come in at any moment.

Anyone could watch.

The thought alone makes me reach for my panties, and I start rubbing myself.

Judging from how his eyes lower to gaze at what I'm doing, he enjoys it too.

But he's not pushing me. Not forcing my lips over his shaft. Not holding the back of my head to push me down to his base.

He lets me do what I want. Almost as if he's curious to see where I'd take it.

I don't mind showing him how committed I am to pure pleasure.

After all, why else would anyone come to this hotel if not to experience just that?

And since he doesn't want a relationship, I might as well enjoy all the benefits for as long as they last.

As I suck him off, his dick grows harder and harder.

Suddenly, the slider is pushed aside, and two eyes are visible. Someone is watching us.

My clit thumps in response.

I don't stop licking him. His moans put me in a trance.

Until Declan suddenly pulls out.

With two fingers, he tips up my chin. "Do you want to know why the door isn't locked?" he asks.

I nod. "So others can watch?"

A devilish grin spreads on his lips. "So others can join."

TWENTY-FOUR

Kat

The man who was watching us opens the door and steps inside. My breathing stops as he closes the door behind him and approaches us.

"Are you scared?" Declan asks as he steps aside to allow the man to see me.

I shake my head. "Intrigued."

Declan releases my chin and gazes at the man until the man steps forward and unzips right in front of me. I feel naked, vulnerable, used. In all the right ways.

His dick is long, thick, and already throbbing with need.

I stay, awaiting Declan's command.

"Up. On your hands and knees," he says, and I immediately follow his instructions. "Open your mouth."

As my mouth opens wide, the man slides his cock onto my tongue.

I don't protest. All I feel is a hunger for more. An insatiable appetite for sex and cum.

A full-blown slut, as Declan would say. And I'd wear the label with pride.

The man uses my throat like I'm not even there, and I accept every inch of him like the greedy girl I am.

I don't even know his name.

From the corner of my eye, I watch Declan pull some things out of a drawer. Lube ... and a toy with thick rings. A butt plug.

He positions himself behind me, shoves up my skirt, and squirts the liquid over my ass. Then he pushes in the butt plug slowly. Every inch makes me squint, and my nails dig into the wooden floor. But I refuse to quit.

He continues until it's completely buried inside me.

Within seconds, the tip of his dick is against my pussy.

Slowly, he pushes inside. I gasp and then hold my breath as he goes deep. It's my first time ever feeling two things inside me at once.

No ... three.

One in my pussy, one in my ass, and another one in my mouth.

"Take it deep, Kitten," Declan says. His voice makes me purr like a real fucking kitty in heat.

When he begins to thrust, I feel it everywhere. It's so damn full, I can barely breathe, but I still manage to let out a moan.

God, it feels so fucking good to have him inside me … skin to skin.

No condom. Nothing between us except the hot air. Three bodies in sync, fucking like madmen, sweat mingling, lust building.

It's so fucking sexy that I'm on the verge of exploding.

But so is the man who's fucking my face. I can feel it from the way his veins bulge and his speed intensifies. I'm struggling with his deep thrusts that poke the back of my throat while Declan's heavy strokes push me closer to his base.

Briefly, a man and a woman appear in the tiny window in the door. I don't know how long they've been watching, but I only notice them now. Maybe they've been watching this whole time. Or maybe many people have already. It doesn't even faze me anymore.

When Declan slaps my ass between thrusts, a primal cry escapes my mouth, and it sets Declan off.

His groans as he releases warm cum inside me, bringing me to the edge.

"Come when he does, Kitten," he growls, still inside me.

And he does. So fucking hard.

Cum jets onto my tongue and against the back of my

throat right when I come undone, and it's the most intense pleasure I've ever experienced.

The man doesn't stop until he's unloaded everything he has inside me, filling my mouth to the brim until it almost runs over, until I'm desperate for air.

"Swallow like the slut you are," Declan commands.

His cock still rests on my tongue as I do my best to make everything go down without a fight.

But once I've succeeded, I feel renewed. Empowered. Proud.

Like I could wear the name slut as a badge.

Declan pulls out, and I can feel his cum drip down my legs.

The unknown man pulls out too and zips up, then leaves.

Not a word. Not a name. Not even a goodbye.

I'm left trying to comprehend what just happened. What I just did voluntarily. And how much I fucking enjoyed all of it.

Cum and saliva cover my face and body as I sink to the floor and breathe in and out slowly while resting my back against the bed. Declan pulls up his pants and goes to his knees in front of me. He places a hand on my cheeks and says, "Well done."

It's all my soul needs to feel fulfilled.

Declan smiles briefly, then his hand lowers from my face. "Turn around." His voice is stern. Unlike what it was only moments ago.

When I do what he says, he pulls the butt plug out of me. I gasp at the feel of it leaving my body. As I turn around, he goes to clean it, but he doesn't say anything else. I wonder what's on his mind.

After he's done, he grabs the bottle of whiskey from the mini fridge and pours himself a glass. Then he stands in front of the window, his back to me.

I'm still recovering, but I have so many questions right now that I can't stop myself from asking them.

"Are we …?"

"No. It's not done yet," he replies.

Okay. Clear. Yet it's not at all clear. Maybe he's still deciding on the next course of action. But that doesn't mean I still can't ask more questions, right?

"That man … who was he?" I continue.

"A random hotel guest," he replies, placing the butt plug back into a drawer. "Don't worry, everyone is medically screened in advance before being allowed into the hotel. It's part of our policy."

Well, that's good although I already believed that to be the case. Still, I want to know more. "Did you invite him?"

He returns to gazing out the window. "No." He's being rather brief.

"Then why did he come?" I ask.

He takes a sip of his whiskey. "Because he wanted to, and the door was unlocked. The green symbol means anyone is free to enter. When it's red, the room is closed off for further entrants."

"So someone gets to decide how many people join in?"

"Exactly," he says, taking another sip. "In this case, me."

"Can anyone book at this hotel?"

"Yes, but the cost is high."

"Right ... so basically only rich people."

"You're wondering if that man who just fucked you is famous? Perhaps. Perhaps not. No one knows."

"Not even you?"

"We do know the identities of the people who sign into the hotel, but once the mask goes on, everyone is anonymous," he clarifies. "No one is forced to reveal their identity at any point except to the staff."

"So the staff here must be drilled thoroughly."

"Yes. We take privacy very seriously."

No wonder he was so angry when I found him at this hotel and even managed to slip into one of the events. I'd proven his security wasn't as airtight as he wanted to believe, and it put him on edge. That explains why he's been so closed off, so unwilling to let me see the real deal. Why he didn't trust me.

It all makes sense. Yet him telling me all this proves there's more to it. That he's willing to share means he's opening up, and that's admirable.

"Thank you," I say. "For letting me participate."

"Did you enjoy yourself?" he asks, still not looking at me.

"Yes ... a lot, actually," I admit, feeling the heat rise once again just from thinking about it.

That, and the fact that I still have all the jizz on me really isn't helping to cool down. But I guess he wants me to feel that. To be in a perpetual state of arousal.

"What now?" I ask after it's been quiet for a while.

"There's a shower over there." He points at a door to the left. "Clean yourself up. Put on the outfit you brought. And put the mask back on too."

"There's more?"

"Yes … much, much more."

The dark voice with which he says it makes goose bumps scatter on my skin. I love it when he's mysterious.

"And after the shower? What do I do then?"

Suddenly, he places his glass on the window sill and walks toward the door without even looking at me. "Then you wait until I call your room …"

And then he leaves.

Just like that.

No kiss. No wink. Not even a see you later or anything else.

My lips part, but I have no clue what to say. Or if I should even say anything at all. If he'd stop to listen.

It's like he's completely detached.

What is going on?

***

DECLAN

I march through the hallways, determined not to go back.

I *cannot* go back. No matter how much I want to take her, kiss her, own her, I can't allow myself to.

This is what she wants. What I want. What's right.

She loved it. I could feel it from the way she writhed underneath my palm, how she licked up every inch of his cum, and how she moaned out for more. And I could see it on her face in the aftermath.

She needs this complete and utter debauchery as a release. Why, I don't know, but it's not my place to judge.

In a way, she reminds me of myself. Maybe that's why I had to leave the room. It was too confronting to see this woman enjoy her body being used in that way. It made me realize just how addicted I've become to this dirty game, this hotel, and everything that it brings, everything that it means.

Pure hedonism.

And like so many others, she's fallen for its magic.

It should come as no surprise to me. After all, Kat really is a NaughtyKitten who likes to play rough.

What does come to a surprise is the way my body reacted the moment it came into contact with hers. How much I actually yearn for her. For her taste, her touch, her skin, her smoldering lips against mine.

All of this was a test to see if she could handle it, if she'd make it through, because then I'd know she'd be up to joining the full ordeal. The actual event that she tried to sneak into last time.

She passed with flying colors.

Still, it doesn't make me smile and it doesn't make me happy even though it should. This means I get to be even dirtier with her. That we both get to act on our fantasies. The sky is the limit.

But *this* event, this trial isn't meant for me. It's meant for her and her alone.

My fist balls as I pass my own reflection in the mirror and briefly glance at it before I walk off. I need to cool down. Clear my head. Get back into my office and finish the final touches for the event tonight. It's the only way to stay sane and live through this.

And then, I'll finally have proven to myself that she means nothing to me.

She is merely a toy. A pet for me to play with.

Tonight will be the final game.

TWENTY-FIVE

Kat

I've showered and dressed, but Declan still hasn't called, so now I'm on the bed reading a magazine and munching on some cookies I found. The longer I lie here, the more I'm starting to yawn, but I ignore the sensation. I can't go to sleep now, especially not with what's next. It's way too exciting. I'll just have to suck it up and catch up on sleep tomorrow.

I wonder how much longer it's going to take, though. I feel like I'm being watched, especially with that window in the door that could slide open at any moment.

Suddenly, the phone next to me rings, and I immediately pick it up.

"Hello?"

"Come downstairs. Same room as before. I'll be waiting at the entrance."

He hangs up before I can respond.

Why is he being so distant? Is something going on, or is he just nervous like I am?

That definitely makes me wonder what's about to happen.

I get off the bed and immediately walk out the door. Luckily, there's no one else in this hallway because I'd probably draw eyes, considering what I'm wearing. A black see-through baby doll and fishnet stockings along with shiny black heels.

I step into the elevator and press the button to go all the way to ground zero. When I arrive, the whole hall is bustling with people, just like before. Only this time, I'm actually invited. Everyone's wearing masks, even the staff, who are clearly identifiable by their red velvety clothes. Even the number of guards has increased. They've definitely tightened things up since the last time I came to an event like this.

If this is even the same as before. I have yet to find out, and I'm beyond excited.

My heart is racing as I approach the doors. A woman comes toward me, smiling, and pushes a sticker onto my top that says Kitty.

Two men open the huge doors wide and the room reveals itself. But it's unlike before.

Dark drapes cover the whole room with dim lights and no music.

The only things filling the air are moans and the thick fog of heat.

It smells of sex. Wild, raunchy sex.

Just what I like.

My heart beats in my throat as I step inside. Right then, a man steps out from the shadows. *Declan.*

I can tell right away from his stride, his hair, the smirk on his face.

"Are you ready?" he asks as he places a hand on the small of my back while guiding me into the room.

I nod, but I can't stop staring at everyone around me. People are having sex everywhere, but more importantly, this time there seems to be many more men than women. And some of the men are fucking each other too, somewhere in a small room to the left. And to my right, two women are giving a show, squirting while simultaneously having a man lick it up from the floor.

There are more rooms. One of them has a woman sitting on a bench while men fuck her in the ass one by one, leaving their cum behind. Another room has sex equipment lining the walls, and one woman in a leathery suit is using a whip on several men while another lady is milking them and catching it in a bowl. I can only imagine what they'll do with that.

Then we come to the middle of the hall. Three white columns with a woman tied to each one. Blindfolded. Bound by ropes. Unable to move except for their mouths.

And the men each approach to fuck them in the mouth … and come.

One of the girls is already covered in it. From top to bottom, she's dripping in cum.

Declan snaps his fingers at one of the staff members, who immediately walks toward that girl who seems to be gasping for air and starts untying her. She's guided away through the crowd, and at the same time, Declan pulls me toward the pillar.

"Is that my spot?" I whisper. "Will you be joining in?"

He doesn't respond. Instead, he sets me down beneath the column, on my knees, and holds my wrists as he pulls them back, tying them in place. He fishes a blindfold from his pocket and wraps it around my eyes.

Everything goes dark.

I feel as if I'm floating out of my body. As if time has stopped, and I'm left floating in nothingness.

Until I feel *it*. A fleshy tip against my lips, swiping back and forth.

Wet liquid gushes out, splashing against my face.

I hold my breath and wait.

When it stops, I gasp and lick my lips. Salty. Warm.

Immoral as hell.

Suddenly, another stream hits me right in the mouth. I don't know where it came from. I just know it's from someone else because the sound he makes is different from the one before.

I hear more groans and jerking off in front of me. There must be five people, if not more. The jets of seed keep coming. I can't tell from where or when. Everything just happens.

There's no time to process what's going on even though all my senses are on overload right now. Because the next dick is already right in front of me.

It's then that I realize the excitement is turning into something else. Fear.

A burst of panic flows through me, but I don't know why because I wanted this. I love this. I need this. This man in front of me keeps doing what he's doing without restraint. It's exactly what I asked for. What I begged Declan for ... yet ...

Everything's happening so fast. Too fast.

"Wait," I mumble, my lips barely able to pronounce the word because of the constant influx of cum and what else. But it's like they can't hear me. Maybe I didn't speak loud enough.

"Declan?" I say, my voice hoarse, ragged. I try to swallow, but it's almost impossible.

Why won't he respond? He has to be here in the room. These are his events. He invited me here. I thought he'd participate, but now I'm not even sure he's still near. Has he abandoned me?

I hope not. I wanted him to be here. I wanted him to

participate, to let me know that he liked it too. So I do the only thing I can think of. I call out his name as loud as I can, "Declan!"

**

DECLAN

I force myself to watch as the men take their turn. She's beaming while I'm biting my lip. She seems to be enjoying herself, just like before. Despite the flood of emotions coursing through my veins, I stay put, unwilling to move. The longer it lasts, the more she seems to go into some sort of trance.

And still, all I can do is watch.

When a metallic taste enters my mouth, I bring my fingers to my lips and gaze at them. Blood.

The color is such a contrast to the white naked scene in front of me. She looks engulfed in the sexual energy. Like a true hedonist.

And me? I don't even know what I'm supposed to do right now.

I organized this event. I have an obligation to make all my guests feel comfortable, to answer their questions, and to tend to any of their needs.

So I close my eyes and turn around, determined not to

come back until her time is over and another one can step in. After all, she's merely a girl who I met online. All we share is the same interest in filth. Nothing more.

That's what I tell myself as I stride out into the crowd with my head down.

Suddenly, a voice calling my name erupts through the explosion of moans.

My heart stops beating for a second. It's her. And she called out for me.

There's no mistaking the sound. I'd recognize it from a flock of people, so I immediately make my way back through the crowd. Without thinking, I approach, breaking through the circle of men and pushing aside the one who's currently in front of her. No hesitation.

"One second," I tell the man as I focus my attention on her.

I go to my knees and place my hand on her cheek. "I'm here."

"Declan ..." she mutters.

She sounds completely out of breath. Like she's been doing this for hours already, even though it's only been a couple of minutes. But her weariness is showing, as her body is hanging from the ropes instead of remaining upright.

Shit. I have to get her out of here.

"Please take the other girl, Sir," I ask the half-naked man watching over us, and he nods.

I'm lucky he doesn't argue with me because I really

don't want to make a scene right now. If he'd said no, I don't know what I would've done. But I do know one thing … I wouldn't let him anywhere close to her.

Not him, not anyone else.

I quickly reach behind her and untie the knots around her wrists. Her body tumbles against me, unable to sustain the weight.

The ordeal took a toll on her, despite the fact that it didn't last long. Maybe she wasn't expecting it to be this intense. Or maybe all her energy was already drained from the encounter upstairs.

Whatever the case, I can't let her continue.

"Declan," she mumbles. "I'm fine."

"You're not," I say, folding my arms around her.

I pick her up from the floor and carry her away from the pillar even though she's still wearing her blindfold—which is covered in cum, just like her. I won't take it off, though. I don't want her to see the people gazing at her … and me.

This has never happened before.

No one has ever interrupted a scene like this, and now I've done it twice.

Their sharp glares make me hold her even tighter. I'm afraid they might try to tear her away from me even though that thought is insane. I know it is, but I can't stop feeling fiercely protective of this girl in my arms … the girl I invited in to experience the most fucked up debauchery.

This girl who wasn't ready for any of this.

I snap my fingers at Greta, who immediately searches

for a new girl to place in front of the pillars. We can't disappoint the guests, no matter what. Someone's just going to have to do double duty.

With my brows furrowed, I march out the main doors, ignoring anyone who speaks to me. I'll explain it all later and cross my fingers no one gets fired over this. I just could not let this go on. Not with her being in the state she was … the state she's still in because of me.

Fuck.

I make my way down the hall and bring her into the elevator. It feels like it's taking an eternity, but when it finally stops, I take her into my office. I put her down on the chair only to grab a thick jacket, which I fold over her shoulders to cover her up. Then I grab a few tissues, rub her face clean and take off the blindfold.

She blinks a couple of times, clearly out of it. I smile and offer her a cup of fresh water. "Drink."

She gleefully chugs it down, partially letting the water run down her chin.

"C'mon," I say, lifting her up into my arms again.

"I can walk," she says, slurring half the words while coughing too.

"Sure, you can," I reply, carrying her out of my office.

I go to the ground floor using the elevator with her still in my arms. Her head drops to my shoulders halfway through walking, her eyes closed. She's completely wiped out, and it's only making me more anxious to get her somewhere safe.

"But what about the … night?" she mutters.

"Forget about it," I say, walking toward the exit.

"Oh, sir!" the bellhop calls out for me as I walk past the desk, but I'm not even remotely interested right now. They can deal with it on their own, or it can wait.

"I need you to do something for me," I say to him, completely ignoring his question. "Go to the VIP floor and grab the bag and clothes you find there. Get someone to deliver them to my home."

"Of course, sir," he says, slightly confused. "Now that you're here, I have a guest who has—"

"Not now," I growl back, marching out into the dark of night with a girl in my arms.

And not just any girl … it's NaughtyKitten we're talking about. The only girl who's managed to worm her way into my world even though I tried so hard to keep her at bay. Never did she complain about it being too much to handle. She kept pushing ahead without fear, thinking she could take on whatever I threw at her.

And what an idiot I am for trying to push her to the brink.

For trying to prove to myself that she was nothing more than just a toy to play with as I pleased.

I was wrong. Dead wrong.

Biting my lip in rage, I make my way to my car and set her down in the passenger's seat, securing her seat belt tight. Then I get behind the wheel and drive off in a hurry, not giving a shit that the event is still going down.

Everything will go according to plan, just like it always does.

I trust my co-workers to carry out their work professionally and to make the guests happy, whatever the cost. I don't doubt they can handle it.

I only hope that I'm not too late ... with her.

TWENTY-SIX

Kat

I wake up in a bed that smells like warm cookies and syrup and a dash of tropical fruit. Or maybe that's pancakes I'm smelling … I'm not sure. But who could be cooking?

I blink a couple of times and stretch my limbs, feeling refreshed and ready to start the day. Only when I look around do I realize I'm not in my own bed. Or in my home.

What the hell?

"Good morning."

The sudden voice makes me jolt up and down in the

bed.

"Jesus. Fuck."

It's Declan, and he's laughing out loud. "Sorry, did I scare you?"

"Kinda," I reply, immediately tucking my hair behind my ear. When I look down, I notice I'm still wearing that same outfit from when I was at the hotel. Except I'm no longer there ...

"The hotel ..." I mumble as I gaze up at him. "Wait, how did I get here?"

"I took you home," he replies, crossing his arms as he leans against the doorjamb. "How are you feeling?"

"Um ... good, I guess," I say, gazing around while still confused as hell. "So this is your place?"

He nods, approaching me with arrogance and flair. "I took you to the nearest place I knew you'd be safe."

"Huh ..." Interesting.

"Sorry, I didn't want to go through the hassle of finding your keys and trying to bring you to your own house, so I took the easier route. Hope you don't mind." He sits down on the bed beside me, but it's so close. Closer than I'm used to from him.

And I'm suddenly very much aware of the fact that I'm still wearing this ... *thing*. This see-through outfit that doesn't leave much to the imagination. Instinctively, I pull up the sheets.

He's looking at me in such a different way from before.

His smile seems a lot more genuine, and his eyes seem

bigger. Does that make sense? Probably not, but it's almost as if something about him has changed. Or am I imagining things?

"You're safe here," he says, placing a hand on top of mine. "You don't have to hide."

I swallow and lick my lips. Confused doesn't even begin to describe the way I'm feeling now.

I don't remember coming here. I don't remember any of this. The last thing I remember was … *that room.*

Being tied to that pole. All those men. And then … calling out for Declan.

"What are you thinking about?" he asks, tilting his head as if he's trying to gaze deeper into my eyes.

"Last night. I called out your name."

He nods.

"So you heard?" My cheeks flush. "Sorry I—"

He places a finger on my lips. "That's all over and done now."

I nod softly, averting my eyes so I'm not distracted by his. I'm trying to remember what happened, but it's hard. I've only got bits and pieces, and the timeline isn't clear.

"Did I black out?" I ask, worried something might've happened.

"I'm not sure. But you weren't very responsive."

"Fuck," I say, rubbing my face. "God, I'm so embarrassed."

He grabs my hands and lowers them. "Don't be. It's understandable, considering everything I did with you."

The smile that follows is so sweet it makes my heart jump.

Jesus. When did I start to fall for him?

He grabs my hand. "I just want to apologize. If I'd known you were so tired, I wouldn't have let you—"

"I made the choice," I say. "It was my decision. You don't have to apologize."

Since when is he so caring? When did he change and why? I must've missed the clues.

"Right." He smiles gently. Then he gets up from the bed. "Hungry?"

"Uhh …"

He raises a brow. "Don't tell me you don't like pancakes."

So my nose was right after all. "Oh, I do," I answer, biting my lip. "But, um …"

I stare down at the clothes I'm still wearing. Or rather, the lack thereof.

His eyes scan me from top to bottom before he breaks out in a short laugh. "I almost forgot. Hold on." He walks out of the room and comes back in with a velvety white robe. "Sorry, I don't have anything for girls."

I grin as he hands it to me. "It's fine."

"I'll … wait here. Feel free to take a shower. Breakfast is coming soon." He points over his shoulder and awkwardly walks backward, closing the door too.

Only when I'm sure he's not around anymore do I throw off the blanket and put on the robe. It's so soft, I feel like I'm wearing an actual cloud. And it smells like him …

Why do I even recognize his smell? Damn, my easy heart.

I shake it off and put on some slippers that are underneath the bed. Then I open the curtains and let the light in. But good God, I am not prepared for the amazing view. We're sky high above the city. And although I have no clue what building or where exactly I am, I can definitely see Hotel O from here just a few blocks away.

I stretch out again and let out another yawn before going into the bathroom adjacent to his room. It smells like lavender soap and fresh towels in here. I snoop through his things until I find a cologne, spritzing it out into the air. Yup. Definitely his.

I close my eyes and take in the smell. Goose bumps scatter across my skin.

What are you doing, Kat? Shower, remember? Jesus.

I quickly turn on the water and throw off my things, then step under the stream. I lather myself with his soap, and by the time I'm done washing and drying off, I smell just like him. Lovely.

I wrap myself in a fresh robe and open the door. "What do I do with my dirty clothes?"

"Oh, just leave them in the corner," he yells back. "I'll bring them to the cleaner and get them back to you."

A blush spreads on my cheeks. That's nice of him.

"Breakfast is ready!" he calls out.

I bite my lip and reply, "Just a second."

Quickly checking myself in the mirror, I fidget with my hair and tuck my tits in so I look at least a little bit presentable despite still looking like a hooker that was plucked off the street after fucking twenty guys. I wish I was exaggerating. But not even a shower can erase this filth.

I don't even know exactly what went down last night. Only that a lot of it was dirty as fuck. And that I felt like I was losing myself at the moment, which turned out to be my downfall.

I underestimated my own stamina, and for some reason, my first instinct was to call out for help. Or more specifically … Declan.

I wanted him to be there. To watch over me. With him, I felt safe. But the moment he left, my whole sense of self seemed to vanish.

And then he came back. Was it because I needed him? Because I called out for him? Or was there another reason?

Taking a deep breath, I shrug it off and open the door, determined not to let my foolish heart believe in the lies it fabricated. He was only looking out for both our interests, nothing else.

As Declan sets down plates filled with warm pancakes on the table in the middle of the room, I look around his spacious apartment. The bottom half of the walls have warm wood paneling, and most of the furniture looks like it's made from a dark mahogany too. It contrasts nicely with the top of the white painted walls and ceiling, and, of course, the fur rug in front of the long beige couch.

"What do you think?" he asks as he pulls up a chair for me. "Hungry?"

"Oh …" I smile, sitting down on the chair. "You've made it cozy in here."

"Thanks," he says, placing forks and knives on the table too. "Did the decorating myself. I'm quite proud of it, if I say so myself."

"I can imagine," I say while he puts down two cups of coffee.

As he sits down opposite me with a smirk on his face, there's an awkward silence between us. It makes my skin crawl, that's how awkward it is.

"Well … eat up!" he says.

"Right." I pick up my fork and knife and cut off a piece, shoving it into my mouth because I'm famished. But I'm not prepared for how good this tastes … like, oh my God, I want to lick up my plate kinda good.

"Like it?" he asks, cocking his head as he cuts into his pancakes.

I nod profusely, shoving more into my mouth. "Amazing. How did you learn to cook like this?"

He laughs. "It's one of the only things I can do right."

"Oh, don't say that," I say. "There are plenty of other things you're great at. Right?"

"Like what?" He raises a brow.

I mull it over for a while, but then all I can think of is how amazing he is with his hands … his lips … his dick … and then my entire face heats again. "Well, I can think of *something*," I mumble, trying not to make it sound even weirder than it already is.

He lets out a short laugh. "Of course, you can, filthy kitten."

That word makes my heart flutter. I don't know why, but every time I hear it, I'm smiling from ear to ear.

"Speaking of which," he says, picking up his cup of coffee, "tell me what you thought about last night."

I swallow down a piece of pancake that felt like it got stuck in my throat, then I wash it down with some coffee before answering. "Hmm ... interesting."

"Just interesting?" He slurps his coffee.

"I liked it."

"Which part?"

Well, this is starting to feel like a job interview.

"Everything."

He takes a casual bite of his pancakes and swallows it before continuing. "Really? Name some specifics."

I gaze up at him. Are we really going to do this? He's not averting his eyes, though, so I guess we are. "You. Me. That room. That man."

"What about the part when you were tied and used by several men?" He holds his cup of coffee with a certain aloofness, but there's a definite serious undertone in his voice.

I can barely swallow down the last bit of pancake I put in my mouth. "I don't ... remember much."

"Lie."

Goddammit. Why does he see through me so easily?

I lean back and fold my arms. "What do you want me to say?"

"Why did you call out for me?" he asks firmly.

"Because I thought you'd be there," I reply.

"I never said that."

"I just assumed," I say.

He narrows his eyes. "You assumed wrong."

"Sorry." I make a face. "I didn't know you'd get mad."

"I'm not," he says, blinking a couple of times while blowing out a breath. "You wanted this. You signed the agreement."

I nod. "And I was going to go through with it."

He plants his coffee down with a little bit too much effort, and it makes me jolt up from my chair. "You were out of energy and couldn't take any more of it."

"I could've handled it."

"No, you couldn't." His stern voice irks me.

I frown. "You don't know that."

"You collapsed in my arms like a used fuck doll. I carried you all the way out to my fucking office and then drove you back home myself."

I stare at him in disbelief. Did he really just say he carried me out in his arms?

"But … why?" I ask.

He clenches his jaw and looks away. "Because you … called *my* name."

"You could've just given me encouraging words and let

me continue."

"No, I couldn't," he says through gritted teeth. "You didn't see what I saw."

"And what did you see?" I ask, raising a brow.

He sucks in a deep breath and looks away again. "A girl in desperate need …"

"Oh …" I laugh out loud and shake my head. "You wanted to be the savior." I drink the last bit of my coffee. "Well, tell you what … I don't need a savior."

As I get up to put my mug in the sink so I can get out of there fast, he gets up too and follows me into the kitchen. Right before I turn around, he grabs my arm and forces me to look at him.

"Are you honestly saying you could've continued all night long with those men shoving their dicks in your face? Making you swallow their jizz?"

I bite my lip, jerking myself free. "Probably."

"No, you don't want to admit you got in over your head."

"What's it to you? You know what I like."

"This wasn't just pleasure to you, and you know it," he says, still up in my face. "There's something else … something you're not telling me."

Jesus. Why am I such an open book?

He can't know what I'm writing. He just can't; it's not even a possibility. Ever.

"I don't have to tell you anything. This was just an agreement between you and me. A mutual exchange of pleasure, right? That's what you wanted. Nothing more, nothing less," I reply, looking him up and down. I won't back down. I'm not scared of him anymore.

"You just don't want to tell me," he says, trapping me between his arms. "Why? What do you have to lose?"

He's so close now; I can feel the heat prickling on my skin. A word lingers on my tongue, but I don't want to say it. I don't want to face the implications … what it would cause.

Yet it tumbles out anyway. "You."

His grip on the kitchen counter tightens as he leans forward. The air between us feels thick with unspoken desires and promises. Something more than … *this*.

"I can't be in a relationship," he whispers, his forehead almost leaning against mine.

"I know," I say, unable to keep my hands from touching his ironed shirt.

"It would put everything at risk," he adds.

I nod, rubbing my lips together. I understand why he's reluctant, considering his job. It's high risk. The hotel would be ruined if things came out …

He's right. We can't date. We're like opposites, and he always pisses me off. Not to mention the fact that my job is a risk factor too. If he knew what I did for a living, he'd kick me out right now.

Maybe I should tell him. Maybe that'd be the better route for both of us. Except the moment I open my mouth, his lips crash onto mine.

TWENTY-SEVEN

DECLAN

Fuck it.

I tried so hard to stop myself from falling. I fought it with all I had, but these lips ... they're too hard to ignore. I want to taste them. I want her. I want it all.

I told myself I could do this, that I could ignore the growing need inside my heart, but I can't. I can't fucking do it anymore.

Not when I have to watch her get fucked by a million other guys.

Just the thought of them having her pisses me off beyond control. I wanted to punch each one of them—start a fight, I don't care—even though it made no sense because I was the one who put her in that position in the first place. It was all my idea because I wanted to see how far she'd go. And how far I'd go to protect myself and the hotel.

When she called out my name, it felt like she needed me to save her, and I couldn't say no, not even if I tried. But enough is enough. I can't take it any longer.

I need to have her. She needs to belong to me and no one else.

So I kiss her deeply. Hard. Like I should have long ago.

The moment she stepped into my life, I should've known she'd consume my every waking thought. Not only because of the lust or the sexual energy that constantly sparks between us, but because of our connection beyond that. My unshaken need to get closer, intimately, in her life and heart.

Fuck. I don't understand it … Why her? Why now, out of all the times I could've fallen for a girl but didn't? So many of them are there—online, offline, ready for the taking—but I don't want any of them. All I want is her. And it's been pissing me off to the point where I kept lashing out at her.

But she's suffered at my hand. I've treated her like shit, fucked her like she was an object, and she took it all without complaints. She's too fucking perfect, and I tried to ruin it. Tried to make her see how bad of a man I would be for her just so she'd get away.

Just so we'd both be safe. But there's no point in being

safe if you can't have what you want, is there? And I definitely want her.

In fact, I can't even keep my fucking hands off her right now as I'm fondling her tits right through the fabric of her robe. Her moans are what keep me going, her nipples taut and needy, just like me.

But then she unlatches her lips from mine, whispering, "We can't …"

"I know, but I'm doing it anyway," I whisper.

"But why? You said you didn't—"

I silence her with another kiss.

It doesn't make any sense, but it doesn't have to. I can't explain to her what I'm feeling right now. I, myself, don't even know why or how it's happening. It just is.

Instead of thinking about it, I just do it. I claim her mouth, her tongue, the rim of her lips, and everything between.

Right then, the doorbell rings, but I ignore it, going straight for the kill.

It keeps ringing, though. Someone's not letting up.

"Fuck," I growl out loud as her lips unlock from mine once again. "Ignore it," I say, trying to kiss her again, but she nudges us apart.

"What if it's important?" she asks, her lips so red and thick I want nothing more than to ravish them.

"I don't care," I say, planting my lips firmly onto her lips, drawing a line down to her neck to that spot where she can't say no to me anymore.

She giggles, biting her lip, clearly struggling to keep it together. Her body says yes, but from the way she's still pushing me away, I can tell she's really distracted.

"Can we check?" she asks.

It takes all the effort I can muster to pull myself away from her. I grunt and march to the door in my comfy sweatpants, knowing full well my dick is erect as I open the door. I don't give a shit.

Except I do the moment I see Flynn standing right there with a suitcase in his hands.

I frown, confused. "What the …?"

"Bellhop said you needed someone to deliver this in a hurry. Emergency or some shit."

His eyes draw down to my dick, and then he quickly closes them, wincing. "Aw, fuck."

I'm stunned to the point I don't even notice that Kat followed right behind me.

And I'm definitely not prepared for the squeal that follows.

***

Kat

"Flynn?!" My eyes widen, and my jaw drops. "What are you doing here?"

"What the fuck, Kat?" Flynn glares at both me and Declan, and it feels like the rug is swooped out from underneath me. "What the hell are you doing here with him?"

How the hell is he even here? And why?

"Oh, boy …" Declan rubs his face with his hand.

"What's going on?" I ask, raising a brow while I look at them. Then I notice the suitcase in Flynn's hand. *My* suitcase.

Shock ripples through me. No fucking way.

"Why does he have my suitcase that I left at the hotel?" I ask.

Declan sighs out loud, and says, "He works for me."

"What?" My jaw drops. I can't even … My brain feels like it's busted. "No way." I stare at Flynn. "You work for Declan? How? Since when?"

"Since a long time. Doesn't matter. Why are you here at his condo?" he asks, making a fist.

"Because she's mine," Declan says with a smug grin on his face.

I roll my eyes and sigh as Flynn only seems to be getting more furious.

"You're not helping," I hiss at Declan.

"So? This is my home," Declan replies.

"If I'd known this was her suitcase, I wouldn't ever have come here." Flynn harshly puts the suitcase inside and focuses his attention on me. "I can't believe you're with him. This is the asshole who hurt you!"

"It's none of your business," Declan says, stepping forward.

They're up in each other's face, breathing like bulls, clearly getting ready for a brawl I'm not prepared for. So I step between them and push them away from each other. "Whoa. Boys. No fighting. Not on my watch."

"Move, Kat," Flynn growls, still glaring at Declan as if he's the devil himself.

"What are you gonna do?" Declan growls back. "Hit me?"

"I'd like to," Flynn responds.

"No," I say, keeping them separate. "Flynn … Please, can you not?"

"But he's been a giant prick to you!" Flynn says. "Tell me I'm wrong."

I'm trying. Really hard. But I can't because he's right. Declan *has* been an asshole. But that still doesn't erase the feelings I have for him.

Flynn points at Declan. "I told you to stay the fuck away from her!"

"Stop it, you two!" I shove them so hard, they have to move or they'll fall. "What's the matter with you?"

"*He's* what's the matter," Flynn says.

"Forgetting I'm your boss, dipshit?" Declan replies.

"Stop. Now," I growl at them both. I don't have time for this jealousy shit. And Flynn has been keeping this a secret from me? Even though they knew each other? No wonder he ended the phone call when I told him it was Declan Porter.

"You didn't even tell me you worked for him," I say to Flynn, feeling pissed off too now. "You could've told me he was your boss."

"And hurt you even more?" he says. "Fuck no."

"And you ..." I direct my attention toward Declan. "You knew he was my friend, and you still didn't tell me he worked for you."

"I didn't think it would make a difference," he says.

"No, you were just afraid she was going to hate you even more," Flynn says.

"No, you're afraid she'd choose me over you," Declan retorts, continuing to fuel the fire to the point I have to remain between them to keep them away from each other.

"Okay, that's it. Time-out," I say, holding up my hands. "Stop acting like little kids and start behaving like grown-ups. Jesus." I let out a big sigh. "Stop fighting over me like I'm some goddamn prize."

Flynn crosses his arms as Declan puts them against his side. Both still look angry as hell, but neither of them are trying to grasp each other's throats anymore, so I guess that's good.

But fuck … I wish I could've seen this coming. I would've brought some protective gear.

"I thought you were over him," Flynn says.

"I …" I swallow. "It's complicated."

"She can do whatever she wants," Declan interjects. "Maybe you should take her wishes into consideration next time you burst into my office."

"I'm protecting a friend because I care about her," Flynn spits. "Unlike you."

"Please," I say, looking at both Declan and Flynn. "Can you stop this? Do it for me, please." I look at Flynn. "I don't want to lose you as a friend, but I … like him, okay?"

"Tsk," Flynn says. "Because he has a dick? This guy isn't good for you."

"You don't even know me," Declan rebukes. "And you're walking on thin ice here, buddy."

"Listen!" I yell, which makes them lean back and finally focus on me instead of each other. "This isn't your choice," I tell Flynn. "It's mine. Please respect that."

Flynn rubs his lips together, clearly having trouble accepting it, but at least he's not trying to change my mind.

"And you …" I say to Declan. "Stop making this about jealousy. It isn't. Flynn's my best friend. Please, don't be so hard on him. He's listened to me again and again when you pulled all that shit on me."

Declan swallows, visibly shaken too.

"I need both of you to behave like adults, please. Now, I know you might not like each other, but at least pretend, for my sake," I say. "Flynn, I love you, but I need to make my own decisions, okay?"

Flynn takes a deep breath and nods slowly.

"Declan ... I know he's probably crossed the line several times because of me. But please do not fire him," I beg.

Declan cocks his head and closes his eyes, rubbing his forehead.

"Fine. I won't," he says through gritted teeth. "But this has to stop."

"It will. I promise," I say, glaring at Flynn so he gets the point. "Flynn, thanks for the suitcase. I owe you."

"You're welcome," he replies. "But I'm outta here. You gonna stay, or are you coming with me?"

My lips part, but I don't even know how to respond because I hadn't thought about that yet. "Umm ..." I look at Declan, who still looks like he's swallowed a bunch of sour grapes. "Maybe? I don't know."

"I think it's better if we all cool down for a moment," Declan says, clearing his throat.

I nod a couple of times. "True."

"Don't you have to go to work too?" Flynn says with that snobby voice he puts up whenever he catches me doing dumb shit.

"Fuck." I immediately check my watch. "You're right."

"Guess that's settled then," Declan says, folding his

arms.

"Sorry," I say, smiling at him. "I'll see you later then?"

"Of course." An arrogant grin spreads on his lips that makes the butterflies return. "But you're not going to go without a kiss, are you?"

"Oh, fuck no," Flynn grumbles, turning around. "I'm outta here." He slams the door shut behind him.

"Bye," Declan snaps, but I grab his face and make him look at me.

"I'm here," I say, licking my lips.

He grabs my ass and pulls me toward him, kissing me hard and greedily as if he wants to show me I belong to him and no one else. As if he's actually scared to lose me to Flynn. Not that that's ever a possibility … but at least it means Declan cares. Maybe more than he's willing to admit.

When our lips unlock, I bite my lip. "That wasn't just a kiss …"

"Had to show you who's boss," he murmurs.

I playfully slap him on the chest. "Seriously?"

"Go on then. Get dressed. Work is waiting."

"One sec," I say, quickly opening the door so I can catch Flynn before he disappears. "Thanks, Flynn! For the suitcase, I mean."

He waves at me without turning around. "No problem. Glad I could help."

I don't think he's really that happy to help, but I appreciate it. I know it's hard on him to see his best friend date a guy like Declan.

If we're even dating ... At this point, no one knows. Not even me.

As I close the door, I turn and grab my suitcase filled with clothes so I can finally put on something decent before going out. But I can't help say, "So about this kiss ..."

He brings his finger to his lips, and says, "Shh ... Don't tell anyone."

Of course, he'd say that.

Why would I expect anything else?

TWENTY-EIGHT

Kat

At work, I'm writing a few articles that are way overdue. I haven't looked at the one I was writing about my experiences at the hotel in ages, partly due to the fact that I have a conflict of interest now. I still want to finish it someday, but I just don't know when. Part of me desperately wants to see what it'd bring me, yet a part of me can't stop thinking something bad will happen if I do. Even if I remove all the personal details and references, I can't shake the feeling that Declan will be pissed, and that I might lose him.

Before, I didn't really care about any of that, but right now, I don't know anymore.

Which is why I've drowned myself in other work so I don't even have to think about it.

However, I've been typing away so much my fingers hurt. I definitely need a break right about now. Plus, I've been meaning to call Flynn after that recent fiasco at Declan's condo.

I still find it so hard to fathom Flynn's been working there all this time, and I didn't even know it. Why wouldn't he tell me? Was he that ashamed of his work? I wonder what he does then … if he's part of the staff or maybe part of the crew that pleases the guests.

My curiosity takes control of me as I pick up my phone and dial his number. I don't even know what to say, but we have to talk about this.

"Flynn," he says as he picks up.

"Hey, it's Kat."

"Oh … hey." He doesn't sound too happy to hear from me.

"Sorry, am I bothering you right now? I can call back later."

"No, it's fine," he says, clearing his throat. "I just wasn't expecting this."

"What? Me calling you?"

"No, I just … never mind."

"What's the matter?" I ask, leaning back in my chair.

"Nothing. I'm just worried about you, okay? That dude isn't right for you, you should know that."

I sigh. "I know you don't like him, and that's fine. But—"

"You don't like him either, Kat," he interrupts. "You just don't want to realize it."

"Maybe I do. So what?"

"He's not a datable guy. Trust me."

"How do you know?"

"Because he treats you like shit, like all the other girls who came before you."

That's not exactly what I want to hear ... but okay. "Maybe this time is different."

"It's not. Don't fool yourself into thinking he'll change. He won't," he says.

"You don't know that. You don't know him like I do."

"He's my boss. I know him differently."

"In a bad way," I say. "I noticed. And that's okay. I get that you're pissed at him, and rightfully so, considering all the shit he did, but I ..." I sigh. "There are feelings involved, okay? I'm not sure what it is, but I want to find out. I need this right now. I need to know if there's a possibility for more."

"There's not. Trust me. Please." He's being so straightforward ... goddammit. I don't know what's gotten into him.

"I want to, believe me, but I have to follow my heart too."

"Dammit, Kat ... Please, listen to me," he growls.

I don't like the tone of his voice. "Flynn—"

"You're making a big mistake," he interjects. "I wish I could explain, but I can't. Not without hurting you even more."

"Fine, then don't," I say. "I don't need advice. I only called to say thank you. To make things up after how badly shit ended when you walked out of Declan's apartment," I say. "For now, Declan is part of my life, and I'm not going to punt him out just because you say he's bad for me."

I'm not letting Declan go this easily. Not for anyone, and certainly not because Flynn wants me to.

"Wait, Kat—"

I end the call before he can say anything more that'll make me question everything.

Even if he's right, I don't want to doubt what I feel right now.

I've lived in doubt for so long, always searching but never finding what I needed, never finding what I was looking for. From the moment I was born, I've been kept in a room like a fucking pet, always being protected from the big, bad outside world. As if living my life the way I wanted to would be the worst thing that could ever happen to me.

No. I want to be free. I want to do what I like. I want to try everything even if it's bad and wrong and filthy. I don't want to be held back anymore.

First, my parents ... now Flynn.

I've had enough. I need this for my own sake. And now

that I've crossed paths with Declan, I have to know where it could lead. Even if it's only heartache.

At least I'll have known just how bad love can be for me.

And maybe learn a thing or two.

He's not all bad. I mean, the sex is amazing, and he did take me home when I was too tired to even walk. And he was so sweet when he made those pancakes for me, and that kiss …

God, I could just about die for another one.

That's it.

I get up from my chair, pack my stuff, and walk to the door.

I'm going to him. I don't care if it's the middle of the day or that I still have work to do. I'll catch up when I get home tonight. Hell, I'll work all through the night if I have to just to get this shit done.

But I am going to see Declan, we are going to talk about this and what it means, and then we're going to have banging hot sex.

End of discussion.

***

DECLAN

A few days later, I'm having the talk.

Not the talk I was hoping for. The bad one.

The one where your boss basically tells you it's do or die at this point.

"I've heard some complaints with the past two events, Declan," my boss says as he struts around his office.

"I know, and it won't happen again, I promise." I'm trying to remain calm even though I want to scream right now.

Fuck. I wish I hadn't pulled her into the events. That I could erase all of it so my job would still be secure and I'd be able take the bad memories away for her too.

But that's not how life works. I made a mistake, and now I have to live with the consequences.

"How will I know for sure?" he asks. "I hired you because you were the best at what you did."

"I am, sir. Please give me a chance to redeem myself."

He scratches his chin. "Multiple co-workers have expressed that they felt uncomfortable with the way you handled a particular girl ..."

"She's out of the picture," I say.

It's not entirely true, but I know I won't take her to these events again. Not just because my job is on the line now, but also because I couldn't stand to watch her with other men when I wasn't there to enjoy her too. I get jealous around her. A lot. And it says something.

"Right. If you say so," he says, interrupting my train of thought.

I know I fucked up a few times at these past few events, but don't the other successful events outweigh that?

"None of the guests were unhappy, sir." I say. "Doesn't that count?"

"True, true …" he mumbles, gazing straight at me. "But I have a business to run. I can't have these things happening at this hotel."

"I understand, sir. It was a hundred percent my fault, and I take full responsibility."

"Good," he says, his voice as stern as the look in his eyes. "Because I should be looking for a different event coordinator if this keeps happening."

Fuck.

Two tiny mistakes at an event and I'm already on the verge of losing the only job I ever wanted.

The job that would lead me to success, and maybe … just maybe … I'd be able to take over the company in the future.

Guess I'm really fucked now.

***

I arrive at the hotel an hour later. I stopped by my place first to put on something sexy. You know, in case Declan wants to get it on. I wouldn't mind it myself either, as I'm definitely in for a rematch after how I left his apartment. He wanted to jump my bones back then, and I desperately wanted him to. But Flynn had to show up and ruin the mood.

Oh well, at least he brought me the suitcase. At least the clothes in there allowed me to leave Declan's apartment with my dignity intact. And I did thank Flynn for it. I just wish he would've accepted my choice.

Oh well. Now's not the time to think about Flynn. I don't want to worry about it anymore. I'd much rather hang out with Declan and see whether he's ready to commit.

So I happily march into the hotel and go to the front desk because I already know the bellhop is waiting to stop me if I proceed.

"Declan's waiting for me," I tell him before he can even say a word.

"Oh, well, that's strange. He told me no one could bother him."

"It's fine. I'm probably the reason." I wink.

I don't really know if that's true. It probably isn't, but I'm sure he won't mind me interrupting a conversation if I bring the goods. And I definitely brought them.

"Sorry," the bellhop says, laughing awkwardly. "I'm just trying not to upset him. After the last fiasco with me asking a fellow employee to bring the suitcase to his home instead of an actual delivery guy." He snorts again, then clears his throat. "Sorry, that was too much detail."

"It's okay. I get it." I lean over the counter. "You're overworked. Underpaid. Underappreciated." I give him my flirty smile. "But I'm sure he'd give you a pay raise if you'd let me pass."

The bellhop swallows, visibly constrained. "Um …"

"You don't want to make him angry, do you?" I add.

"No, of course not," he says. "Go right ahead, ma'am."

"Thank you," I say, winking as I walk up the stairs.

On my stilettos, I hurry down the hall to the office I've become accustomed to. My heart is already racing from the thoughts of how badly I want him, and how badly he's probably going to behave—slapping my ass, pounding me against his desk, making me swallow.

Fuck, I'm already horny by the time I get to the door.

Too bad.

Because when I open it, all that energy comes to a screeching halt.

Inside the room is none other than my father.

TWENTY-NINE

Kat

"Dad?" I mutter, my voice shaking as badly as my legs.

What the hell is he doing here at Hotel O? Is he a guest? What is this?

When he turns around, I'm positive it's him. Shit.

"Kat?" His jaw slowly drops as does his eyebrows. "What in heaven's name are you doing here?"

My eyes scatter back and forth between Declan and my dad, but the longer I look, the less I understand and the more it makes my head spin.

"Declan?" I mutter, feeling queasy.

He immediately gets up from his chair and walks toward me. He grabs my arms, and whispers, "What are you doing here? You should go."

"I wanted to surprise you," I say. "What's going on? What is my dad doing here?"

"He's your dad?" he asks, his eyes widening.

"Yes," I reply, still in shock myself.

"What's the meaning of this?" my dad says, clearing his throat.

"Let go of me," I say, jerking myself free from Declan's grip.

"How do you know my daughter?" Dad grumbles at Declan.

Declan glares at us both, his face turning red. "It's hard to explain …"

"Dad, what are you doing at this hotel? Are you a guest here?" I mumble, flabbergasted. All sorts of thoughts are going through my head right now. None of them good.

"This is *my* hotel."

I feel like the earth is ripped away from underneath my feet.

Declan covers his eyes with his hand, and I can't stop shaking.

"Why didn't you tell me?" I mutter although I don't even know who to ask.

It's all too much to take right now.

"If I'd known he was your dad, I would have, trust me,"

Declan says.

"What are you doing with my daughter?" my dad says, pinpointing his anger on Declan now. "Explain to me what this is. *Now.*"

"Dad!" I say, demanding his attention. "It's none of your business what Declan and I are doing."

"Yes, it is." They're in each other's face now, and I'm having trouble breathing. "Are you telling me you're *dating* my daughter?"

"Well …" Declan rubs his lips together and leans away from my dad who seems to get fired up just from the thought.

"How dare you." My dad shoves his finger into Declan's chest. "You submit her to your filthiness? She's innocent!"

"Far from it," Declan says, putting his hands against his side.

"What?!" my dad yells.

I step between them. "Dad. Stop."

"Is this true?" he asks me. "Have you two—"

"Yes. And like I said, it's none of your business."

"You had no right," Dad says, his mouth practically spitting fire. "Messing with my daughter …"

"Dad, it was my choice," I say, my voice fluctuating in tone.

"That's over now," he says, directing his attention back to Declan as if I'm not even here. "I don't want you involved with my daughter. End of discussion. She will not be coming here or anywhere near you ever again."

And then he grabs my arm and drags me along.

"Wait," I say, trying to free myself from his grip, but he's too strong.

As he opens the door, he barks at Declan. "You're fired!"

"I'm sorry," I say to Declan, but he's already turned his head toward the window in defeat.

"Dad!" I yell, but he doesn't stop pulling me along until we're in an elevator, and he's already pressed the button to the garage underneath.

"Let go of me," I growl, jerking free.

"I expected better of you, Kat," he says. "How long has this been going on? Weeks? Months?"

"I don't have to explain myself to you," I say, averting my eyes. "I'm a grown woman."

When the elevator comes to a halt, he immediately grabs me again and pulls me outside. "Let's go."

"Where?" I mutter as he drags me along.

"You're coming home with me."

"Dad. Stop! Why are you doing this?" I ask, but he doesn't answer.

Instead, he throws open his passenger door. "Sit. Down."

"Fine!" I do what he asks. Not because I'm afraid, but because we need to have a discussion. Badly.

He gets behind the wheel and drives us to his house. Not mine. His.

Where Mom is probably waiting too.

Fuck. All along he was the boss of that hotel? Declan's boss ... my dad ...

This can't get any more absurd.

"How long?" I ask, having trouble finding the proper words. "How long have you owned that damn hotel?"

"Since I built it from the ground up."

Wait, what? My dad? The sex mogul?

No. That can't be, right? He can't be so dirty he'd come up with something like this.

Mom and Dad never let me do anything, never let me out of their sight, didn't let me go out and date boys. Hell, my dad believed I was still a virgin when I moved out of the house.

And then to find out all these events are his doing? It's mindboggling, to say the least.

"You know what goes on at your hotel, right?" I say through gritted teeth.

"Yes."

"All of it?" I ask.

"Everything."

I gasp. "And you never once thought to tell me?"

"No, and that's exactly the reason," he says.

I think about my youth and how little my dad ever shared about his job and what he did. He never once took me to his business, never even spoke a word about it to anyone. Now it all makes sense.

"You've been lying to me all this time," I say, tears welling up in my eyes. "Were you ever going to tell me?"

He throws a glance at me for a second before sighing. "Perhaps. When you were older."

"Why? Why not sooner?"

"Can you imagine?" He glances my way again while driving. "Telling my daughter that I run a sex hotel?"

I cross my arms. "So you're ashamed of what you do. That's it?"

"No ..." He takes a deep breath. "It's a private matter."

"Really? You can't tell your own daughter what it is that you do for a living?" I make a tsk sound. "All this time, I've been wondering what your job was. You were always gone. Never home. Even Mom hated it. Honestly, I'm disappointed you didn't tell me sooner. It would've saved me a lot of tears. Not that you care."

"I do care." He makes a face but doesn't reply any further, which means he knows I'm right. He should have told me. It could've prevented a lot of heartache and pain.

"This is exactly the reason I didn't tell you," he says after a while. "Because I didn't want you to be subjected to what goes on at that hotel. Because it might turn you into something you're not."

"You mean become like you?" I say.

He swallows. "This job isn't easy, Kat. It comes with responsibility and secrecy."

"Yeah, I found that out firsthand," I say, rolling my eyes.

"I'm serious. I wanted something better for you. I wanted you to be able to follow your own path without

307

feeling the pressure to live up to this. To what I do."

Biting my lip, I look away at the streets. We're closing in on my family home now. But I'm nowhere near done with this conversation.

"I'm not ashamed of who I am, Dad. I love being me. And I love the hotel, Dad," I say, glancing at him over my shoulder.

"What? Seriously?"

"Yes. I mean it," I say. "I've been to two events, and I enjoyed it."

"Please don't elaborate," he says, grimacing. "I don't want to hear it."

I laugh. "I'm an adult, Dad. I can do what I like. I'm just as dirty as any other adult."

"Oh, God ..." he mumbles, making me laugh even more.

"Are you that embarrassed? Why start that hotel then?"

"I started that thing when I was young, but I never thought it would grow this big.Yet it did. And look where we are now," he explains.

"You've been keeping this a secret for so long. I still find it hard to believe."

I shake my head, wishing I knew what to say or ask, but I don't. It's too much of a surprise for my brain to handle right now.

When we arrive home, Dad's the first to undo his seat belt, but I keep staring at him.

"So what now?" I say as he gazes at me.

"Go on," he says, nudging his head as he throws a look at the house.

"Is Mom home?" I ask. "Does she know about all this?"

He lets out another big sigh. "Kat …"

"I guess that's a no then," I say as I get out of the car and slam the door shut.

My God. Just when I thought this couldn't get any worse.

He never brought Mom to the hotel? No wonder she's so pissed at him, if he's been keeping secrets from her too. And then on top of that, he has the balls to tell me how to live my life. I can't believe this.

"Kat … please," he says as he follows me inside, but I want none of it.

"Don't," I say, holding up my hand. "You forfeited the right to ask me for anything when you told my man that I'd never see him again."

THIRTY

Kat

Ignoring my dad completely, I ring the doorbell until someone finally opens. When Melvin opens the door, I hug him tight and say, "Long time, no see, Mel."

"Hello, Miss," he says, chuckling as he hugs me back.

"You're home early, sir," Mel says as my dad comes in too.

He nods without saying anything further, so I do on his behalf. "That's because Dad caught me with my boyfriend at his work."

"Boyfriend?" Dad frowns.

"I'll call him whatever the hell I want," I say, marching inside.

"I'll … go make some coffee," Melvin says, shuffling away like he wants nothing to do with it.

"Did I hear the word boyfriend?" Mom's voice appears before she does as she sashays into the hallway where Dad and I are still having a staring contest.

"Yes," I say with a sour face. "And Dad met him today."

"What?" Mom says with a shrill voice. "Who is it? Why haven't I met him yet?"

"You're not gonna," I interject before my dad can say anything. "Dad told him he could never see me again. Oh, and he also fired him." With my eyes, I throw lightning bolts at my dad.

Mom's face immediately turns dark. "He works at your company?"

Dad grunts, his face looking like he just escaped a five-hour traffic jam. "I don't want to talk about it."

"I do." I fold my arms. "Shouldn't you tell Mom about where you really work?"

It's about time she knew the truth. It's been eating away at their relationship for so long … no wonder she was fed up with him.

Mom cocks her head. "What is this about, Fred?"

Dad's face scrunches up, and he lets out another exasperated sigh.

"She deserves to know, Dad," I say.

"Deserve to know what?" Mom steps forward. "Fred?"

"The hotel I run isn't an ordinary hotel."

"Well, I knew that—"

"There's more. You just always said you didn't *want* to know," he interrupts.

Mom's face tightens, but she doesn't say anything. I guess she truly never did know what his business actually entailed.

"There are certain events organized at our hotel ... Guests who are looking for a spicy evening."

She frowns, clearly confused, so I add, "Sex, Mom. They sell it."

"What?" she says, completely flabbergasted. "I thought you said you had rich clients?"

"They are. It's pricey," I add.

"I don't understand," she says, shaking her head. "You let these people have sex at the hotel?"

"Every hotel has guests that have sex," Dad explains. "But these organized events are specifically meant for that occasion."

Mom seems shaky, so I quickly grab a chair and set her down.

"It's all a bit much to take in, isn't it?" I say to her. "I felt the same when I found out Dad works at that hotel."

She nods. "I never ..." She gazes up at Dad. "Fred, this is so unlike you. A sex hotel?"

"I apologize for not telling you," Dad says.

312

"You should have!" Mom yells, clearly upset.

"You have every right to be angry with me," Dad says.

"Why? Why not just a normal hotel?"

"Because this sells," he says, scratching the top of his head. "I saw a hole in the market and went for it."

"But you never told me anything …"

"You never asked, so I assumed you didn't want to know," he repeats, shrugging. "Plus, look at what it's caused."

"That's your fault. You kept things secret," I retort.

Mom gazes up at me. "And you knew about this?"

"I only just found out it's Dad's hotel," I reply.

"My god …" Mom buries her face in her hands. "I can't believe this."

I place a hand on her shoulder. "I'm sorry, Mom."

"Are you a customer there too?" she asks, lifting her eyes. "At that sex hotel?"

"No, I was there because of my … boyfriend. He works there." I clear my throat as it's awkward to say it out loud and hard to explain to them what we really have.

"He works there?" Mom says. "So he helps organize these sex events, or does he participate?"

"He organizes them," I say. "Or at least, he did, before Dad fired him for hanging out with me."

"Oh," she mumbles, still shaken from learning all this.

"Do you want some time alone?" I ask, because she looks like she needs it.

"No," she says sternly. "I've had enough time alone.

Too much." She glares at Dad.

"I'm sorry, honey. I don't know what to say to you except … I'm sorry." Dad sighs.

"Do you guys want some time alone?" I ask.

Mom nods, so I step away and smile as they continue their conversation. I walk off to the kitchen area where Melvin is pouring coffee into three cups. "Some coffee, Miss?" he asks.

"Oh, yeah …" I mutter as he hands me a cup.

"Rough day?" he asks.

I shake my head. "You don't even wanna know."

Melvin goes out to bring some to my parents although I doubt they want anything to drink right now. They're loudly arguing, and I'm having trouble shutting myself off from it. Still, it's better than complete and utter silence, which is what they've been doing for the past couple of years.

I slurp my coffee in silence and wait until everything's gotten quiet again. When my cup is empty, I place it in the sink and muster up the courage to go back to them.

When I see Mom's face and the tears that stain them, I swallow away the lump in my throat. I don't want to make her feel bad, so I won't mention anything about it. I just hope she can cope with all of this.

"Kat," she mumbles.

"I'm sorry, Mom," I say, immediately coming to her side. "Are you okay?"

"Don't apologize." She gently squeezes my hand and lets go again. "It's not your fault." She glares at Dad. "And

I'm glad you're both finally being honest." She looks at me again. "Now tell me what happened with you two at the hotel."

"I was there to surprise my boyfriend. But I found Dad there, which is when I discovered that he's one who's running the hotel. And then he fired my boyfriend on the spot."

Mom looks confused. "But why? He was your boyfriend."

"Dad didn't like seeing me there … with him," I reply, glaring at Dad.

Mom looks up at me. "I was so looking forward to meeting your first love."

"He isn't my first love, Mom," I say, snorting. "I've had a couple."

Her eyes widen. "Really? I always thought you were still a virgin."

Now I'm blushing hard. "I haven't been a virgin in years."

"What? But you were always home." She seems even more shocked and slightly offended too. "I can't believe this."

"Sorry, Mom, but I needed freedom. I needed to be able to do my thing, but you and Dad just wouldn't let me," I say, looking at them both. "I snuck out. A lot."

Mom gives Dad a puzzled look. "I really don't understand any of this. Is this girl our daughter?"

I laugh. "Mom … Really?"

"What?" she says with a snarky voice. "I just thought you'd be more like me."

I shrug. "I don't know what to tell you, Mom. I'm just … me."

"And you? I feel like I don't know either of you anymore," Mom says while gazing at Dad.

"I'm sorry, Meredith." Dad goes to his knees in front of Mom, grabbing her hand. "I've wanted to tell you for so long, but you always said you didn't want to know, and I didn't want you to feel like I was cheating on you."

"Are you?" Mom almost pulls her hand away.

"*No*," he says. "Of course not. I would never. I love you too much for that." He smiles.

"So these events are only for your guests?" she asks.

"Yes …" And then he glances at me. "But our daughter has apparently been to one of them as well."

Mom's face turns ghostly white. "Kat? Is that true?"

I nod, biting my lip. "I needed to know what they were doing there, Mom. I like to try out new and interesting things. Even if they involve sex, yes."

All she does is stare at me with her mouth wide open.

"I'm not that picture-perfect girl you want me to be," I say. "You kept me cooped up in here for so long … When I finally got my own place, I needed to experience what it was like to live in freedom. To do everything that's forbidden and more."

"So you've been doing all these … dirty things too?" Mom swallows away her disgust.

I nod. I don't like admitting this to my parents, but it's about time we played open cards. "Yes, and I'm not ashamed to say I enjoyed it."

"It's that boy. He made you do it, didn't he?" Dad interjects.

"No," I say, stepping away, shaking my head. "No, I approached him."

"How? When?" Mom asks, her voice shrill.

"Online. It's how I've been meeting men for a while now."

"Men? *Several?*" Mom almost loses it. "But I thought …"

"Like I said, I don't need any help in the dating department," I say awkwardly.

"But for how long?" she mutters.

"As long as I've been living on my own. I'm a grown woman, Mom. I don't need permission to do what I like."

She nods a few times, clearly still trying to cope with the fact that I'm not who she thought I was.

"Please understand," I say, licking my lips. "I am my own person too."

"I know, but …" She reaches out to me with open arms. "You're my little baby."

I smile and go in for a much-needed hug. "I haven't been a baby in a long while, though," I say softly.

She sniffs, and we stay there, hugging in silence for a while.

After a few minutes, she speaks again. "I'm sorry, honey.

I just wanted the best for you. Not any of this. I was just so worried all the time that you'd be exposed to something bad ..."

"It's okay, Mom. But I have to live my life the way I want to. I need to experience everything. Even if it hurts."

She nods again. "All this time, I've been trying to protect my only girl, only to be the one to cause her pain."

"No, it's not like that," I say, almost unable to keep the tears at bay myself.

"Yes, it is. You're our only one. Our miracle baby. I was so hung up on that, I forgot you have your own needs ... your own voice." She places a hand on my cheek. "I love you, honey."

"I love you too, Mom," I say, smiling as a tear manages to escape my eyes.

"And if you want to be with this man, then I will support you all the way."

I rub my lips together. "I do ... but ..." I gaze at my dad.

"You're really hung up on him, aren't you?" Dad responds.

I nod. "A lot. And it isn't just ... physically."

"All right, all right, I don't want to know," he says, holding up a hand. "Just tell me ... does he treat you right?"

"Yes," I reply, trying my best not to sound obnoxious. "He's what I want right now. What I need. Please understand. This is who I am."

He rubs his lips together. "If it makes you happy ..."

"A lot," I say, smiling. "And not just me ... he is amazing when it comes to organizing the events, so you have to keep him. He's so devoted he even opposed dating me because he feared I would expose the hotel."

"Really?" Dad raises his brows. "Well, that would be a concern, considering what you do for a living."

"Dad ..." I make a face.

"I know, I know. You're my daughter."

"And I'd never do that to you," I say. "Now that I know you run that hotel ..."

I'll just have to rework all the words I've already written for the magazine so it doesn't expose anything about the location.

"Please tell me you'll rehire Declan," I say. "Take him back. He's a good organizer. He knows his business. He doesn't deserve this."

Dad sucks in a breath and gazes down at his feet.

"Please?" I place a hand on his arm. "He will do his utmost best, I promise. And it would make me very happy if I wasn't the cause of all his problems."

Dad bursts out into laughter. "You? The cause of all his problems? Why doesn't that surprise me?"

Mom pokes him gently. "Fred!"

"What? You know she never listened to any of your rules. Why do you think I wanted you to let her breathe for a while? You know, let her get her bearings in life."

"Don't start arguing again, please," I say, rolling my eyes. "At least you're honest with each other now. That's a good start."

"Well," Mom mumbles, "it does explain why you were always so busy with work all the time."

"I'm sorry, honey," Dad says. "I'll do my best to be home more."

"See? Communication." I wink. "Works wonders."

And then we all laugh.

Like a normal family would.

THIRTY-ONE

DECLAN

I'm in the middle of unpacking all the things I brought home from the office when someone rings my doorbell.

"Door's open," I say, lackluster.

However, the moment her face appears, I immediately light up. It's really her. I can't believe it. After what happened in the office, I thought I'd never see her again.

A smile forms on my lips. "Kat. You're here," I say, almost unable to believe what my eyes are telling me.

"I am," she says. "Surprised?"

I nod, still unsure of how to react. "What are you doing here?"

I hope it's not to say goodbye. Anything but that.

The door softly closes behind her. "I wanted to see you."

She bites the bottom of her lip so seductively it makes my head spin already, but I have to stop focusing on that. This will probably be the last time I'll ever see her. Fuck.

"You can stop unpacking now."

Her words tug at my heart.

I frown, letting go of the box I was holding. "Why?"

She can't stop the smile from forming on her face. "I begged Dad to keep you on, and it worked."

I stare at her for a few seconds before actual words manage to get out of my mouth. "What?" I'm stunned. "Really?"

"Yup," she says, adding a cute giggle that makes my heart pounce.

"But he caught us. Isn't he pissed as hell I kept bringing you here?" I ask.

"Yeah, but we had a good talk, and we finally came to an understanding."

"Huh." That strict man … having a good talk with his daughter? She continues to surprise me.

"I just wanted to apologize for putting you in that position," she says, tiptoeing around and fiddling with her fingers. "I never wanted you to lose the one job you care about so much."

Even after all this going down with her dad, all the secrets and lies, she still cares more about my feelings than hers? She keeps amazing me.

"You don't have to apologize," I say, smiling briefly as I approach her. "It wasn't your fault."

"Yeah, it was. If I'd been honest from day one about who I really was, you would've told me my dad works here."

With my hands tucked in my pockets, I stand before her. I don't do it because I wanna feel casual. It's to stop myself from touching her because I know that if I do, I won't be able to quit.

"But then … we would've never had the opportunity to bang like we did."

She tries to hide her snorting behind her hand, but it's no use. I can see right through her, just from the way her eyes sparkle. Beautiful. Just like her. Why can't I stop noticing?

Without thinking, my hand instinctively reaches for that loose strand of hair framing her face, and I tuck it behind her ear. Her cheeks slowly begin to glow like mine when I watch her smile.

"So Kat Bronson … or should I say Kat *Mayer* …"

It sounds so strange, especially considering who her father is. I'll have to get used to calling her that.

Her cheeks turn even more red. "I prefer KittyKat."

A smirk spreads on her lips, and it makes me shake my head. "Of course, you do. Why should I expect anything else?"

Not that I'm mad. On the contrary, it's exactly what I was thinking as well.

"Once a slut, always a slut," she says with a certain cockiness I could get used to.

And I definitely like where this is going.

Still I need to know one thing before we proceed. "So about your dad … he never told you where he worked then?"

"No, my dad was very secretive. My mom didn't even know," she replies, chewing on her bottom lip.

"Wow …" I take a deep breath to let it all sink in.

"I suppose it's only normal, considering the line of work," she says. "But anyway, we've talked it all out now."

My eyes narrow. "All of it?"

She nods.

"What does your dad think of all this?" I ask, licking my lips. "Won't he be mad that you're here?"

"I told him to accept me for who I am, and that includes my interest in you." She winks, which makes it hard for me to concentrate on the actual conversation instead of the thoughts swirling in my head about banging her right here on my kitchen table.

"And what about your mom?" I add, clearing my throat.

"She knows … although she prefers to call you 'my boyfriend.'" She uses quotation marks, but that doesn't decrease the gravity of the word. It makes my heart pump faster, but I don't know whether that's good or bad.

"Interesting," I muse.

Up until now, no girl has ever gotten so far as to call me that. But she's gone far beyond what I thought I would be willing to do. A definite rule breaker ... and I'm not even mad.

In fact, seeing her right here in my home reminds me of how much I was starting to miss her. How much she's really grown on me.

But I have to remember that there is still some unfinished business.

"So," I say, clearing my throat. "Kat *Mayer* ... do you work for a magazine?"

Her eyes widen. "How did you—"

"I searched for your name online. Didn't take me long to find you."

Her entire face turns as red as a strawberry. I like the color.

She may have been able to hide her fake name pretty well, but her real name? It showed me everything I needed to know about her.

I cock my head. "Were you writing articles for them?"

"About that ..." she mumbles, almost unable to say the words.

"Just be honest with me." I tip up her chin, forcing her to look at me.

"I was. Actually, I am," she says, sucking on her bottom lip.

"About the hotel? About me?"

"It's not like that. I—"

I place a finger on her lips. "No need for lies. I just want to know why."

She nods a few times. "I did it because I wanted the recognition so badly. So I could get a raise," she explains. "All the extra money I earn I donate to a good cause, but it's so little. I wanted to do more. And when I started on that chat site and met you ... I just knew it'd be an amazing opportunity."

Donates her money? I didn't even know. If that's true, my admiration for her only grows.

She sighs out loud. "I only wanted to get a good story out there, but I promise, I was never going to include your name or the hotel. It was going to be an anonymous thing only."

"Show me," I say, trying to remain headstrong even when I can see she's hurting inside.

She knows what she did was wrong and that it would ruin everything between us, but we've gone so far already ... I'm not even sure we *can* stop. If I want to stop.

She fishes her phone from her pocket and scrolls through an app until she finds what she's looking for. "I saved it in my documents. Here."

She hands me her phone, and I read it all.

A lot of mentions about a secret chat site ... sex with a nameless man ... meeting him again and again at a hotel ... some of the orgies. But she's right. No names. No numbers. No address. No date.

It's completely anonymous, yet I can't stop reading it over and over again simply because of one thing.

Her admission that everything we did—even the

craziest, filthiest, most degrading things—were incredible experiences, and that if she'd known beforehand about all the things that would happen to her, she'd do it again in a heartbeat.

My lip twitches, my body unable to stop the smug smile from growing.

I hand the phone back to her in silence.

"And?" she asks, swallowing.

I nod a few times, thinking about how I'm going to respond. "Are you going to publish it?" I ask.

"If you don't want me to, I'll delete it. All of it. Right now." Her thumb hovers over the button on her phone. "Just say it, and I won't."

I lower the phone and her hand, stopping her from pressing the button. "No need. I've already made up my mind about you."

"I don't want to see you hurt," she says. "I care too much. I'm …"

I grab her face and kiss her, silencing the words that didn't need to be spoken.

I know how she feels about me.

I feel the same for her.

So I kiss her, finally sealing the deal. My job doesn't matter in this equation and neither does the hotel. Not anymore. Neither of them will fall because of her because she'd never allow it to happen and neither will I.

And I don't give a damn if she's writing an article about our thing together because it doesn't change anything about my attraction to her. We've been fighting the pull for no reason, and I've had enough. All I want is her ... All I need is her ...

It's been right in front of me this whole time, and I never truly saw, until now, just how much she means to me. And how badly I've already fallen in love with her.

When our lips briefly part, she mumbles, "I don't understand. I thought you'd be upset."

"I was, but then I decided there's no point," I reply.

She cocks her head. "So you trust me?"

I raise a brow. "Prove it to me. Publish the article."

She nods and a genuine, heartfelt smile forms on her face, making me fall even deeper.

I don't even know why or how. I can't explain it, and I don't understand how it happened, but it did. That's all that matters.

"I love you," I whisper.

The phone drops from her hand.

Her lips part. "What did you say?"

"I love you." I don't have to think twice to say it again.

It feels so natural to finally admit it. I've been fighting it for so long, but not anymore. I need this woman in my life. I just never knew how badly until she almost got ripped away from me.

We're two sides of the same coin. Equally dirty, cocky, and downright bad. But I love her for it. I love how she challenges me, how she pushes me to rethink my boundaries and live in the moment. How she made me risk it all, and it paid off.

Because she's here, right in front of me, and I don't think I could ever let her go again.

So I grab her face and kiss her. Hard. Greedily. Just like I always wanted. I should've admitted my fucking feelings long ago instead of avoiding them like they'd kill me. I should enjoy living a little … and I certainly can with her by my side.

When she pulls back to take a breath, she murmurs, "So does that mean you're actually my boyfriend now?"

I narrow my eyes as a filthy smile spreads on her lips. "Please don't. I despise that word."

"What then? Partner? Boy toy?"

I shake my head, musing, "Declan will do just fine."

"But there *is* something …" she says, pointing at my chest. "You can't deny that."

I grab her finger and hold it. "I'm not denying anything." I bring her finger up to my lips, pressing a soft kiss to the tip before taking it into my mouth to give it a slight suckle. "I think I made that very clear."

"So what now?" she asks, rubbing her lips together.

"Now," I say, lifting her up in my arms, "we fuck."

THIRTY-TWO

DECLAN

I set her down on my table and shower her neck with kisses, unable to stop myself from ravishing her any longer. I need to have her … *now*.

So I rip off the blouse she's wearing, not giving a shit that the buttons are flying everywhere. With one quick finger, I unhook her bra and chuck it away, immediately covering her nipple with my mouth. The other one gets tweaked with my fingers until it's nice and taut.

When her moans start filling the air, I cover her mouth with mine again, eager for more. I probe open her lips and lick the roof of her mouth, and her tongue responds with an equally desperate need.

With just my body, I manage to push her down onto the table and shower her skin with kisses until I reach her pants, which I undo with a quick flick. I zip her down and rip them off along with her panties, throwing them in the far corner of the room. Then I bury my face between her legs.

"Holy shit!" she mewls.

I lap her up with my tongue to lull her surprise of my desire. I need to taste her. Feel her writhe underneath me. And I need her to know she's mine and no one else's.

"Tasty little treat," I moan, sucking her clit.

"Fuck," she mumbles, barely able to talk and breathe at the same time.

"Don't waste your breath, Kitten," I whisper, licking and sucking hard. "Focus on the pleasure."

I love the sounds she's making and use my tongue to make her get even louder. Her body shivers as she gets closer and closer to the edge, so I rub my fingers along her slit and slide them inside her.

Her pussy makes me horny as fuck, wanting to ram my cock inside, but I have to control my urges a little longer. I want to taste her on my tongue as she explodes.

And when she finally does ... goddamn, I could come just from feeling her clit grow thick against my tongue.

She's panting, completely blown away, but I'm nowhere near done with her yet.

I tear off my shirt and zip down my pants, letting all of it drop to the floor until there's nothing left but her and me naked.

"What do you want me to do?" she asks, licking her lips as if she's already excited at the prospect of doing whatever I demand.

God, I fucking love this woman.

I have no shame in admitting it, but she pushes all my buttons in the right way.

A devious grin spreads on my lips. "Whatever I ask from you, you'll do it, and you'll beg for my cum when it's over like the slut you are."

***

Kat

I nod, practically ready to beg. That's what he does to me with that dirty mouth of his. He makes me do things I'm not even sorry for … things they'd say would make me a slut. But I hold that title with pride because it means I'm having fun. It means I belong to him.

"Lift your legs and hold them," he says, and when I do, he immediately shoves his dick inside.

I gasp from the pressure, and he sticks his thumb inside my mouth, forcing me to taste myself.

"Mine," he growls, making my heart skip a beat.

Fuck, I love it when he says that—when he treats me like filth—but only because I'm his little kitten. His only one. That's all that matters.

So I let him fuck me like an animal, slamming his cock into me balls deep until I can barely breathe. His hand wraps around my throat gently, but I welcome the feel of his grasp. My body is his to use and humiliate. I love every second of it, and I can tell from the primal gaze in his eyes that he does too.

His free hand slides down my body, marking my body with saliva as he brings it down toward my pussy only to start rubbing me again. I'm in heaven right now, and I feel like staying right here because God … does it feel good.

He brings me close to bliss, but as my pussy begins to tighten, he pulls his raging boner out of me. Then he slaps my tit, making me squeal.

"Off the table," he says.

I instantly slide off and go to my knees. The gleeful smile on his face makes me feel good about myself and everything he does to me. I love being filthy for him because I know it isn't just about the degradation. It's about the undying need for love beneath both our skins. And the more he treats me badly, the more right all of this feels.

"Hands behind your back, mouth open wide," he says as he walks off into his room. When he comes back, he's holding two things in his hand. A big dildo in one hand and a metallic ring attached to a collar in the other hand.

"Is that a …"

"Ring gag," he fills in. "And a dildo, but you probably recognized that."

My brows draw together. "You have toys here?"

He makes a smug face. "You didn't think the hotel was the only place I ever use them, do you?"

My heart thrums faster as he approaches me with the device. "Scared?" he asks.

I gently shake my head. "Excited."

"Good," he says, "Because I'm going to fuck your pretty little mouth, and you won't be able to stop me."

Oh, God. Those words alone could make me come again.

He puts the gag around my face and locks it in place, forcing me to take it into my mouth.

"Don't move your hands," he murmurs as he positions himself in front of me.

Pre-cum drips from his tip as he circles it around my lips. Then he slowly inches forward, sinking into my mouth with ease. I can taste the saltiness on my tongue, going deeper and deeper, and my clit thumps in response.

Wetness pools between my legs as he buries himself deep inside me until I gag. Then he pulls out again.

"Good kitten," he murmurs, going right back in again.

With every thrust, he goes a little bit faster, until I'm struggling to hold back my hands. But I have to resist … I don't ever want to give up pushing my own boundaries just to see how much filthier things can get. And this definitely reaches the oh-my-God spot.

He bumps against the back of my throat while keeping his eyes on me at all times; as if he wants to gauge my reaction to him claiming my mouth like it always belonged to him. I don't look away.

"That's it, Kitten. Feel my cock go down your throat. Every … filthy … inch," he groans, slamming into me faster and faster.

He grabs my face and holds me down at his base, forcing me to feel him inside me. When he pulls out again, I heave as he rubs his dick on my face, covering me with saliva and pre-cum. Then he goes right back in again, repeating the process over and over until I'm dripping … at both ends.

But I never stop looking him in the eyes as he nears his climax, and I watch him come undone … right in my throat.

His seed jets into me as he roars out loud, pounding into me again and again to cover the back of my throat. I struggle to swallow it down. As he pulls out, some of it splashes onto the floor as I cough and lean over.

He immediately wipes his length across my face and shoves his fingers into my mouth. "Bad Kitten."

He takes off the gag and then pushes my head down onto the floor. "Lick. All of it."

My tongue dips out to gather what I spit out and suck it up. I don't even give a shit that it's humiliating because it's such a fucking turn-on that I'm about ready to come again.

That's when I feel his hand on my ass. The sudden

spank has me jolting up.

"Did I say you could stop?" he says.

I quickly return to licking as he perches himself behind me.

I wonder what he's planning to do. I don't have to wait long for the answer, though … because he pushes the dildo inside my pussy.

I moan out loud from both the taste of his cum and the need to pleasure myself.

"Go on then. Fuck this cock like your life depends on it," he says, still holding it.

And I do. So fucking hard.

"Don't stop until the floor is clean … then you can come."

My tongue feels numb, but I keep going because I don't ever give up what I started. So I lick and suck until I'm shaking with need. And when all the drops of cum have been swallowed, I writhe on the dildo that he's still firmly holding.

"Come on then, be a filthy little kitten. Come all over this cock," he growls.

His words are all I need to push me over the edge.

I come so hard my throat feels squeezed from the moan trying to escape. The shockwaves are too delicious, and when they're all done, I almost collapse.

He pulls the dildo out of me and brings it to the front, saying, "Open your mouth."

Then he makes me lick that off too.

By the time we're done, I'm so tired, I can't even get up from the floor.

"So was that enough play for you, or do you want more?" he asks, pulling the dildo from my mouth.

I'm short on breath as I try to formulate words, but I'm sure it sounds more like gibberish. "Tired …"

He grins and then wraps his arms around my body, pulling me up from the floor. "C'mon then," he says, carrying me in his arms like a knight in shining armor. "A shower it is and then a nap."

What a fucking gentleman.

THIRTY-THREE

Kat

After our little sexy bout, I went back home where I finished work on my story. I haven't decided when I'm going to turn it in yet. I will, someday, but I just don't want to do it when it's not a hundred percent perfect, which requires several edits and maybe even more.

I need to let it simmer, so instead, I've made an agreement with Declan that in order to make things right, we need to have a sit-down with Flynn. I don't want him to be upset about us, and I need Declan and him to get along in order to feel good about this.

So with a cup of strong coffee, I sit down at the table and call Flynn.

"Flynn here," he says.

"Hey, it's Kat. Can we talk?" I don't even know how to talk to him anymore without feeling like things are awkward between us.

"Ahh … right now?" he asks.

"Tonight, if you have time," I say. "Or any other time, if you want." A silly chuckle leaves my mouth, and I instantly regret it.

He sighs out loud. "Right … um …"

Please, say yes. Please, say yes. Please, say yes.

"Say yes?" Flynn muses, and my eyes widen.

"Fuck, did I say that out loud?" I mutter.

"Yes, you did." He laughs again.

I smack myself in the head and immediately slurp up my coffee.

"Well, if you put it like that, how can I not?" he says.

"Yay!" I say, putting my coffee down. "Sorry, was that too exciting?"

"A little," he says. "But that's typically you."

"Overly dramatic girl at your service," I reply. "So tonight then?"

"Your place?" he says.

"Perfect," I say, taking another sip of my coffee.

"Okay. See you tonight then. Gotta run."

He hangs up before I can say anything else. I tuck away

the phone and take a deep breath. No going back now. This is it.

"So he's coming?" Declan asks, raising a brow as he comes out of the kitchen.

"Yup ..."

I finish my coffee and place the mug on the table.

With Declan around, I can't wait for this shit to go down.

Oh, boy. This is gonna be rough.

***

After we've washed the dishes, the doorbell rings, and my pulse immediately skyrockets to infinity. Or at least, that's what it feels like as I open the door and greet Flynn with a hug.

"So glad you could come."

He takes off his coat and puts it on the hanger before saying, "Sorry I'm late."

"It's fine," I say. "Don't sweat it. I'm sure you were busy ... sweating it out." I wink at him and follow it up by a quick jab in the gut.

He smirks, and says, "Well, you seem awfully happy."

"Sure, why wouldn't I be?"

He makes a face. "Well, considering how our last conversation went ..."

Yep. There it is. "That's exactly why I wanted to talk," I say.

Right then, Declan appears in view, and Flynn's eyes almost immediately shoot lightning bolts at him.

"What a coincidence," he mumbles, gazing at me. "Was that part of your plan?"

I grab his hand. "Yes, but please, don't leave." I smile. "I just want to talk things out."

"With him around?" He points at Declan. "He's the whole problem."

"Not anymore," I say, licking my lips. "C'mon, let's sit down."

He reluctantly follows me to the table where Declan sets down three cups of coffee. Flynn sits down opposite of us, leaning back in his chair like he's really not feeling it.

"I get that you're angry, but Declan's changed."

"I doubt that," he says.

"I swear, we're on better footing now. He's not an asshole anymore," I say.

"Well, sometimes," Declan says with a smug smile. "But not often."

I roll my eyes. "He's just trying to be funny."

"It ain't working," Flynn sneers.

"Flynn," I say, directing my attention toward him. "Declan and I had a rough start, but I really want to be with him." Declan places his hand on my shoulder, and I smile at him before I continue. "But I don't want you to be upset either. I value our friendship."

"But why him? Why not any other guy?"

"Because … it just happened." I rub my lips together,

trying to find support in Declan. I'm so bad at handling these things.

"What she's trying to say is we found each other. It happened. We can't do anything about it."

"But you treated her like shit," he says.

"I know, and I'm sorry," Declan replies. "I will do better. I promise. I've learned my lesson."

"Have you? So no side chicks?" he asks. "No more chat room?"

Declan frowns and glances at me, so I say, "I tell Flynn pretty much everything."

"I'm not interested in other girls," Declan says resolutely. "The only reason I couldn't be with her was because of the hotel."

Flynn frowns. "Did you tell her who runs the show? Huh?" He glances at me now. "That's what I wanted to tell you on the phone. Why you couldn't trust him."

"I know," I say, grabbing Flynn's hand. "I'm okay with it. I can handle it."

His pupils dilate. "But your father—"

"He knows about us," I interject. "We're still working through the kinks, but I'm not hiding myself any longer. Not for anyone." I smile at Declan. "I know what I want."

Flynn cocks his head, grinding his teeth. "You sure about this?" he asks after a while.

I nod. "Hundred percent."

He lets out a sigh, closing his eyes as he rubs his forehead. "Okay, if you say so."

342

"Plus, you didn't exactly tell me either, now did you?" I raise my brow at him.

"Sorry ..." he replies, averting his eyes. "I just never knew how to tell you. If it was even my place to do so."

"I understand," I say. "I'm not mad. I just want to start over. Between us three. Please?" I ask him, squeezing his hand. "You're my best friend. I don't want to lose you."

He takes a deep breath, and slowly but surely, a small smile begins to appear. "Fuck it. All right, all right."

I jump up from my seat and hug him so hard he cringes and coughs.

"Choking me."

"Sorry," I say, giggling.

"Thanks," he mutters when I release him from my grip.

"So we good?" I ask.

"Yeah, yeah," Flynn says, rolling his eyes. "We weren't ever *not* good. I just want the best for you."

"I know," I say. "But this feels good, Flynn. This." I glance at Declan. "Us."

The way Declan smiles back at me makes the butterflies flutter in my stomach.

"Well, if it makes you happy, then who am I to stand between that?" Flynn says, shrugging.

"Thank you for understand," I say, squeezing his arm. "And I can personally guarantee Declan will keep you on payroll at the hotel."

Flynn doesn't respond. All he does is raise his brow at Declan in a taunting way.

343

"It's true. I swear to God," Declan says jokingly. "I've never had the intention. Ever."

"Not even for getting in your way?" Flynn says.

"No. You're her friend. Of course, I wouldn't fire you." He clears his throat. "Besides, you're valuable to the hotel. You bring in a lot of customers."

Flynn gives us both a smug face. "How long did it take you to make him say that?"

I laugh. "He came up with it himself."

"Really now?" Flynn says.

Declan shrugs. "I can't fabricate numbers. Her dad would kill me."

"Right," he responds.

"I have no intention of starting a fight. I promise. I just want her to be happy, that's all. And she wants us to get along, so ..." Declan says, holding out his hand. "Peace?"

It takes him a while, but eventually, Flynn shakes his hand. "Fine."

"Great," I say, pulling them both in for a super awkward hug. Then I grab their coffees and shove them into their hands. "Now ... let's toast on it!"

***

DECLAN

She lies down on her bed as I undress and prepare to lie down beside her. Tonight, I'm staying at her place, but we've been switching back and forth between both our homes. She's already said she prefers my place, so I figured I'd ask her the big question tonight.

As I get in, she puts her book aside and rolls over, staring at me with a grin. "So am I ever going to be able to go to another event again?"

I frown. "Why are you asking?"

She shrugs. "I kinda liked them."

"You sure about that?" I raise a brow. "You didn't make it through one last time."

"Because you wore me out beforehand," she retorts. "I'm just saying I never got a real chance."

"Do you really want one? With me around?"

"Why not?" She smirks. "We're both filthy. Maybe we could do one together."

"Me? Participate?"

"Why not?" She pokes me. "Or are you saying you don't like sharing me anymore?"

I narrow my eyes. "I'm not jealous if that's what you're asking."

"Yes, you are. You just don't want to admit it."

"I have no problems sharing you. I just don't like to see

others play with you when I'm not part of the game."

"Exactly my point. You need to take part in one of them too."

"I'm a hotel employee, not a guest."

"So? You can have a day off and stay there, right? It's not against the rules, is it?"

I bite my lip. I don't actually know because I've never tried. At least, not before I met her. But if she's that interested in trying it again ... I have to see if there's a possibility.

"C'mon, I don't want to give up our kinky life just because we're a thing now," she says.

"I never said you have to ..." I reply, sighing. "But I'll see what I can do."

"Yay!" She wraps her arm around my neck and hugs me, practically pressing her tits right up in my face. I'd be lying if I said it didn't make me hard as a rock.

"So you're not interested in other girls anymore?" she mumbles.

"Where's all this coming from?" I ask.

"You said that when Flynn was here. Something about the chat room ..." She pokes me.

"Ahh ..." I raise a brow at her. "You're wondering if you have competition?" Is she getting jealous? Nice. It means she's as attached to me as I am attached to her.

"Well, not per se, I just wanna know whether you still intend to use the chat room," she says.

"Right ..." I don't believe her, but I'll give her the

benefit of the doubt. I lick my lips, watching her intently. "That depends if a certain KittyKat is on there or not."

She giggles, her fingers circling on my chest. "Maybe. Depends if a certain Big D is going to play."

"Oh ..." I groan, grabbing her wrist and pinning it above her head as I roll on top of her. "You bet your ass I will. But first," I mumble, planting a kiss on her cheeks and neck until she's practically moaning, "I need to know how committed you really are."

"I'll do anything you want me to do," she replies with a hoarse voice as I keep kissing her everywhere.

"Good. Then you can pack your bags tomorrow, and we can bring everything over to my place."

As her eyes spring open, she turns her head. "What? Are you asking me to move in with you?"

A devilish grin spreads on my lips. "Think you can handle being in the same home as this asshole?"

Before she even says a word, she's already squealing and hugging me. "Yes! Fuck yes."

I laugh. "Well, that was quick."

"Sorry, I already made up my mind long ago." She winks. "But I'm happy you finally came to that conclusion as well."

"Are you telling me you think you knew sooner than I did that we had feelings for each other?"

"Maybe ..." Her brows lift in a taunting way that pushes all my buttons.

"You wish," I reply, flipping her over on the bed so I

can rip down her panties and fuck her into oblivion. "I'll prove it to you right now just how much I fucking love you. But first, you're going to prove to me how much of your morals you're willing to sacrifice."

"Oh yes ..." she moans, as I start to finger her while holding her down on the bed. "Make me filthy."

"You already were from the beginning," I whisper into her ear, nibbling on her earlobe. "A filthy fucking toy for me to play with ... forever."

EPILOGUE

Kat

"And? What do you think?" I ask Crystal, who's reading the story I typed up. It's been thoroughly edited, but she's still the first one to lay eyes on it besides Declan, and I'm nervous as hell.

Her eyes are still scanning the document, and she's biting her lip at the same time, but she won't reply. Not until she's finished. Her eyes widen.

"Oh, my God, is this for real?" she asks.

I don't know if that's positive or not. "Um … yes?"

"Where did you even come up with this?" she squeals.

"I didn't. It's all true."

"What? No! I can't believe it. Really?" She seems hyper.

"Yup," I say, laughing it off like it's no big deal.

"You *did* all this?" she says, still clutching the paper tight.

"Well, yes ..." I can already feel the heat rise to my cheeks. "Is it bad?"

"No! Holy shit, this is amazing!"

I grin. "Well, I'm glad you think so. Do you think Ellen will think it's good enough?"

"Fuck yes. If she doesn't print this, she's nuts."

I laugh. "It's kinda out there, though."

She sits down on my desk, totally up in my space. "Where did you meet this guy? And that place where the events were done, does it really exist?"

"Yeah, but I have to keep it a secret," I say. "I don't want anyone finding out."

"Aww ... why not?" She puts up a pouty face. "I'd love to try it out myself."

"Can't ever reveal my sources, Crystal," I say, winking. Plus, I'm really not interested in seeing her there too.

"Boo!" she says, jumping off my desk again. "Well, I'm sure you'll do great with this." She places the document in front of me.

"You think I should take it to Ellen?"

"Of course. This is big. I just know it," she says as she opens the door. "Let me know how it goes. All the juicy details."

"Will do!" I say as she leaves my office.

I pick up the document and stare at it a few more seconds. Crystal's right. This should get published, and Ellen would be crazy to turn this down.

So with that in mind, I make my way through the building to my boss's office.

***

DECLAN

A week later

"You sure it looks okay?" I ask, readjusting my tie.

"It's fine. Stop worrying about it." She grabs my hand and laces her fingers through mine. "You look sexy." She pinches my ass, and I immediately swat her away.

"Jesus, Kat. Not here."

"Who cares?" she jokes.

"Your parents," I say, just in time before someone opens the door.

"Welcome, Miss Mayer." Melvin holds out his hand to me. "Hello to you too, sir. I'm the butler. You can call me Melvin."

"A butler?" I say, raising my brows at Kat.

Her face flushes. "Yeah …" She rolls her eyes.

"Convenient," I say, to make her feel less embarrassed.

"Sometimes," she says, smiling as we walk inside. "Plus, he's one hell of a listener." She winks.

"Thank you for the compliment, Miss," Melvin says.

"Oh, Mel," she says, nudging him in the side. "Stop being so perfect."

Melvin shrugs. "Can't help it, Miss."

Kat's laugh makes me smile too. I don't think I'll ever get used to loving that sound so much.

Melvin takes our coats, and says, "They're waiting for you in the dining area."

As we walk there, I whisper to Kat, "Dining area?"

"Sorry, did I mention my parents are kinda …"

"Rich?" I fill in. "The house gave it away."

She makes a face without saying anything else, but it's enough.

I place a hand on her back and pat her gently. "No need to feel guilty. It's not a problem."

"Eh, for you it might not be." She bites her lip. "But to me? Ugh …"

"Why? Hard growing up?" I ask as we walk through the hallway.

"Let's just say there's a reason I'm so in love with the freedom I have right now."

We enter the room together. Her parents are sitting at the long table, which is already set. "Hi!"

Her mom gets up and greets her first, giving her two

kisses on the cheek, before holding out her hand to greet me. "Meredith. But we already met."

"I'm still amazed you're her mother," I say, shaking her hand.

"Oh, stop it," she says, nudging me in the arm. Then she glances at Kat. "Is he always this smooth?"

"Like butter," she answers, making me grin.

Her dad gets up too and pats me on the shoulder instead of shaking my hand. "No need for introductions, right?"

"Right …" Nothing's more awkward than this. Meeting your boss when you're not at work.

"C'mon, let's have a drink," her mom says, guiding us back to the table where we all sit down.

Melvin quickly hobbles into the room with a tray filled with cups of tea and coffee. "Dinner will be served shortly," he says, after giving everyone their preferred drink, and then he scurries off just as fast as he came inside.

"Does he always do that?" I whisper into Kat's ear.

"What? The randomly appearing and disappearing thing? You'll get used to it."

I don't know about that. I've never had a butler. Or rich parents. Then again, I can understand it's hard when you're the only child and they don't let you do your thing. Which is what probably happened to Kat. Sheltered to the point of feeling suffocated.

Lucky for me, she was too naughty to stop looking for more, and here we are.

"So you're together now?" her dad says, and I almost

choke on my coffee.

"Yes," Kat replies.

"So is he your boyfriend or just a friend?" her mom asks. "I'm so confused."

Kat's face flushes. "Boyfriend, I guess?" She looks my way for confirmation.

"Yeah, sorry about the confusion." I put down my coffee and look at both her parents. "I'm very serious about your daughter."

"Good. She deserves the best," her mom says with thin lips.

"Did she tell you where I work, though?" I say. I just want to get it done and over with.

Mr. Mayer clears his throat. "He works for me."

Mrs. Mayer asks, "At the hotel, right? And you're okay with that?"

"He's not the one to decide, Mom," Kat says before her father can even open his mouth. "I made this choice. I want Declan." She grabs my hand and squeezes tight.

"Right, of course." Mrs. Mayer licks her lips, sucking on her bottom one. "Well, if you're happy with him, that's all that matters. Right, Fred?"

"Right." He nods, taking a large sip of his coffee. It's all so damn awkward.

When everything's gone silent for a while, I speak up. "Sir, I would just like to apologize to you for finding out this way that I was dating your daughter."

Mr. Mayer glares at me. "Well, it would've been better if

you'd told me beforehand."

"I didn't know she was your daughter. I found out when you did."

"How's that even possible?" he asks.

"I gave him a fake name," Kat mumbles, stirring the spoon in her cup as she looks up at both of us. "Sorry."

"Aha," her dad says. "So you lied?"

"If he knew my name, he could look me up and see where I worked," she explains. "Which means he'd probably have kicked me out for trying to write about the hotel."

"Is that true?" her mom asks.

I nod. "I always have the reputation of the hotel in my mind. It's the most important thing to me, and I don't ever want to jeopardize that. Not for any girl."

"Not that I'd ever expose the hotel, knowing my father owns the place," Kat adds.

"Good to know," Mr. Mayer says. "I'd rather not have any of my business leaked to the public. It'd mean the end of everything. My whole life's work."

"I understand," Kat says, smiling. "I know it's important to you, and it's important to me too. I like the place. I don't want to see it fail."

"Sounds like a marvelous hotel to visit someday," her mom suddenly says.

We all gaze at her with wide eyes. "Please don't," Kat says. "You'd probably have a heart attack."

I try not to snort, I really do.

"She's right, though," her father agrees. "Best not at our

age."

"But you're there too," her mom says with a high-pitched voice.

"It's my hotel. I work there. It's my job," he says. "But I'm not a guest. I don't participate in any of the events."

"I have, and I'm pretty sure it's not your thing, Mom," Kat adds. "Trust me."

Her mom makes a pouty face as she picks up her coffee. "Well, I was looking forward to finally seeing the business … but I guess you're right." She takes a sip.

Everything grows quiet again.

"So is everything cool between you guys now?" Kat asks her dad, who looks around as if he's pretending not to know she's talking to him.

"It seems so," he replies after a few seconds.

"So I can keep my job?" I ask tentatively.

"As long as you can do it without too many mistakes," he says. "Customer happiness is always the number one priority."

"I'll give it two-hundred percent, sir," I reply. "You can count on it."

"Good," her dad says resolutely.

Everything goes quiet again, which seems to happen a lot.

I clear my throat. "I hope we can still keep things professional between us, of course," I say to him. I don't want things to get anymore awkward than they already are.

"Yes, yes. If it's what my daughter wants"—he smiles—

"then I'm happy for her."

Kat places a hand on her dad's arm. "Thanks … I really appreciate you approving of this."

"But the guests come first, always. Got it?" he says.

"Got it," I say without a shred of doubt.

"He'll keep doing his best like he always has," Kat says, jumping in for me. "Nothing will change."

"Good," her dad says, taking the last sip of his coffee before putting the cup down. "Now, where's the food?"

"Calm down, Fred," her mother jests. "It's not like you don't have enough reserves to last a week or more."

I rub my lips together to stop myself from laughing.

"What?" Mr. Mayer says, gazing down at his belly. "This isn't filled with food." He gazes at her intently. "It's filled with love and adoration."

Kat almost dies from laughter while her mother rolls her eyes.

"Really, Fred?" she mumbles while Kat and I can barely keep our shit together. But then her father leans over to kiss her mom on the cheeks, and it brings a warm smile to my face.

"I'm guessing you two have made up then?" Kat asks, winking.

"We have our ups and downs," her father says, sighing, "but being honest does help."

"It definitely does," her mom reiterates. "I finally know where all those missed nights went."

"I only did it for all this, honey," he says as he looks

around at the room he's in. "Money doesn't fall from a tree."

"Neither does being home during dinner," she retorts, and they both raise their brows at each other now.

I lean toward Kat. "Tell me we're not gonna end up like that," I whisper.

She snorts. "I hope not."

"It's all in the communication," I say, winking at her.

"Oh, and you think we've got that covered?" she muses.

I shrug. "Maybe. But I'm not ashamed to admit there's always room for improvement."

She narrows her eyes. "On your end or mine?"

After thinking about it for a second, I reply, "No comment."

"Of course, you'd say that." She pokes me in the side with her elbow. "Asshole."

"Aren't you used to that, with your magazine and all?"

"Oh, your magazine!" her mom suddenly yells. "How's that going?"

"Good, good." Kat nods. "I actually have some news."

Everyone's hanging on her words now, including me. She never said a word. Not through the phone, or the chat site, or anywhere else.

"I actually wrote a story about my experience with the hotel and how I met Declan," she says, holding up her hand so no one interrupts. "Don't worry, I didn't name any names or companies, so no one knows where or what it actually is."

"Okay," her dad says.

"And my boss just approved it to be in a spread."

"Oh, my God, really?" Her mom quickly gets up to hug her tight. "That's great news, honey!"

"Thanks, Mom."

"I'm proud of you," I say, adding a tiny wink.

Her dad seems a little less pleased. "Will this expose the hotel?"

She shakes her head vehemently. "Nada. I keep my sources a secret. I don't mention the hotel itself, any staff, or any names of anyone. Everything is with pseudonyms. Oh, and no times or dates or anything like that."

"Good," he mutters, mulling it over for a while.

"Are you mad?" she asks. "This story … it means a lot to me."

Mr. Mayer takes a deep breath. "If you're sure it won't result in *any* media attention, then I'm happy for you."

Kat gets up from her chair and hugs him softly. "Thanks, Dad. I appreciate it."

"But it better not become a regular thing," he adds.

She laughs a little. "Of course not."

"Except the part where you spend time with me, I hope," I add. Everyone's looking at me now. "As we're gonna be living together."

"Really?" Her mom brightens up.

Kat's face turns as red as a beet. "Yup."

"I love that," her mom says. "You're finally settling down and making something of your life."

Kat rolls her eyes. "Really, Mom?"

"Sorry, I'm just always so worried about my little baby."

Kat looks away, completely mortified. "Please don't call me that again," she whispers even though her mom probably can't hear it. I can. And she can hear me laugh too.

"Stop laughing," she says, poking me in the shoulder.

"Sorry, can't help it. This whole thing just makes me laugh."

"Glad we're so hilarious," she says.

"Dinner!" her dad suddenly says, his eyes flickering with enthusiasm as Melvin walks into the room with several plates filled with what looks like roast lamb and curry.

"Smells delicious," I say as he places it down in front of me.

"Enjoy," he says, winking, and then places down the plates for everyone else. "Bon appétit!"

"Mel," Kat says as he's about to walk off. She grabs an empty chair next to her and drags it back, patting the seat. "Come eat with us."

Melvin gazes at her, then her parents, probably unsure of what to do.

"C'mon," Kat says, still patting the chair.

Her generosity still amazes me to this day. She's so casual about it even though many wouldn't even think about inviting their own butler to dinner. She does because she loves him. And I love her for it.

Melvin stammers, "Are you sure—"

"Mom and Dad won't mind, will you?" She side-eyes

them both.

"Um … sure, why not," her dad says awkwardly, clearing his throat as he gazes at Melvin. "You deserve to enjoy your own cooking. It is amazing, after all."

Melvin smiles and approaches the table, gently sitting down like he's afraid his mere presence will break the table.

Kat quickly runs to the kitchen and comes back with a plate filled with food. "There you go." She places it down in front of him, smiling.

She looks up at him like others would look at their parents. Maybe Melvin has been more of a dad to her than her real dad ever was.

"Thank you, Miss," Melvin says, grabbing his fork and knife.

"Don't thank me. Thank yourself." She pats him on the back. "You did all the cooking."

She winks at him then sits down again. When things get silent, she adds, "Well, dig in, everyone!"

So we all start eating. The moment the food hits my tongue, it's as if I'm in heaven. Fuck, this is some good shit. It's so good, it almost makes me groan.

"That good, huh?" Kat says, snorting.

"What?" I mutter as I'm chewing.

She swallows down the food and licks her lips. "You moaned a little."

"Shit, did I?" Guess who's fighting the embarrassment now? Me.

However, everyone's laughing, so I guess I am too. I'm

normally never this at ease, but with Kat around, it all comes so naturally.

Suddenly, Kat flings herself around my neck and kisses me on the cheeks.

"What was that for?" I ask, surprised.

She shrugs. "No reason. I just love you."

It's the first time she's said that to me. It makes me want to grab her, pin her down, and kiss her hard. But that wouldn't be appropriate in front of her parents.

So I smile and say, "I love you too."

But as we're continuing our dinner, I take out my phone and quickly send her a chat message through the same old site we always went to. The one where we met.

D: I'm going to make you prove that to me. You know that, right?

It takes her seconds to grab her phone and glance at me from the corner of her eyes before tapping on the screen to send something back. I won't look. I enjoy surprises.

NaughtyKitten: You're still on the site?

D: So are you.

NaughtyKitten: Touché. I guess I like the excitement just a little too much. I won't talk to other men, I swear.

D: I trust you.

NaughtyKitten: Yay <3

D: No reason to give up something we both enjoy. I wasn't kidding about the proof part, by the way.

NaughtyKitten: Oh, I know … I wasn't expecting

anything less than complete degradation from you.

D: Good, because when we get home, your ass is gonna be mine.

As I tuck the phone away, I grin and so does she.

That's when I realize … everything will turn out just fine.

Especially when I look at her. My KittyKat. The girl who makes my heart stop every time I look at her. The girl who takes my breath away and makes my cock hard time and time again. The girl who keeps me guessing … who always manages to surprise me with her quirks and kinks. The girl who stumbled into my life like it was no big deal … even though it was. The biggest deal of a lifetime. And I can't wait to find out what else this naughty kitten has in store for me.

EPILOGUE TWO

Kat

When someone sticks the keys into the locks, I quickly open the champagne bottle and pour two glasses. As Declan comes in, I hold them up and say, "Surprise!"

He smiles, confused as he closes the door. "What's this about?"

I nod my head in the general direction of the cabinet next to him. He gazes over it and picks up the magazine. "This?" He sifts through it for a moment until he finds what he's looking for, and a smug grin spreads across his face.

"Well, hello there, Miss NaughtyKitten ..."

I squeal and run over to him, pushing one of the glasses into his hands. "Isn't it amazing?"

He's still reading while simultaneously taking a drink. "Looks good."

"I got the whole spread! And people are already talking about it," I say. "Crystal said she's never got this many emails about it. And there's even rumors that Ellen is going to ask me to do another piece."

"That's fantastic, Kitten," Declan says, pressing a kiss to my cheeks. "I'm proud of you. We should celebrate."

I grin and take a sip of my champagne. "Exactly why I bought this expensive bottle." I chug more down. Don't want to waste the good stuff while it's still cold.

He grabs my glass and puts it down on the cabinet, then places his hands on my waist. "I was thinking of something more .... explicit."

"Oh, I'm intrigued," I muse, licking my lips at the thought.

I wonder what he has in mind.

He pulls me closer and wraps his arms around me completely. "How is your schedule looking for tomorrow?"

I raise a brow. "Depends on why you're asking ..."

"A little bit of play, if you're up to it," he says with that same dark, chocolatey voice that makes everything tingle.

"I think I could work you into my schedule," I reply with a bit of snark.

"I'm honored," he says.

Suddenly, he spins me on my feet. Before I know it, he has my hands pinned behind my back, and my body is pressed up against him as he whispers, "For the next twenty-four hours, you belong to me."

"What now?" I ask as he gently pushes me forward.

"No ifs. No buts. You said yes. Now you do what I say," he says with a gruff voice as he nudges me all the way to the bedroom.

I giggle as he puts me down on the bed and says, "Sit."

I love it when he's all broody and needy at the same time.

He grabs a thick scarf from the cabinet where he keeps all the toys as well as a set of handcuffs. He wraps the scarf around my head and ties it behind my head. Then he binds my wrists together behind my back, effectively making it impossible for me to stop him.

Not that I ever had the intention. I'm too curious to see where this is going.

"Up," he says, and I do what he wants.

Something cold and metallic curls underneath my shirt and pushes against my skin. A few snips to the top and my shirt drops to the floor.

"I still wanted to wear that," I say.

He places a finger on my lip. "Ah-ah … No backtalking. Or do you want me to stuff your mouth too?"

Maybe. I like being manhandled and humiliated. Then again, knowing him, that's exactly what he's going to do regardless of my intentions. And I already know I'm going to enjoy every single second of it.

He puts the scissors aside and leaves my pants for what they are. However, he grabs my nipples and pinches them, then attaches something else ... clamps. There's constant sizzling pain as he gropes my breasts and attaches a metal wire to each of the clamps, which weighs them down.

He covers me up with just a small blazer that barely hides I'm half-naked underneath.

Then he grabs my arm and tugs me through the living room of his condo. "C'mon."

"We're going outside? Like this?" I mumble as he opens the door. "But I'm half naked!"

He covers my mouth with his hand. "One more word, KittyKat ... and I'm going to have to muzzle you."

Goddamn him and his infuriating style of control. But I love him for it anyway. Fuck.

He leans in close to me and whispers into my ear, "You're going to walk all the way down to the car and do whatever I want you to wherever I want you to ... because you're a good little slut, remember?"

That's all I need to melt into a puddle right there and then. Fucking hell. Why does he always have this effect on me? It's like he literally put a spell on my body, and it listens to him, regardless of what he asks, even if it's the most degrading thing.

"Now let's go," he says, not even waiting a second before pulling me along through the corridor.

I'm trying not to blush as I hear other people pass, but

there's no mistaking it. I know they can see my cuffed wrists. They'll probably start asking questions, maybe even call the cops, even though none of that is needed. But Declan doesn't even seem fazed. Maybe he knows just how to deal with it because he's done it before ... or maybe the neighbors already know just how much of a kinky fucker he is.

When we finally get to the car, I hop in quietly, letting out a sigh of relief because we didn't bump into anyone I knew. Declan starts the car and drives off. Meanwhile, I'm left listening to the sound of his controlled breathing, painfully aware of how my own heart is beating faster and faster the closer we get to wherever we're going.

But I'll probably know soon enough ... it's only a matter of time.

After a while, the car comes to a stop, and he helps me out again. He guides me along until we come to a stop, and the beeping sounds of an elevator are audible. The sound is familiar, but I can't place it yet.

We go up all the way, and Declan drags me through a hallway until we come to a room. He opens the door and pushes me inside. I don't hear it get locked.

I stay put as he positions himself behind me. I can tell from the breath rolling down my neck, making all my hairs stand. With gentle but rugged fingers, he takes off the scarf around my head, allowing me to see again.

It's Hotel O. I'm sure of it.

Why?

Because we're in a room without windows. There are only black walls and wooden floors. There's no bed. Just a chair and an open closet, not filled with clothes but with BDSM toys.

And in the middle of the room is a wooden pillory.

***

DECLAN

Excitement rolls through my body as I watch her react to the object right in front of her.

"What is that?" she murmurs.

I undo the blazer and pull the button on her pants. "You're asking the wrong question."

Her breathing stalls. "What are you going to use it for?" she asks a few seconds later.

I rip down her zipper and pull down her pants and panties, throwing them away so she's naked in front of me.

I place my hand around her throat, reminding her of my dominance. "I'm not going to use the pillory … I'm going to use *you*."

The sound of her struggled breath gets my cock hard.

I release her from my grip and grasp the top part of the pillory, pulling it up. Then I shove her down head first and lock it into place. Her hands can remain right where they are, behind her back, where I can use them as reins.

She's bent over so far it's the ideal height for a few fingers shoved up her pussy … and for giving a perfect BJ. But I've got much more in store than just that.

"Comfortable?" I ask as I walk around to her face.

She cocks her head, a smile spreading on her face. "Could be worse."

"Yes, indeed …" I reply. It's like she can read my mind.

I turn toward the closet and take out a red mask, which I pull over her head so no one will recognize her, but it will still allow her to see. Then I grab a big dildo and some lube. She smiles broadly, but she doesn't even know what's going to happen. If she did, that smile would dissipate immediately.

I position myself behind her and liberally squirt the lube onto her ass and the dildo. Then I slowly shove the dildo into her ass. She gasps, and a soft puff escapes her mouth as she tries to contain her squeals.

"Don't fight it, Kitten," I say as I push it in all the way to the base. "You've trained for this."

"Never this big," she says.

"You know I like to push your limits," I reply.

When it's fully in, I flick her nub and make her aware of how good it feels when I fill her up. "I'm not done yet, so enjoy it while you can," I say as I rub her slit and then slap her ass for good measures.

She bounces up and down against the pillory and every single touch makes her acutely aware of what I'm doing even though she can't see a thing. Or do anything about it for that matter. She's under my complete control.

"I've been meaning to celebrate for a long time," I say as I toy with her clit and the dildo inside her ass until she struggles to stay on her feet. "Now I finally have an excuse."

"You had this planned, didn't you?" she asks. "Are we even allowed to do this at the hotel?"

I spank her ass so hard that she squeals out loud. "No back talk, Kitten … I always get what I want."

"Even when it comes to this hotel," she mumbles, so I slap her again, this time harder than before. When her ass cheeks turn red, I grin and pull out the dildo, only to shove it back in again.

Then I position myself behind her and unzip, taking out my cock. My tip is right at her pussy as I mumble, "I don't want to hear anything but moans from your mouth tonight …"

***

Kat

He pushes inside with no shame, no holding back. I'm left gasping for air as my lungs struggle to take in the oxygen while I'm chained up in the most humiliating way. I feel him inside me, filling me up completely right alongside the dildo. It's so full, I can't even think straight. My mind is turning to mush as my body cries out with lust and pain at the same time.

The sounds I make only make him go deeper.

When he's inside all the way to the base, his cock pulses, and he pulls out for just a second. More lube is added and then he thrusts back in again, this time faster than before.

I feel used. Relentlessly fucked into oblivion. And I'm loving every second of it.

The more he slams into me, the closer I am to exploding right there and then. However, the moment my pussy tenses, he pulls out of me, and I never reach that edge.

"Fuck …" I mutter.

He smacks my ass, making me jolt up and down in the pillory. "I never said this was *your* celebration. It's mine."

"What?" I mutter as he approaches me from the front. "For what?"

"You'll find out when I'll tell you," he says with a wink. "Now, open that pretty mouth, Kitten."

When I do, he jams his dick inside my throat with no remorse. I practically choke on him until he pulls out again, allowing me to breathe for only a second before pushing back inside again.

Suddenly, the door behind me opens, but I have no clue who it is. I can't see. This must be one of the VIP rooms on the top floor of the hotel where people can come and go into scenes as they please. And Declan has left the room unlocked. My pupils dilate. *He wants to share me?*

Our eyes lock, an intent stare follows. He pulls out and murmurs, "This is what you asked for, remember?"

"I thought you didn't—"

He shoves his dick right back into my mouth again before I can say another word.

"What I want is what I'll make you do, slut," he responds, making me even wetter than I already was.

Whoever entered the room places his hand on my ass. It's definitely a man, as the hands are coarse … and the dick he swipes against my skin is clearly real.

He pulls out the dildo inside my ass right when Declan thrusts into my throat, making it impossible for me to react. Especially when the man then replaces the dildo with his own cock.

I can feel *everything*. Him going deep into my ass. Declan filling up my throat. The whole thing is making me quiver, and I can barely stay standing.

I feel like I'm fading. Like my mind is drifting off into happy land where there's nothing but bliss. The only thing keeping me in the here and now are Declan's firm eyes focused on mine. With his hand locked around my jaw, I have no option but to gaze right back at him.

Every time he pulls out, he rubs a mixture of pre-cum and spit across my face, adding a devious grin as he watches me suck in the air.

He loves seeing me dirty. Filthy as fuck. *His.*

No matter whether it's one man fucking me or a multitude, Declan always reminds me who I belong to. Him and no one else.

He's the one deciding who comes in, who fucks me, and who uses me like he does. And he does it all for my pleasure … and his.

Soon, the door opens again, and another man steps inside. He sits down on the chair next to me. I can't see him, but I know it's a man simply from the grunts coming from his mouth. He's already jerking off, that much I can tell. And I don't even know if he's the only one watching or not.

How many more will come? And how many will come all over me? The mere thought is making my pussy thump.

The man behind me groans, and then I feel it … his seed jetting into my ass. All while Declan keeps his cock inside my mouth as if he wants to assure me of the fact that I have no control whatsoever.

The unknown man pulls out of me, and cum runs down my legs. A zipper is pulled up. The door opens and closes again. The man in the chair gets up and walks to my back. He too positions himself behind me and pushes inside.

I feel like I'm being used as a fuck hole. And I don't even mind.

The man thrusts hard and fast, his shaft much thicker and longer than the one before. I'm lost in delirium with both men using me, and it barely even registers when two more men step inside the room.

As the man behind me howls, releasing himself inside

me, my eyes barely stay open. Still, Declan's cock inside my mouth is the one thing keeping me afloat.

The two men replace the single man who was inside me; one of them forcing himself up my ass while the other one toys with my nipples. They're banging me so hard, front and back, that the pillory is making loud noises. I wonder if the people next to us can hear.

The man slamming into my ass suddenly pulls out and comes all over my butt cheeks, spraying me with his cum. The other one jerks himself off until he's close to the edge.

Declan invites him toward my face. And I gleefully accept the full load he unleashes over my face.

I don't know his name. Nor can I see his face, which is hidden behind a mask. But none of it matters. No one knows who I am, and no one knows who they are. Everyone is anonymous here. Everyone is safe and able to fulfill their dirtiest fantasies.

And this was definitely one of mine.

When all the men are gone, Declan pulls out of my mouth, and says, "When I come, so do you."

He jams back inside again, this time pinching my nose so I can't breathe. I count the seconds until he pulls out again. I suck in the oxygen immediately, right before he goes back in again.

His length pulses on my tongue, and he groans out loud. Salty cum hits the back of my throat, and the sexiness pushes me over the edge.

Right then, he tugs on the chain tied to my nipples,

freeing them from the clamps.

I cry out in both pain and pleasure, a flood of endorphins washing over me. I'm riding so high the tears stream down my face, and my body convulses with each wave.

When it's subsided, I'm literally hanging from the pillory. My feet have given up the fight.

"Good girl," Declan murmurs into my ear, as he takes off the handcuffs and unlocks the pillory.

He catches me before I fall to the ground. In his arms, he carries me to the shower, laying me down in the bathtub as he turns on the faucet and lets the warm water stream.

The calm after the storm.

***

DECLAN

"And?" I ask as she leans back in the chair and sips her Cherry Coke.

"What?" she says with a smirk, cocking her head so she can face the sun.

We're in the garden on the terrace on the first floor, where there's a bar and a pool for the guests to enjoy. After our bath together, we had a good night's sleep in one of the luxury rooms. But we haven't talked about anything that went down yet. First, I wanted to get her to relax again after such an intense experience. But still, I need to know if she's okay. If this is truly what she wanted and needed.

Because it definitely hit all my buttons a million times and more.

"Did you enjoy yesterday?" I ask, admiring her beauty when the wind casually plays with her hair in the same way I did when I put her in the pillory. Wild. Free. Unchained by rules.

There's a definite grin on her lips. "Maybe." She puts down her drink. "But didn't you say you weren't sure if you wanted to share me again?" Her brow rises. "Something to do with … jealousy."

"I said I didn't like seeing you with other men …" I lean in toward her. "I never said I didn't like sharing you when I can also have fun with you at the same time."

"Hmm …" She hums in a naughty way, the same sound she always makes when she's thinking of nasty things.

"I don't mind it at all. Not a single inch …" She puts emphasis on the word inch. Of course, she'd like the dicks. No surprise there. Especially when there's a multitude. Fake, real—doesn't matter as long as it's raunchy as fuck.

I'm glad she shares my fetish. After all, I love seeing her filled up. Still, she's my woman, and I only share her because *I* want to. Because it gets me excited. Not because of what other people want with her.

I grab her hand and hold it up to my face, pressing a soft kiss to the top. "I love you … you know that, right?"

She giggles. "Of course, I know that. And these nights are the exact reason." She takes another casual sip of her Coke.

My eyes narrow. "You always see right through me …"

"Or maybe I'm just as filthy as you," she says, licking her lips. "But you said you wanted to celebrate something else?"

Guess she remembered, after all. And here I was thinking I'd fucked her brains to mush.

"So? What is it?" she asks.

I pull out my phone and show her the email that I received. It takes her a while to read, but soon her eyes begin to glow.

"What? You got promoted? Seriously?" she squeals.

"Yup. General Manager," I say with a smug smile.

She jumps up from her seat like she's totally refreshed and wraps her arms around my neck, hugging me tight. "Yay! I'm so happy!"

She kisses me right there and then. Her lips are so sugary sweet, my tongue dips out to take a lick. God, she tastes so good. I kiss her back with just as much fervor, wanting every inch. And fuck me … just her lips can get me hard as a rock. Only when she unlatches her lips do I remember to breathe.

I laugh. "So you're not mad?"

She makes a face. "Of course not, why would I be mad?"

"Because my boss is your dad, remember?" I say. "The

higher I get, the more he'll be up in my ass. And that means your ass too, if we're at the hotel doing filthy things."

Now she's the one laughing. "We can handle him. He'll just have to get used to it."

I nod. "True."

"Besides, this promotion proves he trusts you. Who knows? Maybe he'll let you take over the company in the long run."

I cock my head and look her in the eyes. "You think so?"

She nods. "Why not? I think you'd be a great boss."

"But it's your dad's company. Don't you want to …"

"No, nuh-uh," she says, frowning. "I *hate* running things. I'm much better off writing juicy articles." She smiles. "Besides, you know the hotel, and you love working here. You'd do much better than I ever could. Dad promoted you. That's proof enough that the hotel is doing great with you around," she says. "Even though he might not admit it," she adds with a wink.

"He did say the numbers have been growing since I'm around," I say.

"See?" She winks. "He knows you're valuable. This is the reward."

"Hmm … I think I got my reward a long time ago," I muse, nuzzling her when she blushes. "And this one has the biggest value of all to me."

THANK YOU

FOR READING!

Thank you so much for reading Hotel O. I hope you enjoyed the story!

For updates about upcoming books, please visit my website, www.clarissawild.blogspot.com or sign up for my newsletter here: www.bit.ly/clarissanewsletter.

I'd love to talk to you! You can find me on Facebook: www.facebook.com/ClarissaWildAuthor, make sure to click LIKE. You can also join the Fan Club: www.facebook.com/groups/FanClubClarissaWild/ and talk with other readers!

Enjoyed this book? You could really help out by leaving a review on Amazon and Goodreads. Thank you!

ALSO BY CLARISSA WILD

Dark Romance

Delirious Series

Killer & Stalker

Mr. X

Twenty-One

Ultimate Sin

VIKTOR

Indecent Games Series

FATHER

CAGED & LOCKED & CHASED

New Adult Romance

Fierce Series

Blissful Series

Ruin

Erotic Romance

The Billionaire's Bet Series

Enflamed Series

Unprofessional Bad Boys Series

Visit Clarissa Wild's website for current titles.

http://clarissawild.blogspot.com

ABOUT THE AUTHOR

Clarissa Wild is a New York Times & USA Today Bestselling author of Dark Romance and Contemporary Romance novels. She is an avid reader and writer of swoony stories about dangerous men and feisty women. Her other loves include her hilarious husband, her two crazy but cute dogs, and her ninja cat that sometimes thinks he's a dog too. In her free time she enjoys watching all sorts of movies, playing video games, reading tons of books, and cooking her favorite meals.

Want to be informed of new releases and special offers? Sign up for Clarissa Wild's newsletter on her website clarissawild.blogspot.com.

Visit Clarissa Wild on Amazon for current titles.

Printed in Great Britain
by Amazon